A DISCERNING WOMAN

A Tabitha & Wolf Mystery - Book 6

Sarah F. Noel

Copyright © 2024 Sarah F. Noel

All rights reserved

The characters and events portrayed in this book are fictitious. Any similarity to real persons, living or dead, is coincidental and not intended by the author.

No part of this book may be reproduced, or stored in a retrieval system, or transmitted in any form or by any means, electronic, mechanical, photocopying, recording, or otherwise, without express written permission of the publisher.

ISBN: 9798322379041
Cover design by: HelloBriie Creative
Printed in the United States of America

CONTENTS

Title Page
Copyright
Foreword
Prologue — 1
Chapter 1 — 2
Chapter 2 — 9
Chapter 3 — 16
Chapter 4 — 23
Chapter 5 — 31
Chapter 6 — 37
Chapter 7 — 43
Chapter 8 — 50
Chapter 9 — 56
Chapter 10 — 63
Chapter 11 — 70
Chapter 12 — 76
Chapter 13 — 85
Chapter 14 — 92
Chapter 15 — 99
Chapter 16 — 104

Chapter 17	112
Chapter 18	118
Chapter 19	127
Chapter 20	137
Chapter 21	144
Chapter 22	151
Chapter 23	160
Chapter 24	168
Chapter 25	177
Chapter 26	184
Chapter 27	189
Chapter 28	197
Chapter 29	206
Chapter 30	213
Chapter 31	220
Chapter 32	225
Chapter 33	231
Chapter 34	239
Epilogue	244
Afterword	249
Acknowledgement	251
About The Author	253
Books By This Author	255

FOREWORD

This book is written using British English spelling. e.g. dishonour instead of dishonor, realise instead of realize.

British spelling aside, while every effort has been made to proofread this thoroughly, typos do creep in. If you find any, I'd greatly appreciate a quick email to report them at sarahfnoelauthor@gmail.com

PROLOGUE

The blacksmith's wife never heard her attacker come up behind her, hammer held high. It was probably a blessing that she never turned, and so was caught unaware as the improvised weapon slammed down on the back of her head. She immediately crumpled and fell to the ground, blood gushing out of her skull. That one blow had almost certainly killed her immediately, but her killer brought the hammer down twice more, just to be certain.

CHAPTER 1

London, December 1897

Tabitha sighed, shook her head, and then sighed again. Looking at the list in her hand, she wondered how everything on it would be completed by the following day. She considered how her mother had made a similar odyssey at least once a year back to their family estate in Cambridgeshire. Back then, at least to Tabitha's eyes, the planning, packing, and travel itself had seemed to happen almost effortlessly. Tabitha's mother had controlled her household with an iron fist, so there was no doubt that she had overseen every aspect of their moves to and from the country. However, the Marchioness of Cambridgeshire never sullied her hands with anything like actual work. So it was likely that all the stress and labour of such moves had fallen on their long-suffering housekeeper, Mrs Graham, a paragon of her profession. Tabitha had felt far too guilty to place such a burden entirely on the shoulders of her housekeeper, Mrs Jenkins, which was how she found herself with a long list of things to do that morning.

While most people in aristocratic circles would also be retiring to their country estates for Christmas until the start of the social season in the spring, neither Tabitha nor Wolf intended to stay that long. Wolf did not have the warmest memories of Glanwyddan Hall, the Pembroke estate, from his childhood visits there where he would be inspected by his grandfather, the late earl. The earl had died when Wolf was fourteen, and he hadn't returned since. When the plan to spend

Christmas in Pembrokeshire had first arisen, he had confided to Tabitha that his only memory of any kindness during his yearly visits was of the cook, Mrs Budgers, who had always provided a warm, motherly sanctuary for the young Wolf. During planning sessions with Mrs Jenkins, Tabitha had discovered that Mrs Budgers was still in service at the estate. She kept this news from Wolf, hoping to surprise him and help him feel more at home as the new lord of the manor.

The dowager's views on her deceased husband and son's family estate seemed even more complicated than Wolf's. As a rule, the elderly dowager countess did not enjoy the countryside and, for most of her marriage and her husband's brief reign as earl, had preferred to remain at Chesterton House, in London while her husband indulged his love of horses, hunting, and drinking in the country. By all accounts, Jonathan's father was as much of a brute as his son and equally happy to use his wife as a punching bag. Because of this, Tabitha suspected that the dowager had enjoyed the distance between her and her spouse as much as she enjoyed the greater society offered by remaining in London. Once her husband had broken his neck by drunkenly falling off a horse while hunting, indulging his three great passions simultaneously, the dowager never returned to Wales.

While Jonathan had inherited some of his worst traits from his father, he'd had no more love of Glanwyddan Hall than his mother did. Because of this and the briefness of her marriage, Tabitha had never been to the family estate. It seemed that many in their Christmas party would be visiting with very mixed feelings. However, it had been the dowager's suggestion, well, order really, that they all spend Christmas there. Tabitha acknowledged that the woman was right; Wolf needed to present himself to his tenants and step more fully into his role as earl and all that meant as a great landowner.

At least Lord Langley, Bear, Lady Lily, and Viscount Tobias didn't have any prejudices about the estate—or at least Tabitha assumed they didn't. Because, yes, they were all travelling with them as well. Lady Lily was a given; she had been staying with her grandmother, the dowager, for some weeks now.

In theory, the dowager was readying her granddaughter for her first Season. Still, the academically inclined young woman had no interest in going through the necessary aristocratic motions in order to snag an eligible husband. More surprising was how much the dowager's enthusiasm for preparing her granddaughter had waned of late. At the same time, the dowager's godson, the young Viscount Tobias, former rake and wastrel, was seemingly infatuated with Lady Lily, who either didn't realise or didn't mind the attention. Given that the girl's head was always in a scientific book, it was entirely possible that she truly had no idea that the young man carried a torch for her. Either way, her titled godson's interest in her granddaughter gave the dowager the perfect excuse to neglect her duty to prepare her granddaughter. After all, if the girl could bag a wealthy viscount before the season even began, it would save them all some time and effort.

And so, Viscount Tobias was continuing his devoted trailing of Lady Lily. It seemed that the young woman didn't mind his company. At least in part, Tabitha suspected this was because being squired around town by the eligible young viscount kept her out of her grandmother's crosshairs. Tabitha also knew for a fact that Viscount Tobias was a willing escort to the British Library and even some of the Royal Academy's lectures. The things one did for young love!

Finally, there was Maxwell Sandworth, Lord Langley. Tabitha and Wolf had long ago moved on from their suspicions, even dislike of the man, to something that was quickly approaching a trusted friendship. Given that Melody, Tabitha's ward, would, of course, be accompanying them to Pembroke, it was the most natural thing in the world to invite Langley, who was mentoring Melody's older brother, Rat. That Langley had no wife nor children of his own, or at least a child he could publicly acknowledge, meant the man had been happy to accept the invitation. In addition, there was Wolf's private secretary, really his dearest friend, Bear, and their group's gaggle of valets, lady's maids and Melody's nursery maid. Finally, there was Dodo, Melody's King Charles spaniel puppy. Their group would be a large and unruly one.

Some servants remained behind at Chesterton House. However, Mrs Jenkins, their butler Talbot, carriage driver Madison and some other servants had gone ahead that afternoon to supplement Glanwyddan Hall's regular skeleton household staff. Given that no one in the family had visited in years, Mrs Jenkins had been very worried about the state they would find the great house in, and just how undisciplined and slothful its servants might be. She had sent word ahead to Mrs Budgers, the most senior and tenured of the permanent staff, about which additional servants she should hire for the duration of their stay, and the meticulous housekeeper had promised Tabitha she would personally be ready to roll her sleeves up to polish every surface until it gleamed, if necessary. For her sake and Wolf's, Tabitha wasn't too worried. However, she realised that they might not be the main cause of Mrs Jenkin's concerns. She had been housekeeper when the dowager had ruled at Chesterton House and likely had a very good understanding of the woman's expectations and judgement should anything fall short of her exacting standards.

Tabitha's musings and worries were interrupted by Wolf, who had been searching the house for her. After many months of denying her feelings for Wolf and the subsequent unfounded assumptions and ensuant misunderstandings, their recent mutual declaration of love had brought Tabitha peace and happiness. While there had been no further discussion of what might come next for them, Tabitha was in no hurry to change the status of their relationship. The shared looks of longing, stolen kisses, and secret quick touching of hands when they believed the servants weren't looking were delicious and held the promise of much future joy.

For his part, Wolf was less satisfied by the still nebulous state of their relationship. There was no doubt at all in his mind that he wanted to marry Tabitha and spend the rest of his life with her, but he sensed that she still had lingering doubts. He knew the doubts weren't about her feelings for him but rather about ever entering the matrimonial state again. Being married to his cousin Jonathan had traumatised Tabitha, and that trauma wouldn't be easily fixed with kisses and words of love. Wolf knew he had to find a way to assure Tabitha that she would continue to have control over her person, finances and life, even in marriage. He just hadn't yet landed upon the perfect way to make that assurance.

What Wolf didn't know was that there was yet another reason why Tabitha was hesitant to make their love known publicly. While she had grown to realise that she had no desire for society's approval and did not care, at least for herself, about its faux horror that she continued to live in Chesterton House with a single man who was not a direct relative, she did care for Wolf's sake. As soon as any engagement was announced, it would be impossible for them to continue to live together unchaperoned. And who might such a chaperone be? The obvious person was the dowager countess, but that hardly seemed like a satisfactory arrangement for any of them. So, for now, it was easier to enjoy the illicit romance while pretending nothing had changed.

Tabitha looked up and smiled at Wolf's entrance. It felt good to be able to acknowledge her pleasure at his company, at least privately. His returned smile was as full of warmth and love as her own. His words, however, were in stark contrast, "I've just received a telegram from my steward. There have been some incidents recently at Glanwyddan Hall that he wanted to warn me about. It seems that if we weren't already planning to visit, he was going to suggest that I come in person anyway."

"What kind of incidents?" Tabitha asked nervously. After all the worry about Melody's abduction and the dowager's recent disappearance, she did not want to put her extended family in harm's way.

"He didn't go into great detail. It seems that at first, it seemed like nothing more than mischief, and he put it down to high spirits amongst some lads in the village, or even drunkenness. But recently, there seems to have been escalation; a barn was burned down, and Jones is sure it was arson. Then, there have been dead animals."

"Dead animals?" Tabitha asked in alarm. "What kind of animals and where?"

"Dead hares have been left by the kitchen door. When it first happened, Mrs Budgers thought they'd somehow been left there by local poachers, cooked them and thought nothing more about it. But then, a dead raven was found on the front steps of the house. The Welsh consider dead ravens to be a particularly bad omen. The most recent and upsetting incident happened yesterday when they found a dead cat on the front steps. Jones feels that, while any one of these incidents alone might be ignored, together with the burned barn and the prior mischief, there is definitely something of concern happening."

Tabitha's first thought was for Melody and Rat, "Perhaps we shouldn't be going. Or at least we shouldn't all go. I don't want to put the children in harm's way."

"I can't help but agree. While I don't want to be away from all of you over Christmas, I worry that this mischief maker may escalate his efforts if he has a new audience."

With a decision apparently made, Tabitha looked back at her list. If they were to unwind all of their plans, there was much to be done. Should the servants be recalled to Chesterton House? If Wolf was still planning to visit, appearances needed to be maintained. How would it look to the tenants and neighbouring aristocratic families if the new Earl of Pembroke were to reside, even for a few weeks, at an understaffed estate? However, one thing that needed to be done immediately was to inform the dowager. "I must go and telephone Mama," Tabitha explained. "She will not be happy at the change in plans, but the sooner she is told, the better." Wolf could only agree.

Less than ten minutes later, Tabitha re-entered the parlour with a distressed look. "I take it the conversation didn't go well," Wolf remarked.

"That is an understatement if there ever was one. She refuses to see our plans changed. I explained our concerns, and she said, and I quote, 'I refuse to have it said that some country bumpkin rapscallion is able to strike fear into the heart of the Dowager Countess of Pembroke with a few cheap schoolyard pranks.'"

"That does sound like something she would say," Wolf acknowledged. "What I don't understand is why she is so keen to go."

"I know. It's perplexing," Tabitha agreed. "All I've ever heard her say of Glanwyddan Hall over the years is that it's a drafty old pile and that if it weren't for the entail, Jonathan would have sold it off immediately when he inherited. And after hearing what she thinks of the Scots, you can only imagine what she has to say about the Welsh! Yet, she seems determined that we all visit. I do wonder if she has an ulterior motive. I just can't imagine what it might be."

Tabitha's fears remained, but she knew that if the dowager wanted them all to spend Christmas at Glanwyddan Hall, they would, and it was easier to accept that now. With a final shake of her head, she went back to perusing her list.

CHAPTER 2

While shorter than their train ride to Scotland, this trip had been far more stressful. Previously, they had travelled to Edinburgh with a small group of just Tabitha, Wolf, Bear and two servants. That was a very manageable size group to navigate through train stations and carriages. But this group was an entirely different matter, and by the time they arrived in the town of Pembroke, Tabitha was exhausted. The estate owned multiple carriages, and Wolf was pleased to see Madison waiting by one with another two behind. Even so, some of the servants would have to wait with the luggage for one of the carriages to make the trip to Lamphey and back. Lamphey, two miles from the town of Pembroke, was part of the sprawling Pembroke estate that Glanwyddan Hall sat on.

Wolf had still not recovered from his initial shock that he owned the entire village, and now, driving through the quaint hamlet, he was pleased to note that it looked well-maintained and its inhabitants seemingly thriving. He had grown up outside of a very similar-looking village and could appreciate that the rosy-cheeked children playing happily on the village green and freshly painted exteriors of the cottages spoke to a level of good health and comfort. As he'd learned more about the holdings he had inherited from his cousin Jonathan, Wolf had often been appalled at the greedy penny-pinching in which the previous earl had engaged. Wolf was relieved to see such stinginess appeared to have not extended to Lamphey.

The dowager, sitting across from Wolf in the carriage, seemed to intuit his thoughts and said, "My husband loved this village. Apparently, he had very fond memories of growing up on the estate and time spent amongst his tenants here. He made a particular provision in his will so that part of his unentailed wealth maintains Lamphey regardless of what future earls might do." The dowager sniffed, then added, "For my part, I never saw the charm in any of this." She waved her hand dismissively towards the view from the carriage window. "However, for some reason that I never cared to discover, my husband preferred to spend his time here, and that worked out very well for both of us."

"I believe the late earl used to throw a lavish Christmas Eve party to which the entire village was invited," Tabitha said. "Perhaps you can revive that tradition, Wolf."

The dowager sniffed again, "Why on earth would we revive that unnatural mixing of the classes? I never understood the desire to have local labourers swilling down beer in the grand ballroom. I was forced to participate a few times in the early days of my marriage. Still, I luckily was able to remove myself permanently from the estate and my father-in-law's misguided attempt at egalitarianism."

Tabitha was tempted to look at Wolf and roll her eyes, but she managed to resist. However, she couldn't help but reflect on how depressingly normal such comments were from the dowager. After the old woman's stay amongst the prostitutes of London and her shocking continuation of a monthly gathering with a bunch of madams, to say nothing of her delight in the East End Jews they had encountered during their last investigation, Tabitha had held out some hope that with the expansion of her social horizons, the dowager's elitism and snobbery might be tempered somehow. However, based on her comments since entering Wales, it seemed whatever feelings of shared humanity the dowager might have felt towards those outside of her aristocratic circles had the beauty and fragility of a snowflake, destined to shimmer momentarily before inevitably turning to slush.

Less than half a mile outside of Lamphey, the carriage turned and entered through stately wrought iron gates, proceeding down a wide, tree-lined avenue. Tabitha looked out of the window, eager for her first sight of Glanwyddan Hall. While she had technically been its mistress for two years, she felt more kinship for the ancestral home now that Wolf was its master than she ever had before.

For his part, Wolf had such complicated feelings about the Pembroke estate that he found his stomach roiling with anxiety. He had hated his childhood visits to see his grandfather, who used his grandson as a proxy for his disappointment with his son and dislike of the boy's mother. When news of his grandfather's death reached the younger Wolf, his first thought was relief that he would never again have to visit Glanwyddan Hall. Yet, here he was, back again, and this time as the Earl of Pembroke. Was it possible for him to move past the trauma of his early years' association with this house and step into his new role as master and landowner with anything approaching sanguinity?

Jonathan's childhood memories of the estate had been barely better than Wolf's. While his grandfather had harboured specific resentments against Wolf, he hadn't been much more impressed with his heir, Philip, Jonathan's father. Perhaps the old earl sensed the same weakness in his son that the dowager came to despise before the first month of her marriage was done.

The late earl had led a controlled life of moderation, unlike Philip, who gave himself wholly to dissipation and vice when not riding to hounds, and sometimes even when hunting, hence his death only a few years after inheriting when he drunkenly fell off his horse. Determined that his grandson be a more worthy bearer of the Pembroke name than his father, the old earl had tried to rule Jonathan's life with an iron fist.

As soon as he reached his majority, Jonathan spent as little time as possible at Glanwyddan Hall and almost never talked about it, so Tabitha had few preconceived notions of the estate. Given this, her first view of the stately house, dating in parts to Henry VIII's time, was a delightful surprise.

Glanwyddan Hall had originally been an abbey that Elizabeth I had gifted to the first Earl of Pembroke as a reward for services rendered to the crown. While the original building had been added to over the years, these additions did not have the jarring mismatched aesthetic that so often was the case as old estates were "improved" by aristocrats with more money than taste. Instead, the newer wings were somehow blended with the old such that the overall effect was pleasing to the eye even while it was obvious that varying eras were represented.

Clapping her hands with delight, Tabitha exclaimed, "Oh, Wolf. It's beautiful. I had no idea."

While Wolf was glad to hear Tabitha's admiration, he was unable to separate the physical structure from his unpleasant memories and could not conjure up a similar appreciation. For her part, the dowager had her own bad memories from the early years of her marriage; the first time Philip struck her had been in this house.

Sniffing, she said, "Beautiful? Is that what you think? I never saw the appeal of the place."

Looking between the two of them, Tabitha intuited her companions were plagued by demons that one merry Christmas in the house would be unlikely to banish entirely. Nevertheless, she was determined to do what she could to enable Wolf at least to turn a new page at Glanwyddan Hall. There was already much he found burdensome about the earldom; she refused to allow a house to add to that load.

Melody was riding in the carriage with them, and she slipped her little hand into Wolf's much larger one and said in a sweet, innocent voice, "Wolfie, is this your house? It's very big. I'm scared I'll get lost in it."

Looking down at the adorable little girl with her red-gold ringlets and spray of freckles across her nose, Wolf said, "Don't you worry, Miss Melly. I will show you all the best spots. There used to be a wonderful treehouse in a huge oak tree. We'll have to go and see if it's still there. And there was a swing hanging off one of the branches of the tree. I used to love playing on that swing and seeing how high I could go."

"Will you push me high, Wolfie?"

"So high that you'll be able to touch the sky."

Tabitha smiled at this exchange. Initially, Wolf had been very reluctant to have Melody live at Chesterton House, harbouring serious and justified concerns about Tabitha's evident attachment to the child. However, despite his best efforts to remain detached, even he had proven unable to resist Melody. The child was not just delightful; she was very intelligent. So intelligent that Tabitha sometimes wondered how much the charm offensive the little girl directed at Wolf was guilelessness and how much calculated by an orphan who intuited that her magical new life was at his pleasure.

As the carriages drew up to the house, a line of servants waited to greet them. Despite the cold, damp weather, it looked as if the entire household staff had been shuffled outside to greet their new master. Wolf descended first and then helped the dowager, Tabitha and Melody down. Tabitha was pleased to see the familiar faces of Talbot, Mrs Jenkins and some of the other Chesterton House servants.

Talbot approached them, "Milord, milady, and milady, I hope your journey was an easy one. I won't introduce you to every member of staff, but there are a few you should meet now." He paused, then gave a conspiratorial smile in Tabitha's direction, "And one person you might remember."

With that, the sea of servants parted, and a short, very round, elderly woman wearing an apron came forward, a beaming smile on her face. "Budgie!" Wolf exclaimed. "You're still in service here? I had no idea. What a wonderful surprise."

These were the first genuine words of pleasure Tabitha had heard Wolf say in hours, and they lightened the heaviness she had felt throughout the trip.

Mrs Budgers had initially looked a little overawed; the last time she had seen Wolf, he had been a gangly, awkward fourteen-year-old. Now, he was a grown man and her new master. But at his words, she seemed suddenly to see the shy, unhappy little boy she had loved and comforted instead of the tall, handsome man in front of her. She came towards him and clasped him to her bosom in an undeniable breach of social etiquette that was nevertheless heartwarming to behold. "Wolfie, you've come home," the woman said in a soft, local Welsh accent, tears in her eyes.

Tabitha could only imagine what the dowager thought about the new Earl of Pembroke being embraced by one of his staff and called by such a pet name. Luckily, the woman kept these thoughts to herself, even if her facial expression spoke volumes. However, Wolf did not share the dowager's horror and hugged the cook back with equal pleasure. Seeing the looks Talbot and Tabitha were exchanging, he kept one arm around Mrs Budgers and smiled, "Did you two conspire against me?"

"Indeed, milord. After hearing from Mrs Jenkins that Mrs Budgers was still in service here, her ladyship suggested that this might be a pleasant surprise for you."

"I cannot imagine a better one. Budgie makes the best scones I've ever eaten." Turning back to the cook, he asked, "I hope to eat plenty of them while we're here."

The elderly cook blushed and smiled proudly, "I have a batch just out of the oven for you as soon as you're ready, m'lord." The woman seemed to have realised the impropriety of her initial greeting of the new earl.

"None of that, Budgie. I was always Wolfie, and I don't want to be called anything other than that by you. You must never stand on ceremony with me. Do you hear me?" The old woman beamed with pleasure and nodded her head. Turning to Melody, who was standing next to Tabitha, Wolf said, "Budgie, I want to introduce you to the only other person who is allowed to call me Wolfie." He beckoned to Melody, who came over shyly and took Mrs Budgers' proffered hand.

"I'm very pleased to meet you, Miss Melody," Mrs Budgie said, dropping a quick curtsey.

"Can I call you Budgie as well?" Melody asked.

"Of course, you can, Miss Melody," the cook answered.

"Then you can call me Melly."

Wolf laughed, "You know, Melly, when I was your age, I used to sneak down to the kitchen, and Budgie would feed me scones and jam tarts and all manner of other wonderful things. She even let me help her roll the pastry sometimes," Wolf said in a stage whisper.

Melody's eyes lit up, "Can I help you as well?"

By now, Mrs 'Budgers' lined, worn cheeks were wet with tears, "It's been too long since children ran through this house." Looking back up at Wolf, she said, "Far too long, Wolfie."

Standing to the side, watching the scene unfold, Tabitha found her own cheeks wet with tears. It was possible that even the dowager's initial disapproval had thawed. Perhaps.

CHAPTER 3

Glanwyddan Hall was as imposing inside as outside, beginning with the entrance hall's soaring cathedral ceiling. The house had not been updated with any of the modern conveniences enjoyed by Chesterton House, and all the lighting was either gaslights or even candles. A roaring fire crackled in a huge fireplace that dominated one wall of the hallway and provided a much-appreciated warmth after the chill of standing outside talking to the servants for even a short time.

Looking around her, Tabitha found the house to be much as she would have expected. Just as with her family's estate, most of the décor paid homage to the long, illustrious Pembroke line. There were paintings of stern-looking ancestors on the walls, a few marble busts, and a suit of armour in one corner with a display of swords on the wall next to it. Most of Wolf's ancestors were interchangeable with her own: pompous old men and women, glaring disapprovingly at future generations.

The first carriage holding some of the servants had arrived. Once Withers, Ginny, and Melody's nursemaid, Mary, had exited the carriage, Mrs Jenkins showed Tabitha and the dowager to their rooms and then took Melody and Mary to the nursery. Before leaving London, Tabitha had discussed the room assignments with Mrs Jenkins. While it was a given that Wolf would take what would have been Jonathan's room, it was a little unclear who should be offered the bedchamber that would have been Tabitha's by right if she had ever visited before her husband's death. Etiquette probably leaned in the direction of

Tabitha still taking that room, but common sense suggested that she cede the privilege to the dowager. If the dowager had been expecting to be relegated to a lesser bedchamber, she certainly gave no indication. Instead, she paused before the door Mrs Jenkins led her to, turned and asked, "Does this room still have the same hideous wallpaper? I would have ripped it out years ago, but Philip refused me the funds to redecorate."

As always when they travelled, Ginny had prepared an overnight bag that enabled Tabitha to refresh herself without all the trunks being unpacked. And even though her journey had been as long and tiring as Tabitha's, Ginny fluttered around the large, elegant room, ensuring her mistress' comfort with no thought to her own. Given that the house did not have electricity, Tabitha was relieved to find it had enough modern plumbing that she had a private privy. However, it was not so modern that a bath could be run for her without pails of hot water coming up from the depths of the house. Luckily, Mrs Jenkins had anticipated Tabitha's need to rinse the grime of travel off and had sent a stream of housemaids up with water.

Soaking in a warm, rose-scented bath, listening to Ginny in the next room humming to herself as she unpacked, Tabitha was finally able to relax somewhat. Ever since Wolf had received the telegram from his steward, she had been filled with a sense of dread at their trip. It was December 16, less than ten days until Christmas. This would be the first Christmas that Tabitha and Wolf had spent together, and with Melody and Rat. It should be a joyful occasion, and as she lay there, Tabitha resolved that it would be. She wouldn't let some malicious prankster ruin what should be a festive, wonderful time.

Apart from the upcoming holiday season, there was the matter of Rat's birthday. From what Tabitha and Wolf knew, Rat and Melody's parents had died about a year and a half before. Rat had a memory that, sometime before Christmas, his mother used to mention something about him being a year older. When Tabitha first met the young street urchin, he thought he was eight years old, but perhaps he was nine. He had been so malnourished at the time it was hard to make an accurate guess. He seemed more sure of eight than anything, and so that is what everyone had decided to accept. As for his actual birthday, he had nothing more than a vague memory. Because of this, Tabitha, Wolf and Langley had decided that the child needed an actual date of birth, and they had landed on December 24, 1888.

When they had asked Rat if he was happy with this decision, he'd looked rather nonplussed, clearly ignorant of what difference an actual birthdate might make to him. Tabitha had quickly informed him that birthdays meant cake and presents. The boy's eyes had opened in wondrous amazement, and he'd happily nodded his head at their suggestion. And so now they also had an upcoming birthday to celebrate.

Wolf was soaking in a bath at the same time, his valet buzzing around as efficiently as Tabitha's maid. His emotions were even more wildly mixed than they had been on the journey. He reflected on his childhood visits to the estate. His cousin Jonathan had been almost ten years older than Wolf, so even on the few occasions he had been in residence at Glanwyddan Hall during Wolf's visits, he had shown no interest in getting to know the younger boy. By the time Wolf was old enough to begin these visits, the dowager had long since established her only residence as Chesterton House in London, and so they never crossed paths. As for her husband Philip, Wolf's uncle, while he did spend most of his time at Glanwyddan Hall, he did his best to avoid his father at all costs. Sleeping in until past noon most days to recover from his excesses the evening before, the dissolute man certainly had no interest in entertaining his brother's brat.

However, being reunited with Mrs Budgers reminded him that he did have some good memories of his childhood visits to Glanwyddan Hall. While those memories were not of his grandfather or his very occasional run-ins with his uncle, and even his cousin Jonathan once or twice, it didn't mean they weren't there. Budgie hadn't been the only servant to take pity on the quiet, lonely little boy. The butler at the time, Paulson, had taken care to warn the young Wolf of his grandfather's preferences and how best to endear himself to the man. There was the gardener who had restored the old treehouse and built the swing so that Wolf might have a place to escape to. The month-long visit every year had seemed interminable at the time, but Wolf reflected how much worse they might have been without the little kindnesses shown to him by the staff. He made a mental note to ask Budgie if any of the servants he remembered so fondly were still living nearby.

Wolf also thought about the one friend his age he had made during those visits, a girl from the village he had encountered when wandering in the woods abutting the hall's extensive gardens. It didn't occur to him at the time that the girl was probably not supposed to be playing on the estate, but he had just been happy to meet someone his age. Her name was Glynnie, and she'd been a year younger than Wolf.

Even at a very young age, Wolf had intuited that his grandfather would disapprove of his connection with a local commoner, and so the friendship had been his secret. He would escape from the house in the afternoon while his grandfather napped after lunch. Rushing to the treehouse, he would usually find Glynnie already there. Early on in the friendship, Mrs Budgers had caught Wolf taking extra biscuits and scones to his new friend. When he confessed about Glynnie, Mrs Budgers had taken pity on the lonely boy and, from that point, had always made a point of packing a little basket with tasty morsels Wolf could bring to share with his friend.

As Wolf thought about Glynnie, it occurred to him that he had never thought to ask her about her life in the village. While he knew she wasn't someone his grandfather would approve of as a companion, he hadn't really considered just how inappropriate she might be as the playfellow for the grandson of an earl. He had some memory of Glynnie talking about her father's farm, but they were always too busy conjuring up imaginary worlds to dwell in the harsh realities of their actual one.

Wolf's grandfather had died in the winter, and so he hadn't

realised that his time with Glynnie that last summer would be their final one. By that time, Wolf's voice had started to deepen, and he even had the beginnings of some whiskers on his face. For her part, Glynnie had suddenly blossomed into a young woman and when Wolf had first seen her that last summer, he suddenly became very awkward around her. Up until that summer, Wolf hadn't really considered that Glynnie was a girl, but those last few weeks with her, he'd been horribly aware of the fact; unable to stop sneaking looks at her new womanly curves. If Glynnie had been aware of this change, she hadn't shown it. When they had parted, she'd given him a chaste peck on the cheek and said, "See you next summer, Wolf Boy." He hadn't washed his face for three days after that.

Did Glynnie still live in Lamphey? Wolf assumed that, by this time, she was married with a brood of children. Trying to see beyond the early blossoming of a young man's awareness of the opposite sex, Wolf tried to remember what Glynnie looked like. He remembered a golden-haired child with striking, large, chocolate-brown eyes framed with dark blonde lashes. He remembered a wide, generous smile and an infectious laugh. Would he recognise her if he saw her now, more than fifteen years later? He would have to ask Budgie if she knew what had happened to his childhood friend.

Down the corridor in the bedroom that even she knew should be Tabitha's by right, the dowager was sunk in her own memories. As Withers fixed her hair, the dowager reflected on that first punch within weeks of her marriage. She had realised what a weak, pathetic man she had married almost before the wedding night was out. However, it wasn't until that first strike that she realised that what Philip lacked in moral fibre he made up for in brute strength. He was a large man with fists that would have served him well in a boxing ring, and he felt no qualms about his young wife being on the receiving end of the punches those fists were able to deliver so effectively.

The young Julia Chesterton had been so shocked by the first punch that she had put her hand up to the eye that was already swelling and said nothing but, "Oh!" She was not an eighteen-year-old ingenue nearly barely out of the schoolroom. She was a woman of almost twenty-four, almost an old maid by society's standards. Pretty enough, but deemed too much trouble by eligible potential husbands, her parents had almost given up hope of marrying her off. There was no doubt that the life of a spinster would not have given the young woman access to the intellectual and social circles she did not doubt she was born to dominate. And so, when Philip, Viscount Chesterton, paid her some attention, the dowager had been ambitious enough to encourage his suit, even though she was fully aware what a dolt the man was. If she'd been aware that he was not just stupid but also violent, she might have thought twice about the marriage.

Of course, Philip had been immediately contrite. In fact, he'd been quite inconsolable, and his young wife had found that she was expected to soothe him with words of love and promises that things would be better from thereon in. Except, she couldn't bring herself to make herself as emotionally vulnerable as she had been physically. Instead, she had left him to the ministrations of his valet, curled up on the floor of his bedchamber, crying tears of self-pity. She had gone to her room, where her then maid, Peters, had shown for the first time, but not the last, that she had a useful ability to apply face paint to cover bruises.

The following morning, the young viscountess had left Pembrokeshire at the first sign of dawn and returned to London. That might have been the last interaction she ever had with her new husband if there hadn't been the imperative, realised on both sides, to produce an heir. By some unspoken agreement, Philip did not follow his bride to London and instead stayed behind at Glanwyddan Hall. As the years went on, he spent an increasing amount of time in Wales. The dowager, then the viscountess, managed to bring into the world two healthy baby daughters but no son and heir. Finally, when the old earl had finally given up hope of his son being the one to extend the line, a boy had been born. The dowager had barely returned to Wales after delivering an heir and certainly never after her husband died.

CHAPTER 4

As Tabitha made her way down to meet their rag-tag band of friends and family for dinner, she thought about how different this Christmas was from the previous one. Jonathan had still been alive a year before, and she had felt no joy at the approaching holiday season. Quite the opposite, in fact; she had suffered her most recent loss of a pregnancy, and Jonathan had been in a particularly foul mood at this most recent evidence that his wife would be unable to provide him with an heir.

Tabitha's relationship with her own family growing up had been strained. While she adored her father, her mother was a difficult woman, not unlike the dowager at her worst, but without that woman's surprising occasional capacity for compassion. The youngest of four girls, Tabitha had been a bright, inquisitive young girl who found high society's etiquette and unspoken rules suffocating. Despairing of her youngest child, Tabitha's mother had been only too happy to marry her off to Jonathan and wash her hands of any maternal obligations. Of course, Tabitha had not found a warm, loving family in her marriage. However, now, amongst this rather unconventional grouping of lords, ladies, orphaned former street urchins, and even Bear, Tabitha felt as if she was finally surrounded by the love and acceptance she had always longed for.

So much had changed in a year; this Christmas would be filled with childish laughter as Melody and Rat opened the many gifts they would find waiting under the tree. Tabitha would feel the warmth of friendship surrounded by Langley, Bear, Lady Lily, and even Viscount Tobias, who was surprising them all with what a charming young man he could be now he was no longer constantly sullen and moody.

Then, there was the newly declared love she shared with Wolf. More than anything, this warmed Tabitha from within and made her smile as she thought of Wolf's loving gaze. Tabitha even felt affection towards the dowager, who was the one person who had been part of those less pleasant Christmases past. Their relationship might never be totally easy, but Tabitha had been genuinely worried at the woman's recent disappearance and thought that, in return, her erstwhile mother-in-law had perhaps thawed slightly towards her. Perhaps.

Walking into the drawing room where everyone was gathered before dinner, Tabitha smiled indulgently at the scene before her: Langley was playing chess with Rat, Tobias was looking at Lady Lily with puppy dog eyes while she patiently tried to explain a scientific thesis she had just read about. The new ideas of botanical research were clearly wasted on the young viscount, who nevertheless looked adoringly at the brilliant young woman by his side. Not for the first time, Tabitha wondered if there was some kind of understanding between the two. Viscount Tobias made no efforts to hide his feelings for Lily, who, for her part, seemed to indulge him as one might a charming, if slightly slow, child.

The dowager was sitting in an armchair by the fire, nursing a glass of sherry. Bear was sitting opposite her, sketchpad in hand, apparently capturing her likeness with charcoals. Tabitha had been delighted to discover the huge man's artistic talent, and he had already started on a promised painting of Melly. While she was somewhat surprised that the dowager was a willing subject, she also knew that the old woman had a soft spot for the gentle giant of a man. Even now that she had her own huge, even more gruesome-looking protector in Little Ian, a manservant she had inherited from the East End gangster Mickey D, the woman nevertheless still appreciated Bear's ability to strike fear into her neighbours. Tabitha thought it for the best that Little Ian had stayed behind in London. They didn't need to discombobulate the locals any more than Bear's presence might.

Melody would be having dinner in the nursery with Rat, but for now she was sitting on Wolf's lap while he read one of her favourite books, *Alice in Wonderland*. This sight made Tabitha happier than anything. There was a time when she would have easily walked away from Wolf and Chesterton House if he had been anything less than accepting of the little girl. Now, such a situation would break her heart should it ever be necessary. Every sign that Wolf was becoming increasingly beguiled by the little girl brought Tabitha joy and greater peace of mind.

Feeling Tabitha's eyes on him, Wolf looked up and smiled. He wasn't sure how he had ever thought of her as anything but the most beautiful woman in the world. Even more lovely than her glorious, richly chestnut hair, hazel eyes, and gentle smile were the kindness and intelligence that suffused her face. And more than intelligence, strength of character. Tabitha had a fundamental decency to her that inspired Wolf to try to be a better man. She challenged him at every turn with her intellect and bravery. Wolf had fancied himself in love as a much younger man, but what he had felt for Arlene had been a shallow, brittle love compared to his feelings for Tabitha who returned his smile and moved to approach him.

Catching sight of Tabitha out of the corner of her eye, the dowager called out, "Tabitha, call for Talbot and ask how long we will have to wait for dinner. This really isn't good enough. We've been travelling all day and I'm ravenous."

Tabitha sighed. It was nowhere near the customary time for dinner, and she refused to harass the staff, who must be in enough of a tizzy on their first night serving the new earl. As if intuiting the situation, Talbot appeared in the doorway with some canapés. He made straight for the dowager, who harrumphed but helped herself to a salmon tartlet. Tabitha continued over to Wolf.

"Melly, I think we can save the next chapter for tomorrow," Wolf said gently to the little girl.

Melody pouted adorably and said, "Wolfie, just one more. I want to know what happens at the tea party."

Tabitha lifted the child off Wolf's lap and kissed her rosy cheek, "Melly, if you're a very good girl and go with Mary now, perhaps Wolfie will come and play the tickle game with you tomorrow."

This seemed to appease the child, who turned to Wolf and said, "Will you show me and Dodo the treehouse as well?" The puppy had been sleeping in front of the fire, but at her name, raised her head and looked expectantly. While the dog had been an unwanted addition to the household, at least as far as Tabitha had been concerned, she was now quite well-trained and had stopped chewing everything, for the most part. Moreover, ever since Dodo had been responsible for saving her life in Brighton, Tabitha found herself far more warmly inclined towards the dog, who had definitely made herself very at home in their household. Even the dowager seemed fond of stroking the silky, soft, floppy ears on occasion.

"I think that can be arranged, Miss Melly. If you're a good girl for Mary now," Wolf answered.

As the nursemaid rose from her place in the corner of the room and approached her charge, Rat stood and said to Langley, "I'm going to finish you off tomorrow, sir. I already have a strategy for checkmate."

The often quite sombre earl laughed and said, "I have no doubt you will, my boy. I think I see your plan, and it doesn't bode well for me. Meanwhile, remember, your studies do not stop because we're away. I will see you in the library tomorrow morning at ten o'clock sharp."

"I'm going to crack that new puzzle as well," Rat exclaimed confidently.

"I'm equally certain of that, lad," Langley answered affectionately.

Dinner was a lavish affair, with one delicious, rich dish after another. Mrs Budgers had spared no expense or effort for her Wolfie's first night home. The atmosphere at dinner was companionable, and the conversation lively and filled with laughter. This was a group that was comfortable enough with each other not to stand on ceremony and conform to the rigid expectations of how dinner conversation was normally conducted in society. Instead, Tabitha reflected, looking around the table, this felt like a loud, rambunctious family meal. Even the dowager seemed prepared to put aside her normal exacting standards of etiquette and was happily engaged, entertaining Lily and mortifying Tobias by telling increasingly personal stories about his family.

Everyone was aware that the dowager did not approve of women retiring while the men drank port. Rather, she didn't approve of that happening when she was one of the women excluded, so everyone rose together to drink port, whiskey or tea in the drawing room. Lily made her way over to the pianoforte, and Tobias followed her, happy to be of service turning the pages of music. Wolf decided to forgo port in favour of brandy, and Langley and Bear joined him. Tabitha was happy with tea and sat in an armchair by the fire, happily gazing into the flames as she listened to Lily play.

Tabitha felt all was right with the world, and any apprehension she had felt at coming to Glanwyddan Hall seemed as ephemeral as the wisps of smoke that curled up the chimney. Her eyes felt pleasantly heavy, and she was almost nodding off when she heard the drawing room door open and a polite clearing of throat as Talbot said, "Milord, I am sorry to interrupt you, but there has been an incident."

Suddenly, Tabitha was no longer tired. What incident? Were Melody and Rat alright? She jumped out of her chair, and her fears must have shown on her face. Talbot said, "The children are safe. This is, well, it's something else."

The butler paused, and the dowager exclaimed impatiently, "Out with it, man! What has happened?"

"A rock was thrown through the kitchen window and hit the scullery maid in the head. She had a fright but will be fine. One of the footmen ran outside and thought he heard someone running away. He tried to give chase, but it is very dark out there."

"So, local children are causing mischief," the dowager pronounced. "Is that any reason to disturb our evening?'

Talbot paused again, "There was a note wrapped around the rock, milady." The man held out a scrap of paper with something crudely scribbled on it.

Wolf took the paper and read it out loud: "I know what you did." He looked up and wondered, "What does this mean? Who is this even supposed to be for?" Was this message meant for him? He knew Tabitha had never visited Glanwyddan Hall, and as far as he knew, neither had Langley.

"It was thrown through the kitchen window, so it was almost certainly meant for one of the servants," the dowager said definitively. Turning to Talbot, she demanded, "Speak to them all and see who knows what this is about."

Wolf interrupted her, "Talbot, you will do no such thing. I will not begin our visit here with the servants being interrogated for no good reason. We have no reason to believe they have anything to do with this."

The dowager glared at him; he had increasingly been contradicting her recently and refusing her demands. This was unacceptable. She and Jeremy would be having words. It never occurred to the dowager countess that she was visiting Glanwyddan Hall at the new earl's pleasure. She was related to Wolf only by marriage, and he had no obligation towards her beyond what was stipulated in her dower portion. He certainly did not have to tolerate her constant interference in his life. But the dowager was a master strategist. Whatever her understanding of the precariousness of her position, she would never be foolish enough to acknowledge it. She believed that if she projected total confidence in her preeminent status, others would blindly follow.

Wolf continued, "If everyone in the kitchen is alright, if a bit shaken, let us ignore this incident. It is likely yet another prank. Is there a local constable I might speak with tomorrow?"

Talbot nodded, "I believe there is one in Lamphey who reports to the Pembrokeshire police force. I will send a note down to the village in the morning asking him to call on you, milord."

Wolf hoped that decision would calm everyone's nerves. However, it was apparent that the evening's convivial atmosphere had been ruined. Within minutes of Talbot exiting, the dowager announced that she was retiring for the night, quickly followed by Tabitha and Lady Lily. The men followed soon enough. As they all made their way up to their bedchambers, Wolf pulled Langley aside and quickly told him about the other recent incidents.

"A burned barn sounds like more than local lads causing mischief," Langley conceded.

"And perhaps in isolation, it might be, but there have been too many incidents, and now this note. Do you think it was meant for me?" Wolf asked anxiously.

"Can you think of any reason it might be?" Langley asked.

"Honestly, no. I haven't been here since I was fourteen. And in all the summers I spent here, I can't remember anyone I might have offended in any way."

Wolf paused. Langley sensed his hesitation and asked, "Except perhaps one person?"

"Truly, I can't imagine it to be the case. But I had a friend for many years. The last time I saw her, I had no reason to believe it would be the last time. But my grandfather died that winter, and my uncle Philip had no desire to keep the connection to his brother's family. Perhaps she is hurt that I never returned."

"Hurt enough to burn down a barn?" Langley asked sceptically.

"I wouldn't have thought so. I'm not even sure if she still lives in Lamphey. But I'm sure Mrs Budgers knows. I'll ask her tomorrow. If Glynnie is still here, perhaps I'll go and visit. I was thinking to do so anyway."

"If and when you do, I'll come with you," Lord Langley offered.

Wolf looked at the man he had suspected of murder only a few months ago and who had then kidnapped Melody, causing them all to be suspicious of him for some time afterwards. How was it that Langley had won them all over so much that he was now a trusted friend and confidant? Because that is what he was. Wolf had always had a difficult relationship with his father and had long felt he was able to go through life without paternal guidance. However, in Langley, he found an older, wiser man whose opinion he valued and whose warm friendship had somehow surprised both him and Tabitha with its steadfastness.

"Thank you, Langley. I appreciate that," Wolf said sincerely.

CHAPTER 5

Early the next morning, Wolf rose and went to the kitchen in search of Mrs Budgers. He found her with her apron covered in flour, busy kneading bread for lunch. When she saw him come in, she took her hands out of the bread and grinned broadly. "Wolfie, what are you doing in here? You don't need to sneak down to the kitchen to steal biscuits anymore."

Wolf sat down at the kitchen table. There was a pot of tea on the table, and he poured himself a cup. The cook wiped off her hands and went and brought a plate of scones over and a pot of jam. Wolf slathered his scone with the strawberry jam, took a bite and groaned in pleasure, "Budgie, they're even better than I remember." Mrs Budgers glowed with pleasure at the compliment. Wolf took another bite, then said, "Budgie, I don't know if you remember my friend all those years ago, Glynnie."

"O' course I remember the sweet girl," Mrs Budgers answered. "She was Elinor's daughter. God bless her soul."

"Was? What happened to her?"

"Glynda, for that's what she went by when she was grown, stayed in Lamphey and married the blacksmith's son, Rhys Thomas. They had seven children and seemed happy enough. Then, she was brutally murdered just a couple of weeks ago now, it must be. Her husband Rhys was arrested for the murder. He's being held over until the next assize. Terrible business. Just think of all those poor children who will be orphaned when their da hangs for the murder of their mam."

Wolf was surprised at how affected he was by the shocking

news of Glynnie's death. While he hadn't thought of his childhood friend in more than fifteen years, returning to Glanwyddan Hall had brought back memories of how much her companionship had meant to him during those otherwise unpleasant visits to see his grandfather. Wolf wanted to understand more about Glynnie's murder and why her husband was the main suspect, but he knew better than to think that dear Budgie would be a source of anything more than the village gossip. The local constable had been asked to visit that morning, and now there were two things to discuss with him.

Putting aside the topic of Glynnie's murder, Wolf asked Mrs Budgers about some of the other servants who had been kind to him as a boy. The old butler had died, and the housekeeper had been pensioned off and had gone to live with her niece in Swansea. However, there was a maid who had married the grocer's boy and still lived in the village. Wolf had particularly warm memories of this maid, Cadi. She hadn't been much older than Wolf and yet had shown him an almost motherly comfort. Cadi had been responsible for laying the fire in his hearth every morning and bringing him his hot chocolate before he rose. She joined the household a few years before the old earl's death, and for the few years that they overlapped at Glanwyddan Hall, Wolf always looked forward to her sunny smile and cheery disposition when he woke. Wolf asked Mrs Budgers where Cadi lived and determined to visit her.

Tabitha had also awoken early after a restless night. Despite her initial fears when they had first received news of the pranks at the estate, Tabitha had managed to put those fears aside during their trip to Wales and had been determined to enjoy her first Christmas with Wolf, Melly, and Rat. However, the mysterious note the evening before had brought all those fears to the forefront, and she was tempted to suggest to Wolf that she take the children and return to London.

Ginny had brought her some tea and toast, and as she sat in bed nibbling on a crust, Tabitha asked her maid, "Ginny, what do the servants think about all these things that have been happening at the Hall?" Only a few years older than Tabitha, Ginny was an Irish girl who had been her lady's maid since Tabitha was fifteen, and there was a strong, trusting bond between the two. During previous investigations, Ginny had proven herself to be an intelligent, observant woman who had often discovered useful pieces of information from below stairs. Tabitha knew that Ginny's friendliness and willingness to help out usually ingratiated her with other servants and that the woman kept her ears open for any pertinent gossip that she could relay back to her mistress.

"It seems that at first, the consensus was that it was boys from the village. Apparently, there's a gang of them, headed up by the baker's son, who are troublemakers."

"They think these boys burned the barn down?"

"Well, they didn't at first. It seems there have been some problems with vagrants recently. The stableboy had found some evidence that one had been sleeping in one of the barns, and he thought that perhaps he had set a fire and hadn't tamped it down properly when he moved on."

"But now they think it might have been these boys?" Tabitha asked.

"I'm not sure anyone knows what to think at this point. You know how servants can be, particularly ones in the country; rumours fly around, and gossip brought up from the village gives everyone something exciting to think about. I will tell you this: that rock through the window shook everyone. None of the resident servants believe that the local boys would have done that. Talbot wouldn't say what the note said, and now their tongues are wagging, speculating on what it was about."

Tabitha thought about Ginny's words, "What kind of speculation?" Even before she had begun investigating with Wolf, Tabitha had been aware of just how much servants see and hear. Often treated as invisible by the aristocrats they served, servants were often privy to deep, dark secrets and innermost family tensions. Certainly, Tabitha tried always to be aware of what she said and did in front of her household staff.

"It runs the gamut. Most of it is silly stuff."

"Such as?"

"Well, it seems there's a strong belief in fairy folk locally. Mrs Budgers was telling me that fairies are known to be mischievous and that this is typical fairy behaviour," Ginny explained.

Knowing the Irish also to be a superstitious people who gave a lot of credence to similar myths and legends, Tabitha didn't want to throw aspersions on what Ginny was telling her. However, she couldn't help but say, "Do fairies usually throw rocks through windows?"

Ginny laughed, "Not in Ireland, they don't. But perhaps Welsh fairies are more aggressive."

"Well, just let me know if any more serious theories surface in the servants' hall," Tabitha requested.

The dowager had not slept any better than Tabitha. She hated being back in this godforsaken place. Everything reminded her of the past, of Philip, of all the pain and humiliation she had been forced to endure. The day the dowager had learned of Philip's fatal fall from his horse had been the happiest of her life. It was a day she always secretly celebrated, raising a glass of champagne and toasting herself and the woman she was finally able to become when freed from the shackles of her marriage.

The dowager had always claimed that her major complaint against Tabitha was that she had been an insufficiently docile wife and had provoked and enraged Jonathan. However, the truth was, she had witnessed Tabitha's wifely subservience, and it was so much more than the dowager had even managed. Of course, Jonathan was not a drunken fool like his father, and his cruelty was far more considered and far harder to escape. When she considered it now, the dowager wasn't sure why she had so despised Tabitha for falling victim to a similar matrimonial fate as her own. And she certainly wasn't sure why she begrudged the girl her relief at the accident of fate that delivered her connubial freedom. In her more honest moments, she admitted to herself that perhaps she was jealous that Tabitha only had to endure two years with her husband and managed to escape without bearing his children.

Withers had brought the dowager her cup of tea, and like Tabitha, the dowager took the opportunity to question her maid about her impressions of the household. The dowager did not have as relaxed a relationship with her lady's maid as Tabitha did. Still, the dowager trusted and respected her opinion, at least as much as she could ever trust any servant's. Perhaps most importantly, Withers had been with the dowager for almost forty years. She knew some of the dowager's marital history and had accompanied her mistress on her very occasional visits to Glanwyddan Hall before Philip had died, and so she knew Mrs Budgers.

The dowager asked many of the same questions Tabitha had and received very similar answers. Hearing the staff's superstitious explanations for the goings-on, the dowager said derisively, "The ignorant beliefs of the masses! Perhaps there is something to the idea of compulsory education for all children if it lifts people out of such irrational, ridiculous thinking."

Tea was not going to be sufficient, the dowager decided and sent Withers back down to the kitchen to fetch her a cup of coffee. While her maid was gone, the dowager thought about how best to learn the information she wanted without giving more away than necessary. Withers was privy to many of her mistress' secrets, but certainly not her deepest, darkest ones. And the secret the dowager worried was imperilled was her darkest.

Withers returned with the cup of coffee and some Welsh shortbread biscuits that the dowager had always found to be one of the only good things about the region. The dowager took a bite and savoured the rich, buttery taste, then, attempting a nonchalant tone, said, "Before you came to work for me, I had a lady's maid who ended up marrying one of the footmen here. I believe his name was David. Of course, he'd be too old to be in service here anymore, I assume."

"Whether or not he'd be too old, the Hall functions with a very bare staff normally. It's Mrs Budgers, a few maids, the stable boy, and some gardeners. Just enough to keep the place running. My understanding is that your son rarely visited, and so the place hasn't been lived in since your husband's death. When was that now? 1889?"

"1888," the dowager answered. She kept track of how many years she'd been celebrating.

"Yes, that's right. I remember now. Anyway, I believe some of the footmen and other servants were kept on for a few years by the steward. But eventually, they either moved on or were let go."

Hoping to keep the casual conversational tone going, the dowager mused, "I wonder how many of them remained in the locality? I believe there are other great houses not far from here. In fact, I believe that we are hosting some local gentry and others this evening for dinner." Normally, the idea of mingling with untitled gentry was abhorrent to the dowager. However, she had been persuaded that their trip to Pembrokeshire would be quite dull if she refused to socialise with anyone who wasn't at least a baron.

As it happened, recently the dowager had grown to appreciate the company of some of the lower classes, East End gangsters, madams and prostitutes amongst them. She had even started to believe such people to be more interesting companions than her usual society cronies. Tabitha had suggested that perhaps this newfound interest in the masses might extend to the landed gentry. The dowager had doubted this would be the case, but had deigned to mingle with them, nonetheless.

Withers was not as good at gaining the trust of other servants as Ginny and definitely not as adept a gatherer of information. She shook her head at the dowager's question; she had no idea what had happened to the estate's prior servants and hoped her mistress wasn't going to task her with finding out. Luckily for the maid, her mistress had other ideas about how to glean the information she was after. Suddenly, very eager to be up and dressed, the dowager commanded, "Get my green walking dress. I believe I will go and find the children and see if they would like a tour of the gardens."

CHAPTER 6

Throughout her few visits to Glanwyddan Hall over the years, the dowager hadn't had any cause to visit the nursery. When she had brought her children to Wales for the occasional visit, the nursery had been the nanny's domain. As they were when they were in London, the children had been paraded before their parents, or at least their mother, in the drawing room every afternoon at four. The dowager had inspected them as they stood to attention, perhaps had one of the girls play an air on the piano, and then dismissed them with a curt nod of the head. However, now she needed to find out where the nursery was; the dowager wanted to maintain a low profile for her conversation with Rat and went in search of him and Melody.

During her recent solo investigation, the dowager had found the young boy to be an intelligent and discreet confidante. At the conclusion of that case, Tabitha and Wolf had spoken to the dowager in a stern tone that she felt wholly inappropriate. They had expressly forbidden her from involving Rat in any further investigations that she might take on. All she had heard was their acknowledgement that there would be future investigations. There had been no doubt in her mind, but it was satisfying to hear it from them. In fact, unbeknownst to Tabitha and Wolf, the dowager had already had cards made with the inscription, The Investigative Countess, Rapier Sharp Logic paired with Great Insight and Boldness. A Private Inquiry Agent. It was quite a long title to fit on a card, but the dowager was thrilled with how it looked and sounded. Because the cards had to be larger than her usual calling cards in order to fit all the wording, she had ordered a specially made sterling silver case, which she had taken to always carrying in her reticule; one never knew when a situation might arise in which one needed to present credentials.

As she dressed, the dowager had casually asked Withers where the nursery was located and now made her way to the floor above, where the sound of childish laughter assured her she was going in the right direction. That laughter was accompanied by barking. Even better! Dodo would give her the perfect excuse to take the children outside. Walking into the nursery, the dowager found Melody and Rat eating breakfast while Dodo ran around in circles, trying to catch her tail. As a rule, the dowager was not an animal lover. Anything with four legs and fur reminded her far too much of her husband, who had never met a dog or horse he didn't like more than any human. But even she had to admit there was something quite loveable about the puppy, particularly now she had learned some manners and was able to sit and lie down on command.

Looking up as the dowager entered the room, Melody cried out, "Granny, look at how silly Dodo is being."

The dowager felt no strong attachment to any of her children and, until her recent extended exposure to Lady Lily, hadn't felt any warmer towards her grandchildren. However, for reasons the dowager couldn't quite explain, Melody had quickly and decisively brought out a grandmotherly urge in her that surprised her as much as it did everybody else. The orphaned former street urchin was an adorable child; the red-gold ringlets, freckles and large blue eyes gave her the appearance of a perfect china doll. However, the child's charm went far beyond appearances; she was very intelligent and had an astuteness that the dowager recognised and respected. Her own grandchildren didn't call her Granny, yet she not only permitted but delighted in hearing it when said by Melody.

Rat stood as the dowager entered the room. She was very fond of the boy and was impressed by how Lord Langley had improved his manners and speech. She knew that the earl, who worked for British Intelligence, was hoping to train Rat for some kind of security-related role. The dowager agreed that the boy was worth the time and effort. Thinking about Langley reminded the dowager that Rat was supposed to be meeting him in the library at ten to continue his studies. Glancing at the clock on the mantle of the nursery, she realised that if she wished to go for a walk with him, she should get to the point with all haste. "Rat, Melody, how would you like to come for a walk around the grounds with me? It certainly seems as if Dodo could do with some exercise."

Melody jumped up and clapped her hands with gleeful anticipation. For reasons that Tabitha couldn't really fathom, the old woman was a particular favourite of Melody's. However, Tabitha recognised the advantages that being championed by the Dowager Countess of Pembroke could bestow on the child and so gladly enabled their relationship, even if it mystified her somewhat.

Rat looked less excited about the walk and glanced nervously at the clock. "I know that you have an appointment to meet with Lord Langley, and I promised I will not cause you to be late," the dowager assured him. "We will not walk far."

Nodding his agreement with the plan, Rat said he would go and fetch his coat and meet them in the imposing entrance hall. Not ten minutes later, the dowager, Rat, Melody, Mary and Dodo set off for their walk. It was a cold but crisp and dry December morning, and the dowager breathed in the clean air; it was one of the only redeeming features of the countryside.

Melody and Dodo ran ahead, with Mary in pursuit. The dowager wasn't quite sure how to begin the conversation. In truth, she wasn't even entirely sure what she wanted to ask the boy to do. Finally, realising that she was wasting precious time, she began, "Rat, I never got a chance to thank you properly for your help with my last investigation."

Rat looked sheepish. He had been persuaded to confess to Tabitha and Wolf about the dowager's investigative activities, her visit to one brothel, and her expedition to Villiers Street. Rat might have been his name, but it was not his nature. The young boy had spent enough time on the harsh streets of Whitechapel to understand his transgression in not keeping the dowager's confidence.

Realising some of the boy's apprehension, the dowager assured him, "I know why you told Lord Pembroke what you knew, and I don't blame you. In fact, I'm grateful that you did. Who knows how things might have turned out if he had not found me when he did." Rat looked relieved. The dowager paused, considered how best to phrase her request, then continued, "You were so very helpful on that case. If it were not for your insights, the case might never have been solved. I can see why Lord Langley believes you worthy of his time and effort; you are a very observant and resourceful young man."

Indeed, Rat was a very observant child, and he intuited that this conversation was more than a friendly chat. The boy had a very strong sense of how lucky he and Melody were; one day, they were orphans living hand-to-mouth on the harsh Whitechapel streets, and the next, they were living in Mayfair mansions, well-fed, dressed in nice clothes, sleeping in warm, comfortable beds, and loved and cherished. They were safe and secure. Rat hadn't minded his Whitechapel life so much for himself, but he had been consumed with fear and worry for his little sister ever since the death of his parents had forced him into the role of protector and provider. Knowing that Melly was not only being taken care of but would be raised as a proper lady was beyond anything Rat could have ever dreamed of. He was also astute enough to realise the power the dowager countess had to make their lives easier or more difficult if she chose. Given this, he was predisposed to help her in any way he was able.

The dowager said as casually as she could, "You must miss spending time with boys your own age."

What was the answer she was looking for, Rat wondered. In truth, it had been a long time since Rat had the luxury of playtime with other children. Even when his parents were alive, money had always been tight and, from a young age, Rat had done odd jobs wherever he could find them. Rat sensed that the dowager wanted him to say that he did miss it, and so answered, "Maybe it would be nice. Sometimes. Not that I'm complaining. I'm very grateful to Lord Langley and I enjoy my studies very much."

"Of course, of course," the dowager said. "You know, the village of Lamphey is very close, and I'm sure there are boys your age down there who might make good playmates." Where was she going with this?

"Maybe when you are finished with your lessons for Lord Langley today, you could take Dodo for a walk down to the village. I am sure no one would object to such an outing." She paused again, then said in as casual a tone as possible, "There used to be some servants at Glanwyddan Hall who got married. I wonder if they're still living locally. I would love to pay them a visit. One of them was my lady's maid."

If Rat wondered why the dowager didn't just ask Mrs Budgers, he kept that thought to himself. Instead, he asked, "Would you like me to ask around and see if anyone knows?"

Smart lad, the dowager thought. "What a wonderful idea, Rat. Why did I not think of it?" She shared her maid's first and maiden names. She said she didn't remember the name of the footman her maid had married, then added, as if it was an afterthought, "Of course, such inquiries would have to be made with great discretion."

Again, Rat was bright enough not to ask why such discretion might be needed. For her part, the dowager was very satisfied with how the conversation had gone; Rat was quick on the uptake and wise enough not to ask questions. If the dowager felt any twinge of guilt at yet again pulling Rat into a situation she knew Tabitha and Wolf would not approve of, she managed to put it to the back of her mind, telling herself that she was not asking the boy to do anything wrong or even remotely dangerous. She had merely asked him to ask around for the whereabouts of people who had once worked for her. Really, it was all so innocent she could almost imagine confessing her request to Tabitha. Almost.

They walked for a few minutes more, but grey clouds had started to gather and threaten rain. Aware that Rat needed to return to the house to meet with Langley anyway, the dowager had him run ahead to get Melly and Mary, who were throwing sticks for Dodo to chase. The group managed to make it back into the house just as plump raindrops began to fall. The dowager silently hoped that the weather had cleared by the afternoon so there would be no delay in Rat fulfilling her request.

CHAPTER 7

At eleven o'clock sharp, the local constable, PC Ian Evans, presented himself at Glanwyddan Hall. PC Evans prided himself on his strict timekeeping. He had been the Lamphey constable for the past twenty years, and up until the last few weeks, this had been an easy job that primarily consisted of making sure the peace was kept in the village after a particularly rowdy night at the local hostelry, the Stag and Hounds. Every so often, there was a dispute over sheep that required him to weigh in with Solomon-like wisdom, and once, a body had been found floating in the stream on Brynn Davis' land. Luckily, it was quickly determined that the body was a well-known drunk and troublemaker from a nearby village. A decision was made that whatever had befallen the man must have happened there, and the body merely drifted down to Lamphey, relieving PC Evans of any responsibility.

Ian Evans was a ruddy-faced, stocky man who most enjoyed the parts of his job that involved stopping in to chat with villagers and taking a cup of tea and a slice of fruitcake while he was there. It was quite a few hours since Mrs Evans had sent him off with his usual breakfast of sausages and eggs, and PC Evans did wonder if the earl would offer him some refreshments. He had tried Mrs Budgers' scones when she had brought some to the local church fair in the summer, and he wouldn't mind one or two of those.

The constable was shown into the drawing room. He had only ever been in the servant's hall and was quite overawed with the magnificence of the grand reception room. There were many rooms Wolf could have received the constable in, but Tabitha had persuaded him that the drawing room was the most formal and the most likely to set the appropriate tone. Wolf hadn't wanted to ask what tone that might be; left to his own devices, he would have been happy to receive the man in the more comfortable morning sitting room.

The constable had never met the last earl, Wolf's cousin Jonathan. However, he had known Jonathan's father, Philip. This was mostly because the man liked to escape his father's critical eye and drink in the Stag and Hounds, surrounded by curious but friendly villagers. PC Evans hadn't thought much of the then viscount and hadn't been surprised at how he met his maker. At first blush, this new earl seemed to be a more serious-looking, respectable man, even if his hair was a little too long.

There had been plenty of gossip in the village about the new earl's visit, particularly about his companions. Mrs Morris at the bakery was sure that the younger Lady Pembroke was the earl's wife, but Mrs Thomas, who cleaned for Reverend Lewis, said that she knew for a fact that the earl was unmarried. Mrs Evans had sent her husband out that morning with strict instructions to gather intelligence on the matter so that she might reclaim her rightful spot as the preeminent gossip in Lamphey, and possibly beyond.

There were people in the village who had some memory of the dowager countess, and there was some talk amongst the older villagers about happenings when she visited in the past. There hadn't been a lot of details, rather just whispers and a few old women crossing themselves when her name came up. That had been enough to make PC Evans happy that it was the younger Lady Pembroke with the earl in the drawing room rather than the elder.

"PC Evans, isn't it?" Wolf said, approaching the nervous constable with his hand outstretched. PC Evans hadn't been sure if he was expected to bow and so was relieved the decision was made for him as he grasped the other man's hand. "Thank you for coming so promptly." He gestured towards Tabitha, "This is Lady Pembroke." Well, that didn't clear anything up, did it? PC Evans resigned himself to Mrs Evans' displeasure when he returned home that evening.

Tabitha sat, and Wolf indicated that the constable should take a comfortable-looking armchair. Constable Evans was a mild-mannered man who had never entertained ideas above his station. Once seated, he patiently waited for the earl to begin the conversation.

Wolf decided that as much as he wanted to learn more details about Glynnie's death, the more pressing issue was the disturbing happenings at the Hall. "Constable Evans, I'm not sure if you are aware of some of the mischief that has been directed towards Glanwyddan Hall over the last few weeks."

Constable Evans was relieved to be able to answer in the affirmative, at least to some extent, "I did come out and take a look at the burned barn. To tell you the truth, m'lord, I didn't see any evidence that it was arson. We've had a problem with vagrants of late. Ever since so many of the quarries were crippled, there have been a lot of men out of work who've lost everything. I feel bad for them. I really do, but not bad enough to turn Lamphey into a vagrants' camp. And so many of them aren't even local but came in from all over during the boom. We take care of our own here, but these men came for the good times and never bothered to integrate in. Now they've fallen on hard times, seems to me they should go back to where they came from."

Wolf was not interested in hearing the constable's views on the state of labour and immigration in Wales. Given the subsequent incidents, he did not doubt that the barn burning was arson. He quickly brought the constable up to speed on the string of incidents ending with the note thrown through the window the previous evening.

Partway through Wolf's story, Talbot entered with a tea tray laden with scones and cake. PC Evans was determined to string his visit out long enough that he could have at least one scone, maybe two. And if he wasn't mistaken, the cake was Teisen Lap, a delicious Welsh fruitcake that he was quite partial to. While it was hard to imagine that Mrs Budgers' baking could hold a candle to Mrs Evans', Teisen Lap was not part of Mrs Evans' regular repertoire, and her husband was willing to put any spousal cake loyalty aside to partake of Mrs Budgers'.

Tabitha must have seen him look longingly at the tea tray, for she said, "Perhaps you would like a cup of tea and a scone or piece of cake before you give Lord Pembroke your professional assessment."

PC Evans agreed that a cup of tea would be very welcome and that he'd not insult Mrs Budgers by refusing one of her famous scones. There was strawberry jam and cream provided, and Talbot ensured that the constable was amply supplied with both and then added a slice of fruitcake to the plate for good measure. PC Evans' eyes gleamed with gustatory anticipation. Seeing this, Wolf suspected it would not be hard to persuade the constable to return to the Hall if necessary.

A few eager bites of his scone later, PC Evans realised that he had likely kept the earl and countess waiting long enough for an answer. He washed his scone down with a large gulp of tea and said, "I will ask around in the village and see what I can find out. There is no reason to believe there is any ill will harboured towards your family. Indeed, it's been so long since anyone was in residence here that I wonder how many people have ever interacted with any of you."

Gesturing towards Tabitha, Wolf confirmed, "Lady Pembroke never visited while my cousin, her late husband, was alive."

Ah! Thought Constable Evans. Mrs Evans was going to be delighted with that titbit.

Wolf continued, "And, of course, I visited when my grandfather was still alive, but that was more than fifteen years ago, and I was no more than a child at the time." He considered his next words, "As far as I know, the older Lady Pembroke was never a frequent visitor and certainly stopped coming altogether when her husband died, if not earlier. It's hard to imagine that any of this is directed at any of us personally.

However, after that note last night, it's equally hard to believe these are harmless pranks."

PC Evans was not normally particularly astute, but his desire for another scone spurred him to think more deeply than he was usually wont to do. "From what you've said, most of the dead animals were left outside of the back door, and the rock was thrown through the kitchen window. Perhaps none of this is aimed at the family but at one of the servants."

This was an interesting idea, and both Tabitha and Wolf were surprised that it had come from the seemingly rather dull-witted policeman. "Constable Evans, can I tempt you with another scone?" Tabitha offered by way of a reward for the insight.

Another piece of cake followed the second scone, but if Tabitha had hoped that PC Evans might be inspired to any more feats of intellect, she was to be sorely disappointed. When it became evident that there was nothing else useful to be gleaned from the greedy constable, Wolf thanked him for his time. "Do let me know if your inquiries in the village uncover anything," Wolf said as he rose.

PC Evans took the hint and left quickly with one last longing glance at the scones. He would certainly do what he could to uncover enough information to justify a return visit.

Wolf turned to Tabitha and asked, "So what do you think of the good constable's suggestion?"

After considering the question for a moment, Tabitha replied, "There may be something to what he suggested. However, the timing seems a trifle suspicious. Our visit has been planned for two weeks now, and I'm sure every tradesman in the village and beyond was aware of our imminent arrival. Extra staff were hired, so I'm sure there isn't a person in a five-mile radius who didn't have some awareness the Earl of Pembroke would be spending Christmas at the Hall."

Wolf agreed, but he also thought it was too soon to discount the constable's theory. Thinking over what PC Evans had suggested, he asked, "Are there any of the Chesterton House servants who have ever been here before?"

Tabitha considered the question. Before her marriage to Jonathan, the dowager's butler Manning had been the butler at Chesterton House, and so had likely been to Glanwyddan Hall on multiple occasions. However, Manning was not with them for this visit. Though, would the locals have anticipated that? "Mrs Jenkins has been on staff for many years. But it is very hard imagining her having offended anyone enough to inspire such actions. I am not sure how long Withers has been Mama's lady's maid." She thought about the quiet but rather stern maid. While she didn't know Withers well, Tabitha had always thought she was precisely the kind of person who could survive decades with the difficult dowager. It wasn't impossible that such a person might have made a few enemies along the way. Voicing this thought, she said, "It may be worth asking Mama about Withers and any other servants who were with her back then."

"Drat," Wolf exclaimed. "I forgot to ask PC Evans about Glynnie."

Tabitha raised her eyebrows. She had no idea who this Glynnie was and why Wolf might need to talk to the constable about her. Wolf had told her very little about his visits to Glanwyddan Hall beyond his affection for Mrs Budgers. Was this Glynnie another servant?

Seeing the unspoken question play out on Tabitha's face, Wolf explained, "Glynnie, or Glynda as she apparently was called as an adult, was a girl from the village who was my only playmate during my childhood visits. I met her that first summer I was here, I could not have been more than five or six years old. We used to meet in the treehouse, every day if we could both get away. I haven't thought much about her since my last visit here before my grandfather's death. Coming back has stirred up lots of memories, most bad, but some less unpleasant. And some of the best memories are of the times I spent playing with Glynnie. I asked Mrs Budgers if she still lived in the village. She told me that she had, but that about two weeks ago, she was brutally murdered and that her husband has been arrested for the crime."

Tabitha gasped. Whatever she'd been expecting Wolf to say, this wasn't it. "I am so sorry, Wolf. That must have been so upsetting to hear. What were you planning to ask PC Evans?"

"I am not entirely sure," Wolf admitted. "I suppose I wanted to understand more about what happened and why Glynnie's husband is the main suspect. Budgie told me Glynnie has, I mean had, children who, of course, will be orphaned if their father hangs for the murder of their mother. Perhaps I thought that if I could do anything to disprove his guilt, it would be a way to repay Glynnie for her companionship to a very lonely boy all those years ago."

Tabitha had been sitting on an armchair next to the sofa Wolf had sat on during their conversation with PC Evans. Now, she rose and came and sat next to him, placing her hand in his. "I suspect that dear PC Evans would not have been a source of much useful information. That does not mean that we cannot try to perform Glynnie that final service. I am sure Mrs Budgers knows who the local magistrate is. Let us pay him a visit and see what we can learn."

Wolf brought her hand up to his mouth and kissed it. Then, throwing caution to the wind, he gently cupped her face, stroking her cheek with his thumb before leaning towards her and brushing her lips with a kiss of gossamer lightness. As gentle as the kiss was, it nevertheless caused Tabitha to flush with a heat that Wolf's every touch seemed to generate. Leaning into him, Tabitha kissed Wolf back with an urgency that surprised them both. The kiss deepened, and they both forgot that they were sitting in the drawing room and might be discovered at any moment. A sudden sound from the doorway caused them to spring apart.

CHAPTER 8

The dowager countess had a pretty good idea of what she had just walked in on. If she hadn't had strong suspicions before that moment, the guilty looks worn by Wolf and Tabitha were confirmation enough. She hadn't spent much time around the pair of them together since the conclusion of their last investigation, but in the time she had been in their company, the observant old woman could tell there was a change in their relationship. Did they really believe that the longing glances and secret smiles fooled her? The dowager had been tempted to say something at some point during the trip to Wales, but there had never been a time when the three of them were alone. Certainly, Melody was far too intelligent for them to have had the conversation in the carriage without her being aware of the topic.

The dowager had complicated feelings about the obviously burgeoning romance between Tabitha and Wolf. Her knee-jerk reaction towards Tabitha was disapproval. However, the dowager admitted to herself, indeed, had even admitted to Tabitha when they were in Brighton, that the younger woman was the devil the dowager knew. It was inevitable that Wolf would marry; he was a young, handsome, rich aristocrat. Once the season was underway, the scheming mamas would be throwing their daughters in his path at every turn. Tabitha was a known quantity as a daughter-in-law. It seemed she might even harbour some affection for the dowager. Certainly, even the dowager had to admit that Tabitha had been very accommodating of the dowager's desire to spend time with

Melody. However, if Wolf were to marry someone else, Tabitha would have to leave Chesterton House and would take Melody with her. A different future Lady Pembroke might be far less accommodating towards the dowager's self-appointed role as family matriarch.

"Mama, you are up and about early," Tabitha said, desperately hoping that the dowager hadn't noticed anything untoward.

"I am not sure why you would say such a thing," the dowager said, sniffing in faux high dudgeon. In truth, she didn't usually emerge from her bedchamber much before noon if she could help it. However, that was not for Tabitha to comment on. Even as she thought this, the dowager realised that Tabitha had said the first thing she could think of in an attempt to distract the dowager from anything she might have thought she witnessed. A lesser woman might have generously allowed the couple such a charade; the dowager was not so easily played and continued, "I am quite insulted by your suggestion. In fact, I have already been out for a walk in the gardens with Rat, Melody and even the dog."

The dowager was under no illusion that her morning stroll with the children would not come to Tabitha and Wolf's notice and so decided it would attract far less notice if she were the one to mention it.

Tabitha narrowed her eyes. She was suspicious. The dowager was not known for her love of exercise. However, perhaps her dictates against walking only applied in London. Certainly, Tabitha couldn't imagine what ulterior motive the dowager might have, and so she decided not to question the statement.

The dowager continued into the room, noticed PC Evans' plate and cup on the side table next to the chair he had sat in, and asked, "Was there a visitor this morning? I was not informed of any caller."

"Yes, Lady Pembroke. If you remember, I sent a note down to the local constable asking him to call on me this morning," Wolf said.

"Ah yes, I do remember now. And did the gentleman have

anything illuminating to say?"

Wolf replied, "The constable suggested a twist on what you mentioned last night: that this mischief targets not the family but the staff. His thought was that it might be aimed at one of the servants who has been in service long enough to have visited in the past."

The dowager didn't answer immediately. Instead, she took the seat recently vacated by the constable, steepled her hands, lightly tapping her fingertips together as if contemplating Wolf's words. At first glance, it seemed as if she were genuinely considering the suggestion. However, there was something in her attitude that made Tabitha wonder what was really going through the old woman's mind. Tabitha knew better than to play chess with the dowager countess, who could think many moves ahead of even the most nimble-minded opponent.

Finally, the dowager said, "Of the servants with us on this trip, only Withers and Mrs Jenkins have ever previously visited Glanwyddan Hall. I find it hard to believe that either woman managed to engender such hatred."

"I think it best that we talk to both of them, just to be sure. If nothing else, there may be something one of them remembers," Wolf suggested.

Tabitha watched the dowager's face as the suggestion was made and was surprised by the emotion she saw flash briefly across the woman's face before being quickly replaced by a forced insouciance: fear. "Is there some reason we should not talk to Withers and Mrs Jenkins?" Tabitha asked.

"I believe it was Jeremy who said, just last night, that we should not be interrogating the servants about this matter," the dowager countered defensively.

Wolf pointed out, "What I said was that we should not interrogate them for no good reason. That certainly was not a blanket statement."

"I cannot have any say over your treatment of Mrs Jenkins. She is your housekeeper now. However, I can and will have dominion over my servants." The dowager was almost certain that Withers knew nothing, but she would not take that chance if she could help it.

Tabitha glanced at Wolf, wondering if he was thinking what she was. Originally, talking to Withers had been a long shot at best, but the more the dowager fought it, the more it seemed that the lady's maid might know something.

A similar thought had crossed Wolf's mind, and he now found himself in a delicate situation. The dowager was correct; she did have authority over Withers. However, she didn't have the final say at Glanwyddan Hall or within the Pembroke estate, he did. Wolf knew the dowager well enough to realise that if he insisted on his pre-eminence in this situation, there was a good chance the old woman would counter by packing her bags and leaving. If Withers was somehow the target or cause of the pranks, this might cause them to cease, but at what cost? Certainly, if he forced the dowager countess out just before Christmas into the wilds of Wales, he would never hear the end of it.

Tabitha's thoughts had run in a similar direction. Hoping to save Wolf from an escalation of hostilities, she replied, "Mama, of course, we will not talk with Withers at the moment if that is what you desire. However," Tabitha put a heavy emphasis on this word and paused briefly before she continued, "if we cannot make any progress with getting to the bottom of this mischief, and more importantly, if there are any further incidents, then Wolf may have to insist."

At this final comment, Tabitha looked to Wolf, worried that she may have overstepped in speaking for him. She needn't have worried; he flashed her a grateful smile and concurred, "Indeed, Lady Pembroke, as Tabitha says, we will put this aside for now, but I cannot promise that we will not revisit the topic of Withers later."

The dowager knew when to hold her fire and take a tactical win. She nodded her acceptance of Wolf's conditions. The wily old woman also knew that she had inflamed Tabitha and Wolf's suspicions, and she silently berated herself for showing her hand. Perhaps she should have let them speak with Withers.

The woman had certainly proven her discretion and loyalty over the years. However, to rescind her prohibition now would be an unthinkable retreat. No, she would merely regroup and consider her next move. Depending on what Rat was able to uncover in the village, perhaps the threat was not what she thought it was.

Deciding to change the topic to one less uncomfortable, the dowager asked, "And what of the arrangements for this evening's festivities? If I am to be subjected to the Welsh masses, I should at least be able to prepare myself."

Tabitha sighed and said, "Mama, how is it that you are perfectly happy to socialise with your Ladies of KB and even Mickey D, and yet the idea of spending the evening with the local landed gentry and other notables is beyond the pale?"

The question was a fair one to which the dowager didn't have a perfectly rational answer. Why was it that she so enjoyed the company of a Whitechapel gangster and a group of colourful lightskirts, and yet the thought of the middle classes, or even the lower echelons of the upper classes, was so abhorrent to her? Her only justification was that, in truth, she also found most of the aristocracy to be crashing bores, but at least they were her peers. However, being bored by lesser mortals was more than she could endure. Unwilling to state this so baldly, she answered, "Tabitha, it goes without saying that I will be a gracious hostess no matter how many local solicitors and mercers risen above their station parade through the drawing room tonight. Just know, I will not be happy about it!"

"In reviewing my steward's suggestions for possible invitees, I saw no one likely to offend your sensibilities," Wolf observed. "I believe there is a pair of spinster sisters whose father was a baron, the local vicar and his wife, a Mr Prescott and his daughter who live on the neighbouring estate, Squire Partridge, who is the local magistrate, and finally, Sir Jerome and his wife, Lady Anna."

"If reciting this list was supposed to placate me, Jeremy, then you do not know me very well at all," the dowager told Wolf. She accompanied her statement with her signature sniff of disapproval. "The local vicar? A man whose only claim to any standing is the good fortune to have land abutting the Pembroke estate? Is Pembrokeshire truly such a social wasteland that Jones could not even conjure up an actual baron and instead presents us with the spinster offspring of one?"

"Mama, you were one of the strongest advocates for Wolf presenting himself to the local populace," Tabitha pointed out.

"Indeed I was, and I stand by that suggestion. The new Earl of Pembroke needed to be seen taking command of the estate by his tenants. However, at no time did I suggest that he should lower himself to mixing in whatever passes for society in this godforsaken place. Certainly, I did not foresee that I would be expected to join him in this lowering of the family standards for acceptable dinner companions."

It was evident to Tabitha and Wolf that this argument was going nowhere. It was futile to point out the dowager's contrariness in happily having Mickey D as a dinner companion but being offended at the thought of sharing a meal with the local landowners. Tabitha only hoped that the dowager would keep her abhorrence of their guests to herself that evening.

CHAPTER 9

Rat had finished his lesson with Lord Langley at twelve thirty and had then gone to the nursery to have lunch with Melody. The morning rain had passed, and Rat thought he might as well go to the village as per Lady Pembroke's request. Telling Mary that he was going to take Dodo for a walk down to the village, he attached the dog's lead to her collar, scooped her up, and headed down to the kitchen. There was no reason why Rat couldn't come and go through the Hall's front door, but he still felt more comfortable leaving the way the servants did.

Having left word of his destination with Mary, Rat didn't worry that he would be missed, at least until dinner. Walking through the kitchen, he couldn't help but be distracted by the wonderful smells. Mrs Budgers was busy baking for afternoon tea. Seeing the young boy, the kindly cook asked, "Would you like a shortbread? I have scones in the oven, but they won't be done for a bit."

Rat nodded eagerly and gratefully accepted two shortbread biscuits. Unable to resist trying one, he took a bite. "These are delicious, Mrs Budgers. Thank you."

"You're very welcome, young man. Where are you off to?"

Rat thought about the dowager's warning to be discreet and shrugged his shoulders, saying, "I'm going to run down to the village with Dodo."

Mrs Budget wiped her hands on a towel and looked at the young lad. Mrs Jenkins had given her the rough outline of the story of how Rat and his sister had ended up living at Chesterton

House. Tabitha and Wolf had worried that their household staff would hold some resentment towards the street urchin who had entered the household as the lowliest of servants and had now become Lord Langley's ward and mentee; they needn't have worried. The entire household was in thrall to Melody, and Rat was such a nice, helpful boy who never flaunted his good fortune that the servants could be nothing but happy for the children. The affection in which the Chesterton House staff held Melody and Rat had communicated itself to the staff at the Hall.

Even if that hadn't generally been the case, Mrs Budgers was a warm, motherly woman, and Mrs Jenkins' story of how Rat had taken care of his little sister after their parents died warmed her heart. She was sure that if the lad could survive on the streets of Whitechapel, he was more than capable of handling himself in the village. Nevertheless, she felt compelled to say, "Watch yourself, lad. There's been goings on here recently, and it seems the Hall and its inhabitants have rubbed someone or something the wrong way." Rat wasn't sure what the cook meant, but he caught the tone of warning and nodded.

Before coming to Chesterton House, not even six months before, Rat had never visited the country. He'd barely seen grass or trees during his short, harsh life in Whitechapel. However, since then, he'd visited Scotland and Brighton and, during the train rides to and from both, had marvelled as the verdant British countryside had flown past the train's window. Even so, clean, fresh country air and fields and woods, as far as his eye could see, had not yet lost their novelty. Rat ran through the gardens with Dodo happily running beside him.

Rat remembered how the carriage had brought them to the Hall through Lamphey the day before. While he was sure there was a shorter way down to the village over the fields, he thought it best to stick to the road so he didn't get lost. It didn't take Rat long to walk the half a mile to the village. Just as its stone cottages with their thatched roofs came into sight, he heard a whistle off to his left. Looking around, he couldn't see where the sound had come from. Before he knew it, there was an answering whistle from up ahead. Rat's head spun around, but again, he couldn't see either of the whistlers. He kept walking, but after a few minutes, he got the sense he was being followed. Rat hadn't lived in Mayfair long enough to have lost his street smarts, and he also knew how to use his fists. Balling them up in anticipation, he walked more deliberately, listening carefully to see if whoever was following him was getting closer.

Just at the edge of the village, there was a medium-sized copse of trees that would have provided a quicker route. Rat thought about what he would do if the situation were reversed, and realised that he would ambush someone from the trees. Attacking him out on the open road was far too risky. Out of the corner of his eye, he thought he saw a streak of motion and assumed that whoever was following him had sped up to beat him to the trees. Rat slowed down and considered his next moves. For all he knew, he was being stalked by thieves hoping to steal whatever they could find from him. Rat knew that his fine clothes and well-shone shoes indicated that he was part of a well-to-do family. He would have changed his clothes before leaving the Hall but hadn't brought any of his old clothes with him. There had been no reason to assume he would need to sneak out in disguise.

Rat knew he couldn't hope to defend himself against a grown man. Certainly not against more than one of them, which the multiple whistles had indicated. However, he did have a certain element of surprise in his favour. He assumed that whoever was planning to attack him believed him to be some fancy toff. It would never have occurred to them that he had spent most of his life doing whatever he needed to in order to survive on the rough streets of the East End of London.

While he hadn't brought his Whitechapel clothes, Rat had never lost the habit of keeping a knife in his boot. Even if he had never needed it for more than peeling an apple for Melly up until then, it was always good to be prepared. Rat didn't want to alert his would-be attackers to his weapon and so made a show of saying loudly that he thought he had stepped on something.

A DISCERNING WOMAN

Bending down to supposedly check his boot, he surreptitiously slipped his knife out of his boot and held it upside down so that the blade was hidden up his sleeve. This was an old trick he'd learned on the streets, and he was adept at quickly flipping the knife around when needed.

As he stood back up, Rat considered the copse. It wasn't very large, and while there was a path through it that very clearly led to the village, it was the quickest but not the only route. The carriage had come through the village on the road, which seemed to wind around. Rat assumed that if he stayed on the road, he'd end up in the village. He was a brave boy but not a foolhardy one. He was ready for a fight but shrewd enough to avoid one where possible. Particularly one where he suspected he was outnumbered. He stayed on the road, seemingly facing straight ahead, but his eyes darting back and forth, always aware of the shadowy figures that were following his progress. At one point, he caught a decent look at one of the figures and realised, with relief, that he was a boy not much larger than he was. Rat did not doubt he could take on a couple of village boys who probably didn't even have knives on them.

Finally, at the edge of the village, Rat lost sight of his shadowy companions. Perhaps, disappointed at the missed opportunity to ambush him in the woods, their interest had waned, and they'd moved on to other mischief. However, Rat didn't let his guard down, just in case. Now that he was in the village, he wasn't sure what to do next. The dowager had been so circumspect in her request that he had no idea how to begin. Rat thought about what he might have done in Whitechapel if he wanted to learn something; he'd go into a local store and chat up the storekeeper. That had only worked occasionally in the days when his clothes were ragged and his face smeared with dirt. Now, he was in fine, clean clothes, and he had coins in his pocket that he could use to purchase something. Rat was sure any storekeeper would be far more inclined to gossip about their neighbours to a customer dressed as a toff than they had been to give the time of day to a penniless street urchin.

The first store Rat saw was a butcher's shop, but he couldn't imagine what he would buy in there. Next to it was a bakery and that was far more promising. Strolling over to look in the shop window, Rat was thrilled to see iced buns laid out for display. He had a particular fondness for iced buns. As he opened the door, a bell rang, causing a very round, cheery-looking woman with a face full of freckles and bright orange hair to look up. As he'd hoped, the woman, Mrs Morris, the baker's wife, immediately took notice of his smart clothes and asked, "What can I do for you, m'love?"

Rat knew he wanted an iced bun, but he also wanted to engage the woman in conversation, so he pretended to be unsure. "I'm not sure what I fancy," he said. "What do you recommend?"

The woman had been busy putting a fresh batch of cream puffs in the display case and, indicating to them, asked, "What about a nice cream horn?"

Rat wasn't fond of cream cakes and shook his head. Considering how to engage the woman in conversation, he said, "I think one of those might be too filling, and I'll get into trouble if I return to the Hall too full for tea."

This got Mrs Morris' attention. "You'll be staying up at Glanwyddan Hall, will you?" Rat nodded again. The woman continued, "It's been a long time since any of the family have been up. Are you the new earl's son then?"

Rat had thought carefully about how to introduce himself. He didn't want to lie, but he had also learned over the last six months the power of an aristocratic title, so he said vaguely, "No, I came with the Earl of Langley."

"Two earls? What do you know? And I hear the old countess is with them, and the younger one, who isn't the wife of the new earl." PC Evans had returned home for lunch, reporting to Mrs Evans the news he had discovered that morning. It was almost two o'clock by the time Rat walked into the bakery, and Mrs Evans had long since done a tour of the village, spreading the intelligence her husband had gathered during his successful mission to research the inhabitants of the Hall for her. PC Evans had received an extra slice of meat pie for lunch as a reward and Mrs Evans was able to reassert her dominance in the village gossip hierarchy over Mrs Morris.

Rat seized on the mention of the dowager countess to say casually, "I believe that the dowager countess used to have a lady's maid who might still live in the village."

Mrs Morris had been quite put out by Mrs Evans' gleeful gloating about her gossip scoop and had tried to downplay it. However, Mrs Evans had only received second-hand gossip through her husband, but Mrs Morris would be a first-hand witness to some juicy titbits if she played her hand right.

The baker's wife considered what she wanted to ask the boy and decided to give up a piece of information in the hope that it would encourage the lad to be more open. "Yes, indeed. Elinor Hughes, as she is now. Married a local lad, David Hughes, must have been about forty years ago now. I was just a nipper myself. David had been a footman up at the Hall, but not long after they married, he came back to the village and took up farming with his father on the estate. David died last year, but Elinor still lives up at the farm." Mrs Morris was about to mention the tragedy that had recently befallen the Hughes family with the murder of Glynda. Still, looking at how young the boy must be, she reconsidered saying anything.

Rat thought about what Mrs Morris had told him. He was sure the dowager would be pleased that he had discovered that her lady's maid was still living locally, but he felt sure she would be more pleased if he could report back on exactly where the farm could be found. Mrs Morris was happy to relay that information and was now focused on what she might extract out of Rat in return.

Rat had met many a Mrs Morris in his time, and he was fully aware that the woman was hoping to mine him for gossip about Wolf, Tabitha, and the dowager. The boy had no intention of revealing anything private but wanted to keep Mrs Morris as a possible future informant, and so said as innocently as he could, "The dowager countess will be so happy to hear this news. I know that she's very happy with her current lady's maid, Withers, but will still be happy to learn what you have shared of Mrs Hughes."

This was Mrs Morris' opening, and she seized it, "From what I've heard, the old countess is quite the dragon of a woman. Even back when I was young, stories would come back from up at the Hall about what a terror she was."

Rat was sure that the dowager would love nothing more than to have word spread of how terrifying she still was, and so replied in a stage whisper, "Oh, she is, trust me. I am quite terrified of her, and I'm sure all the servants are. I believe she is the most feared woman in London." Mrs Evans smiled like the cat that had got the cream. Just wait until she spread this tasty morsel around.

With Mrs Morris' appetite for gossip assuaged, at least temporarily, Rat was able to return to the task of choosing a tasty treat. He pointed to the iced buns and thought to take an extra one back for Melly.

Mrs Morris was just selecting two buns when the bell rang again. "Billy, what have you been up to?" Mrs Morris said sternly. "I told you to sweep the yard and deal with the sacks of flour, and the next thing I know, you'd disappeared."

Rat turned around to see a stocky boy a few inches taller than him with freckles and orange hair that matched Mrs Morris'. "I'll get to it, Mam. Stop your nagging," the boy whined in a particularly nasty tone.

Rat looked into the boy's eyes and just knew that he'd been one of his earlier stalkers. Curious about what this boy had intended, Rat decided not to rush from the bakery.

CHAPTER 10

Billy Morris had a reputation as a troublemaker that wasn't entirely undeserved. More than anything, he was an intelligent, lively boy who was bored and felt constrained by village life and the assumption that he would follow in his father's footsteps and work in the bakery. At eleven years old, Billy was supposed to be in school, but like so many working-class children, his education had mostly stopped once he had a rudimentary grasp of reading and writing and could count well enough to give the correct change on the purchase of a loaf of bread. As his mother's nagging indicated, Billy was supposed to be working in the bakery, but took any opportunity to slip away.

Most of Billy's mischief was harmless enough, but recently, he had started to think about how he might escape the drudgery of life as a baker and decided that a life of petty crime might provide him with the escape from Lamphey he so desired. Billy had two friends, young Kenny Evans (PC Evans' nephew) and Griffith Thomas, Glynda the murder victim's oldest son. Ever since his mother's murder, supposedly at the hands of his father, Griffith and his older sister had been taking care of their younger siblings, and so the gang was just Kenny and Billy. It had been Kenny who had been Rat's other stalker earlier.

Billy and Kenny had been talking about how they might make some money, and then, as if by magic, they had spotted Rat walking down the road in his fancy clothes with his fancy dog. He seemed like the perfect victim; Billy had assured Kenny they wouldn't even have to hurt the younger boy. The young toff would be so scared that he'd give them whatever money he had. What Billy hadn't expected was to come face to face with his prey or that his intended victim would have such a determined and knowing gaze.

Mrs Morris, seeing Rat and Billy eyeing each other up, said, "Billy, this young gentleman is staying up at the Hall as a guest of the new earl." Billy knew the tone his mother was using and understood the warning that lay beneath her words: leave him alone.

Rat paid for his buns, making a point of taking out a large handful of coins with which to pay. Even though he had his back to Billy, he could sense the other boy's avaricious eyes on the money. Rat had known plenty of boys like Billy Morris back in Whitechapel. In truth, if Rat hadn't tried to pick Wolf's pocket that fateful day more than a year and a half ago, it was likely he would have become one of those boys: shifty, always on the hunt for their next victim, never thinking much beyond what they could nick next. Within a few years, those boys graduated from petty crime to working for one of the East End gangs. As he accepted his change from Mrs Morris, Rat wondered what boys like Billy in rural Wales graduated to.

Tabitha had intended to shield Rat from the disturbing happenings at Glanwyddan Hall. However, the lad paid close attention to what was happening around him, and he'd heard the servants whisper about the dead animals and the rock thrown through the window. He'd also heard the suggestion that the baker's son might have something to do with these pranks. Having met Billy Morris, Rat considered that these rumours might be correct. Perhaps that's what boys like Billy graduated to, but to what end?

Once Rat made this connection, he was even more determined to talk to Billy Morris privately. He knew Billy would follow him out of the bakery and make another attempt on his purse. The other boy had an advantage over Rat; he knew the village and Rat didn't. Rat didn't consider the other boy's age and size an advantage. He doubted that an eleven-year-old country boy was any match for him. Perhaps if Billy still had his sidekick with him, but the second shadow seemed to have disappeared. One-on-one, Rat felt even more confident. He was sure that Billy would have to wait at least a few minutes before following him so as not to arouse his mother's suspicions. Billy now knew where Rat was headed back to. Knowing all the routes to the Hall, Billy would imagine he did not need to rush.

Rat left the bakery and untied Dodo's lead from the tree he had left her by. He didn't want to do anything that would put the puppy at risk, but after the climax of their adventures in Brighton, he knew that the spaniel was very protective when roused. Billy Morris had no idea what he was walking into.

Looking around the small village, Rat considered where might be the best place for an ambush. He was sure that Billy Morris was watching him from within the shop and wanted to make sure that his actions were exaggerated and deliberate. The most obvious answer was to walk back through the copse, but having avoided it on his way into the village, Rat considered that to take it on his way back was too obvious a ploy. The village church and its graveyard caught his eye.

The church was a charming stone structure, and while Rat was no judge of such things, it looked old. Rat had spent a fair amount of time over the course of his short life hanging about graveyards. When he was very young, not much older than Melly, his grandfather used to take him to Bunhill Fields burial grounds and point out the graves of the famous writers who were buried there. After his grandfather's death, Rat would still trek over to Bunhill on occasion and talk to his grandfather as if he were still alive. He would have liked to have visited his grandfather and parents' actual graves, but they were thrown in a paupers' communal plot.

Rat thought about his visits to Bunhill as he casually sauntered over to this village graveyard, making a point of talking loudly to Dodo about where they were going. He didn't want to look behind him, but quickly sensed he was being followed. When Rat had bent to untie Dodo's lead, he had again taken his knife out of his boot, where he had replaced it before going into the bakery. Keeping it hidden up his sleeve as he had before, Rat walked at a steady pace, as if he didn't have a care in the world. The graveyard reminded him of Bunhill; it was maintained but not well-manicured. Ivy grew on the surrounding walls, and dry leaves carpeted the ground. Glancing at some of the gravestones, Rat saw that, while some of them were quite new, many were hundreds of years old. Rat decided it was safer for Dodo to leave her tied up to a tree by the entrance rather than risk her getting involved in any fight with Billy.

The leaves on the ground would make it difficult for Billy to follow without making a sound. Even better, Rat thought. This would ensure that Billy kept his distance. Over to the side of the graveyard, next to a particularly ivy-covered, crumbling section of wall, Rat could see what looked like a monument with a statue of a person lying down on top. Rat remembered seeing one of these at Bunhill Fields and his grandfather telling him it was a grave for special, famous people. In the case of Bunhill, a famous poet. There were words engraved on the large, white marble base, and Rat strolled over as if to read what was written. Pausing briefly, he then wandered around to the back of the monument as if to see if anything was written there.

Once he was behind the monument, Rat realised he would have to hope he would hear Billy approach because he couldn't take a chance of being seen peeking around it. Luckily, Billy was a total amateur at tracking people and made more noise than Rat could have hoped for. Rat turned his knife around in his hand and stood ready. Billy's footsteps got closer; then, suddenly, he was quiet. He was clearly waiting for Rat to re-emerge from behind the monument. Fair enough, Rat might have done the same himself. There was no one else around, and Billy was quite sure he had a size, age and experience advantage over what he thought was a milk-soft toff.

Rat took a deep breath, then, as if he didn't have a care in the world, strolled back around to the front of the monument. As soon as he appeared, Billy went to jump him, but in the split second before he launched himself, he caught sight of the gleaming, sharp blade Rat held in his hand.

"Woah, what are you planning to do? Fillet me like a fish?" Billy yelled.

"If that was what was needed, sure," Rat answered.

"Why would you do that? I haven't done anything to hurt you," Billy protested, attempting to inject a plaintive, innocent note in his voice.

"You stalked me into the village and were planning to ambush me in the woods, and then you followed me here and were just about to attack me," Rat said plainly.

Billy narrowed his eyes suspiciously as he looked at Rat in a fighting pose, knife in hand. The other boy looked like he knew how to use the weapon and perhaps had used it in the past. Billy knew he had misjudged the situation. Billy was tall and stout for his age and had always relied on his size to intimidate other children. His actual fighting skills were quite negligible, and he certainly had no idea how to go up against someone with a knife.

Putting his hands up in surrender, he admitted, "Well, perhaps I was. But only to get a few coins off you, nothing more."

Rat wasn't sure he believed he wouldn't have been subjected to anything more. However, even if that was the truth, his hardscrabble days weren't so far behind him that he could view the loss of coins as insignificant. Straightening up out of his fighting pose but keeping his knife out in front of him, he said, "I will be staying at the Hall for a few weeks. During that time, I may take walks down to the village. If you see me, keep your distance. I always have this knife on me and I'm pretty good with my fists as well. You may have some inches and some pounds on me, but I learned how to defend myself on some of the most dangerous streets in London."

Billy wasn't a fool; he knew he had met his match. Keeping his hands up, he began to back away, saying, "You've got yourself a deal. I'll stay out of your way, and you stay out of mine."

With Billy gone, Rat retrieved Dodo and made his way out of the village. Confident that Billy had been sufficiently scared off,

Rat took the shortcut through the woods, certain he was in no danger of being ambushed. He thought about his afternoon and his encounter with Billy Morris. Now he'd met the boy, he could believe he was responsible for the dead animals and even the rock through the window. However, he didn't think Billy would do it out of boredom, he was too sharp to take such a risk for no reason, but Rat could imagine him doing the pranks for coin.

Rat wanted to share his insights with Wolf, but he needed to think about how to explain his visit to the village without revealing the task the dowager had given him. Was it believable that he wandered down to the village with Dodo for no particular reason? Rat supposed it might be. The boy felt that he had managed to disappoint the dowager, Tabitha and Wolf during their last investigation. He had broken the dowager's confidence when he'd revealed what he knew about her activities, but he had also kept vital information from the very people responsible for rescuing him and Melody from the streets. Rat didn't want to find himself in such a situation again and resolved to tell Wolf what he could while keeping the dowager's secrets, whatever they were.

Arriving back at Glanwyddan Hall, Rat deposited an exhausted Dodo back in the nursery with Melody and Mary and went to find the dowager. He eventually located her in the aptly named Green Room at the back of the house. The Green Room was decorated in various shades of its namesake colour. If she'd had any interest in the Hall, the dowager would have long ago insisted on redecorating the room. However, as much as she disapproved of the colour scheme, the room was part conservatory with a glass roof and exterior wall. Because of this, it was a suntrap and usually warmer than the other rooms in the house, even on a chilly December day. Philip's father, the old earl, had been an avid collector of orchids, and in his day, the conservatory had been filled with the flowers. It was a long while now since the room housed any exotic plants, but there were still some low-maintenance specimens that added to the greenness of the decor.

"Ah, Rat, come and join me," the dowager said, indicating that he should close the door behind him. Rat was still clutching his bag with iced buns and wondered whether it would be a social faux pas to eat one in the dowager's company. A tea tray with a plate of treats was on the table. Seeing the bag Rat was clutching, the dowager asked, "Would you like a biscuit, or do you have something tastier in the bag?"

Rat sat and pulled out one of the iced buns. The dowager, well aware of the boy's predilection for the baked goods, smiled indulgently. She allowed the boy his first couple of bites and then asked, "So, how was your trip to the village?"

The boy finished chewing his bite of the bun and answered, "Very interesting. Mrs Morris, the baker's wife, was very helpful." While Rat knew that they were alone and that, with the door closed, they were safe from eavesdroppers, he was nevertheless very aware of the dowager's wish for secrecy. So, in a casually innocent tone, he added, "You'll never guess what she told me? Your lady's maid still lives just outside the village." Seeing the approving look in the dowager's eyes, he continued, "She married a man called David Hughes, who is dead now. But she still lives on the Hughes farm."

"Does she now? How interesting," the dowager murmured.

CHAPTER 11

Tabitha had discussed possible eveningwear for their party that night with Ginny at great lengths. She recognised that she needed to look the part of the Countess of Pembroke and that tongues would wag if she were decked out in anything short of the appropriate sartorial splendour. However, she didn't want to seem to be lording it over the locals. Together with Ginny, a decision was made to be stylishly simple in dress and jewels. They chose a gown of grey silk trimmed around the hem and neckline with delicate, intricate embroidery. The bodice was covered with a pattern formed from pearls, and the sleeves were flounces of lace. Her jewellery was a simple strand pearls interwoven with pink sapphires.

Putting the finishing touches to Tabitha's hair, Ginny stepped back and admired her handiwork. The maid had always thought her mistress beautiful. She had silently chafed against Jonathan's attempts to dim his wife's magnificence with his insistence on stern, unflattering hairstyles and clothing. Over the last few months, Tabitha had really come out of the shell that two years of marriage had forced her into and had found her style, no longer a demure debutante nor an oppressed wife. Instead, Tabitha had grown increasingly comfortable with a more playful, even flirtatious style. She would never be one to flaunt her assets, except in the cause of an investigation, yet the more tailored cut of her dresses and tasteful hints of decolletage showed her slim yet womanly figure off to fine form.

For her part, it had been many months since Tabitha had

silently judged every outfit she wore by Jonathan's exacting standards. She couldn't help but worry what critique the dowager would pass, but even those concerns had faded to brief flickers of doubt that quickly dispersed. Now, she was more likely to wonder about the bright glow of appreciation she anticipated seeing in Wolf's eyes. Even more than considerations of his admiration, Tabitha felt she was finally dressing as she wanted to, and that the only person's appraisal that really mattered was her own, and maybe Ginny's.

Tabitha had dressed early because she wanted to go down and check on the evening's preparations. Normally, she would trust that the very capable Mrs Jenkins and Chesterton House's equally capable cook, Mrs Smith, would have everything well under control, but Mrs Budgers and her skeleton staff, hastily augmented by local villagers, hadn't catered a lavish party for many years. In hindsight, Tabitha realised that hosting a party on their second day in residence at the Hall was probably overly ambitious. Mrs Jenkins had assured her of Mrs Budgers' competence and was confident everything would run smoothly. Nevertheless, Tabitha was worried. At the very least, she hoped that their guests' standards might be less exacting than a bunch of aristocrats in London, and, if there were any hiccups, they would either go unnoticed or at least unmentioned.

After checking in on the housekeeper and cook and being assured that everything was under control, Tabitha wandered into the drawing room and was pleasantly surprised to find Wolf alone. As she had hoped, his eyes lit up with love and appreciation as she entered.

"You are down early," she remarked teasingly. In reality, she knew that Wolf despised all aspects of dressing up and much preferred to be in more comfortable clothes with his jacket off and shirt sleeves rolled up. Every second that his valet, Thompson, insisted on spending primping him and teasing his cravat to perfection ratcheted up Wolf's irritation. He suspected that Thompson, knowing this, went out of his way to extend the grooming even longer than he felt necessary.

Wolf smiled and said, "I decided it was quicker and easier to allow Thompson free rein rather than wasting time debating with him. We both know that, in the end, he will win. My valet is a terror and rules me with an iron fist. Remind me again why I allow it."

They both knew why Wolf allowed it; his valet was not merely good at his job but didn't hesitate to help dress his master in all manner of disguises. He was as comfortable dressing him as the Earl of Pembroke as he was outfitting him as a dissolute, disgraced fifth son who now spent his nights in various gambling hells. Wolf did not doubt that if he were to request an outfit for an even more louche character, Thompson would be equal to the task and would dress him with barely a raise of an eyebrow.

Wolf was learning on the mantelpiece, a glass of brandy in his hand. As Tabitha crossed the room to him, Wolf set the glass down and held out his hands for her much smaller ones. They stood there for a moment, looking into each other's eyes, smiling conspiratorially at the secret that warmed them both.

A discreet clearing of the throat disturbed their romantic moment, and the couple sprung apart. Talbot didn't bat an eye at whatever he thought he had witnessed. As it happened, it was a given amongst the Chesterton Hall servants that the earl and countess were in love and would eventually acknowledge their feelings for each other. As Mrs Smith often said, "How could they not be in love?" Whether or not Talbot was aware of the acknowledged nature of their mutual feelings, he was far too inscrutable a butler ever to let on.

"Your lordship, you have a visitor," Talbot said in a neutral tone. However, if Wolf wasn't mistaken, there was just a slight raise of one eyebrow that gave the very faint impression that there was something questionable about this visitor. Wolf barely had time to consider who such a guest might be when a booming Scottish accent could be heard in the vestibule, Before they knew it, Uncle Duncan had pushed past Talbot into the drawing room, beaming with bonhomie more than likely brought on by an excess of Scotch whisky.

Uncle Duncan was, strictly speaking, Lily's uncle on her father's side, so he was not a blood relative of Wolf's. Nevertheless, both Tabitha and Wolf had grown quite fond of the old rascal on their trip to visit Lily's parents in Edinburgh. This fondness was only enhanced by the incorrigible man's tormenting of the dowager by flirting outrageously with her, seemingly blind to how ill-received his attentions were.

Uncle Duncan was a large man who shared a jovial gruffness with his nephew, Hamish. He had a shock of snow-white hair, twinkly blue eyes and a wide, toothy grin. It had never been clear to Tabitha and Wolf where Uncle Duncan lived or whether he instead led the life of a perpetual houseguest, moving on when it was clear, even to him, that he had outstayed his welcome. What was he doing in Wales, and more to the point, in Wolf's drawing room?

Tabitha glanced at Wolf questioningly; she was sure that he would have mentioned if Uncle Duncan had been invited or invited himself to Glanwyddan Hall for Christmas. As far as she knew, the two men were not even correspondents. Wolf gave a little shake of his head to indicate he was as bemused as she was. Despite her confusion, Tabitha walked towards Uncle Duncan, holding out her hand and saying warmly, "What a lovely surprise. To what do we owe this visit, Uncle Duncan? How did you even know we were here?"

Taking off his great coat and almost throwing it at Talbot, the florid man took her hand and said, "I've been in Cardiff, staying with an old friend and attending tae some business matters. It seems I may have o'erstayed my welcome. Then, a letter arrived from Lily, informing me of your plans tae visit Pembrokeshire for Christmas. It struck me then, why not join ye all and spend the festive season with my favourite great niece?" the man said in his Scottish burr. It seemed it had never occurred to Uncle Duncan to let them know of his plans or inquire as to whether his visit would be welcomed.

Neither Tabitha nor Wolf had to ask how Uncle Duncan might

have overstayed his welcome; they could imagine plenty of reasons they might be feeling the same if he stayed more than a few days. Given that there was just over a week until Christmas, it was probably unrealistic to expect his visit to be any less than that. It was even possible the man was planning to impose on them into the new year. Still, he was Lily's family, and Tabitha was sure the young woman would be thrilled to see her ne'er-do-well uncle. If nothing else, Uncle Duncan would liven up the evening's proceedings.

Lily and Tobias were the next people to enter the drawing room, and indeed, Lily was genuinely thrilled to see her uncle. Shyly, she introduced him to Tobias, "Uncle Duncan, I'd like to introduce you to my friend, Viscount Tobias."

"A viscount, eh? I'm no' sure how I feel aboot my niece gallivantin' wi' an Englishman, even if he is a lord," Uncle Duncan said sternly, then smiling and winking at Tobias.

The young man was utterly nonplussed by this unexpected relative and stammered, "I'm very pleased to meet you, sir. I promise, there is no gallivanting. I am merely happy to escort Lady Lily wherever she should want to go."

"So, ye're content tae be her milksop, are ye, lad? Tak' ma word for it, put yer fit doon early, firmly, and often," Uncle Duncan advised.

Tobias blushed deeply at Uncle Duncan's words, but Lily merely laughed them off, saying, "Uncle Duncan, you are as bad as ever!" as she kissed him fondly on the cheek.

Wolf offered Uncle Duncan a brandy and apologised for the lack of whisky. "'Dinnae bother yersel', I hae a couple o' bottles in ma trunk, and I'll be sure tae bring some down wi' me the morn," the man answered, taking the offered brandy.

Just then, there was the sound of tapping outside the door, and the dowager entered, leaning on her cane, escorted by Lord Langley.

"Tabitha, you really must have words with Mrs Jenkins about the maids. I swear I have more idea how to lay a fire than they do," the dowager said grumpily before pulling up short at the sight of their surprise guest. "What on earth is that awful man doing here?" she demanded, pointing her cane at Uncle Duncan.

Ignoring the hostility in her voice, Uncle Duncan replied, "Dinnae pretend ye're no' pleased tae see me, lass. I ken that yer bark is far waur than yer bite. No' that I'd be unhappy for ye tae hae a wee nibble if ye want."

CHAPTER 12

The dowager was rarely lost for words, but there was something about Uncle Duncan's outrageous lechery that left the normally outspoken dowager countess gasping for a rejoinder. Tabitha, recognised that she needed to soothe the troubled waters, at least for their party that evening. She quickly moved over to take the dowager's arm and said, "Mama, I think that this armchair would be the perfect place from which you can observe our guests as they enter and then ensure you can be fully involved in conversations." The dowager narrowed her eyes and looked at Tabitha; was she being called a nosy busybody and a lover of gossip?

Regardless of Tabitha's true intent, the armchair was deemed an acceptable spot, and the dowager allowed herself to be led to it. Gesturing to the armchair near it, she said loudly, "Lily, come and join me."

Before Lily could react, Uncle Duncan moved over to claim the chair, saying, "Leave the lassie alone. She disnae want tae spend her evenin' wi' us auld folks. But I'll be happy tae keep ye company."

"I have no desire for your company, sir. Please remove yourself immediately!"

Uncle Duncan merely chuckled and said, "I've told ye afore that I like ma women feisty. I willnae be put aff that easily."

The look the dowager gave him indicated an imminent eruption, but luckily, whatever she was going to say was forestalled by Talbot re-entering the room and announcing, "Mr and Miss Prescott, milord."

All eyes were turned towards the door and the first of their guests for that evening. Mr Prescott looked like what he was: a solidly prosperous businessman. His clothes were well-made but spoke of practicalities rather than luxury. He looked to be in his mid-fifties, with silver hair swept back off his forehead and clusters of crow's feet around his eyes. Everything about how the man carried himself spoke of a prosperous middle-class merchant who did not have ideas above his station. The same could not be said of his daughter, Miss Maureen Prescott.

Miss Prescott looked to be on the wrong side of thirty, certainly old enough to be considered a confirmed spinster. As such, she might have been expected to dress with a certain practical modesty. Instead, she wore a mauve silk dress with pink lace trimmings that, while it was clearly meant to exclaim wealth and status, instead spoke of someone trying far too hard. She had a pink feather secured with a large diamond clip in her hair. To top the outfit off, she carried a pink and mauve reticule that seemed to be shaped like a flower. Everything about the woman, from her jewellery to hair that seemed a rather unnatural colour to the rather artificial voice she seemed to assume as she made her greetings, was just too much.

Tabitha was the first to go to greet Miss Prescott, introducing herself and saying, "I am Lady Pembroke, the widow of Lord Pembroke's cousin, the previous earl."

At these words, Miss Prescott's eyes lit up, and she surveyed Wolf, who was greeting her father, so greedily that Tabitha was surprised the woman didn't lick her lips. "There were local gossips who were sure that you and Lord Pembroke were man and wife," Miss Prescott explained. "How delightful to hear that my intelligence was correct and that he remains a bachelor." Tabitha didn't bother to ask why that was delightful; Miss Prescott's thoughts were not hard to deduce.

Throwing one last look at Tabitha, Miss Prescott said, "I do not doubt that Lord Pembroke will prefer a fine cognac over sour ale." Tabitha was quite stunned at the woman's blatant insult and wasn't sure what to reply. Luckily, Miss Prescott negated the need for a rejoinder. Turning abruptly from Tabitha without another word, she moved over to where her father and Wolf stood and offered her hand, "Lord Pembroke, we're so delighted to have you here. I can only hope you can be persuaded to extend your visit," she paused, glanced at Tabitha, and continued, "with or without your entourage."

Her meaning was so blatant and outrageous that Tabitha almost gasped, managing to control herself only because more guests were entering the room, and she needed to greet them. For his part, Wolf darted a confused look at Tabitha, who returned it with a tiny shrug of her shoulders. Wolf took Miss Prescott's outstretched hand and replied graciously, "I am certainly delighted to be in Pembrokeshire again. It has been many years. As to how long we will all be here," he put particular emphasis on the 'we', "I cannot say."

Miss Prescott, who hadn't let go of Wolf's hand, took a step closer and said, in what she clearly believed to be a seductive voice, "I am sure we can find reasons to entice you to remain, milord."

What was the woman's game? Tabitha wondered. Did she believe she was auditioning for the role of the next Countess of Pembroke? Clearly, her performance had not gone unnoticed by the dowager who had observed the parlour play in which Miss Prescott was engaging and rose from her seat and crossed the room with surprising speed. Arriving at Wolf's side, the diminutive old woman's steel grey eyes glowered at Miss Prescott.

Maureen Prescott was blessed with a fulsome amount of unwarranted self-confidence and a corresponding lack of self-awareness. Unlike the gossips of Lamphey who had worked hard to piece together the biographies of the various members of Wolf's party, Miss Prescott had been focused solely on the new earl himself. While she knew broadly speaking who the members of the Chesterton family were, she hadn't bothered to familiarise herself with the details of their party.

Miss Prescott looked the old woman over dismissively. Visibly unimpressed with what she saw, she took her hand from Wolf's, where it had rested for far longer than he was comfortable with, and held it out to the dowager. She said in an aloof voice, "I am Miss Maureen Prescott, and you are?"

The dowager ignored the proffered hand and replied in a booming and strident voice, "I am the Dowager Countess of Pembroke, and it is customary for commoners to curtsey when greeting me." Maureen Prescott's eyes widened in shock at the dowager's tone and words. While the use of the word commoner was strictly correct, having it directed at her felt as if she had been slapped across the face. Maureen Prescott was always quite vocal in her dismissal of aristocrats, saying she cared nothing for inherited rank and instead reserved her respect for men like her father, who built their wealth and status from nothing. However, it was one thing for her to dismiss the importance of a title and another to be lumped together with the hoi polloi by some dried-up toff who thought herself better than everyone else.

Miss Prescott hesitated as she considered her next move. To comply with the dowager's words would be to acknowledge an unbearable obsequiousness. To ignore them would be a breach of social etiquette so outrageous that, even if it didn't get her removed immediately from the dinner party, would surely guarantee no more invitations would be forthcoming. Maureen Prescott was nowhere near the dowager's equal in battlefield strategy, yet she held her own amongst her peers. Recognising the longer-term gain to be had from compliance, she quickly bobbed a curtsey that conveyed as little deference as possible. As she dipped down, she refused to lower her head, instead maintaining eye contact with the dowager throughout.

Occasionally, the dowager had some approbation for people with enough backbone to stand up to her; this was not one of those occasions. Everything about Miss Prescott offended her, from the woman's gaudy costume to her blatant flirting with Wolf. Finally, but not least, Miss Prescott's disgraceful lack of respect towards her betters. While the dowager was not usually inclined to defend or support Tabitha in any way, the idea that this flibbertigibbet was making advances to the Earl of Pembroke was insupportable. She straightened her already stiff spine, threw back her shoulders even more, and said in her most imperious voice, "As a leading member of the so-called entourage of which you dare to speak, let me assure you that our stay in the area will be brief, and any extension of it will surely not be the result of persuasion by any person so wholly insignificant to the Pembroke name."

This was such a clear insult to Miss Prescott that Tabitha would not have blamed the woman for leaving the party, but Maureen Prescott was made of sterner stuff. While she did colour up at the blatant insult, she nevertheless never broke eye contact with the dowager, made another curtsey that was even briefer than the first and into which she managed to imbue an impressive amount of insubordination somehow, as she said, "Milady."

The dowager knew a thing or two about superficially fulfilling the niceties of social etiquette while managing to insult instead. She wasn't fooled by the seemingly respectful greeting for a moment. Tabitha, who could see that the exchange had the potential to become an even more flagrant escalation of hostilities, caught Mr Prescott's eye. The mild-mannered man understood the look immediately and, stepping forward, took his daughter's arm and said, "Come, my dear, others are waiting to greet his lordship, we must not hog the reception line."

As it happened, with the entrance into the room of the spinster sisters, the Miss Edgars, there were others suddenly waiting, so Miss Prescott was given a graceful way out. She took this, if not happily, with the resignation of someone who knew when she had met her match. Tabitha sighed in relief and turned to meet the rest of their guests.

The Miss Edgars were virtually indistinguishable from each other. Tabitha's first thought was that they must be twins, but they quickly dispelled this notion; it seemed it was a common mistake. Apparently, there were barely nine months between the sisters, who looked and sounded as similar as any twins Tabitha had ever met. Not only were they identical, they finished each other's sentences in a rather disarming way. The sisters were no taller than the dowager and probably of a similar age. In contrast with the dowager countess, who had a demeanour to rival the greatest generals, the sisters seemed to have an almost nursery-like childishness about them, along with a frailty that made Tabitha wonder if their locking of arms was as much about propping each other up as anything.

The sisters were quickly welcomed and escorted to a comfortable sofa at the side of the room, where they sat giggling together until dinner was called. The next to be greeted was the vicar, Reverend Marshall and his wife. Everything about this couple seemed exactly as one might expect from a rural man of the cloth and his spouse. Following closely on Reverend Marshall's heels was Squire Partridge, a large, red-faced man with a bulbous whiskey nose that spoke of a drinking habit to equal Uncle Duncan's.

The Squire also seemed to share Uncle Duncan's loud affability. Tabitha wondered whether it was better to keep the two men apart if possible or encourage a friendship, thereby localising the fallout from any possible misbehaviour throughout the evening.

Squire Partridge bowed as he greeted Tabitha and said in a booming voice, "Good to have Glanwyddan Hall occupied again. I have fond memories of hunting with your father-in-law, Lady Pembroke." He held his hand up to his mouth and spoke in a conspiratorial stage whisper, "To say nothing of our evenings carousing. Fine man, fine. Jolly bad job that accident. I was there, you know."

Tabitha did not know this and wondered if the dowager did. Luckily, after her standoff with Miss Prescott, the dowager had retired back to her armchair. Tabitha suspected that Squire Partridge's friendship with Philip Chesterton would not endear him to the man's widow. She wondered how to warn him off rhapsodising about the late earl's habits in earshot of the dowager. Any chance she might have to suggest this was cut off by the arrival of their final guests, Sir Jerome and Lady Anna.

From the notes the steward had efficiently provided about each guest, Tabitha knew that Sir Jerome had been knighted after having been mayor of Pembroke for more than twenty years. He had given up his mayoral duties a few years before and had retired to a small holding just outside of Lamphey to enjoy his elevation in status surrounded by people who didn't have immediate memories of his early days as a butcher's boy.

Sir Jerome bowed over Tabitha's hand with an unctuousness so extreme that it took all Tabitha's self-control not to shudder and pull her hand back unceremoniously. Lady Anna was only slightly less off-putting. She was a very plump matron. Her highly decorated dress, bright pink satin dress, covered in embroidery, lace and trimmings, would have been unflattering on the most lithe and youthful figure. On Lady Anna, it was a riot of unflattering inelegance. Tabitha could only imagine what the dowager would make of this couple and hoped she managed to keep a civil tongue.

By the time all the guests had arrived and been greeted, it was almost time for dinner to be announced. It seemed all their guests were well acquainted with each other. After greeting Wolf in as cringing manner as he had Tabitha, Squire Partridge had made straight for the grouping of Reverend Marshall and Mr Prescott, who were gathered to the side of the room. Miss Prescott was chatting with Lady Anna, though they both looked as if they'd rather be doing anything else.

Wolf had not said more than a greeting to Squire Partridge when they first met because he'd been hoping to talk to him discreetly without drawing attention to their conversation. Wolf couldn't say why he felt this was called for. Perhaps it was nothing more than a long habit of cautiousness. As he watched the little group of local men, he saw Reverend Marshall called over by his wife, at which point Mr Prescott moved across the room to examine a landscape painting on the wall. Hurrying to take advantage of Squire Partridge's solitude, Wolf crossed the room to speak to the other man.

With Mr Prescott's exit, Squire Partridge had been considering which group he might attach himself to next. Mr Prescott's sudden interest in art was a poorly concealed attempt to remove himself from the squire's presence. The men had known each other too long to be much good at pretending enjoyment in the other's company. But to whom would the squire prefer to talk? He knew better than to try to engage the Edgar sisters in rational dialogue, and he had heard more than enough of Reverend Marshall's ravings on the joys of lepidopterology over the years. Sir Jerome was a crashing bore, and his wife was not much better. Miss Prescott wasn't boring, but her delusions of grandeur were almost as outrageous as her dresses. He had noticed Uncle Duncan sitting nursing a brandy and thought the man looked like a potential kindred spirit. He had just decided to make his way over to introduce himself when he saw the new earl moving his way.

Squire Partridge had known Philip Chesterton his whole life and had a genuine appreciation for the man's company. They had shared a mutual love of riding to hounds, fine bottles of claret, and buxom wenches in their beds. Together, the men had spent many a happy day and evening indulging in all three to excess. Squire Partridge had a particularly fond memory of a couple of local dairymaids, sisters if he remembered rightly, whose bounteous assets had been on wonderful display when he and Philip had come across them out in the field. Easily tempted back to one of the barns on the estate, the men had each enjoyed both women's charms excessively.

The women had been so delicious that the men had sought them out the following evening, where the ravishment had been even more satisfying. Squire Partridge licked his lips just at the thought. It had been far too long since he had ravished a buxom wench, far too long. After Philip's accident, such exploits hadn't seemed as much fun, for a while. Then, once the gout set in, it was harder to chase the saucy lasses down. Thinking of his old friend, Squire Partridge decided that he wasn't in his grave yet.

There was a delightful new maid in his own servants' hall whose uniform could barely contain her delights. Just the thought of cornering her as she tidied his bedchamber brought a gleam to his eye.

The squire had never met Philip's wife before; the then countess' visits had been infrequent and short enough that her husband had never felt the need to expose his friend to her sharp tongue. Looking over at her now, Squire Partridge remembered his friend's description of his harpy of a wife and shuddered at the thought of interacting with the shrew. He could see she must have been a fine-looking woman in her time. Nevertheless, the most appealing feature a woman could have, even beyond a voluptuous body, was to keep a still tongue. From everything he had ever heard of Philip's widow, not only was her tongue not still, it was rapier sharp.

As Wolf made his way to the squire's side, the older man sized him up. He hadn't known Wolf's cousin, Jonathan, well, and their few interactions had been brief and uncomfortable. Jonathan had despised his father's many weaknesses and knew that Squire Partridge had been his confederate in many of his degenerate exploits. Did this new earl resemble the father or the son more?

Wolf spoke first, "Squire Partridge, I'm glad to have caught you alone. I understand you are the local magistrate?"

Squire Partridge nodded and wondered where this conversation was headed.

"Might you do me the privilege of calling here tomorrow so we might speak privately?" Wolf asked.

"Of course, my lord. Would eleven o'clock be convenient?"

"It would. Thank you. Meanwhile, enjoy the evening," Wolf said, wondering what else he could talk with the man about now that the request had been made. Luckily, just at that moment, Talbot entered the room and announced dinner.

CHAPTER 13

Wolf excused himself and went over to the dowager to lead her into dinner. Lord Langley accompanied Tabitha, Viscount Tobias Lady Lily, followed by the other guests. Tabitha had spent some time pondering where to seat her guests. Not knowing much beyond their titles, she was unsure who might best survive either side of the dowager. She had been tempted to put Viscount Tobias to the right of his godmother. Still, she knew that she should be interspersing their guests evenly between the family around the large round table.

Without having met the vicar, she knew better than to subject him to the dowager's views on the Church of England. She claimed to have the ear of the Archbishop of Canterbury, and Tabitha could well imagine how Reverend Marshall could be cowed by the woman's threats to give the Archbishop a piece of her mind on the state of his clergy. Beyond this, Tabitha knew something of the nonconformist movement in Wales, which chafed against the Church of England's teachings and dominance. The last thing she wanted was for Reverend Marshall to unwittingly subject himself to the dowager's views on splinter denominations.

Finally, she had decided to put Mr Prescott on the dowager's right and Sir Jerome on her left. Now that she had met the oily Sir Jerome, Tabitha felt that when he inevitably brought the full force of the dowager's scorn upon him, she would feel little guilt at the placement. The plan had been for Bear to join the dinner party in order to round out the numbers. However,

Tabitha saw that the ever-efficient Talbot had somehow made Bear aware of their last-minute guest and so he, almost certainly gratefully, hadn't joined the party. Instead, Bear's name card had been replaced with one for Uncle Duncan. She also noticed that although the original intent had been to seat Bear opposite the dowager, Talbot had wisely moved the name cards around so that now she was facing her godson, Viscount Tobias. Uncle Duncan had been moved to Tabitha's left, as far down the table as possible from the dowager. Tabitha sighed in relief and appreciation for Talbot's quick thinking.

Wolf was seated between Miss Prescott and Lady Anna. Not only were their dresses individually in poor taste, but the colours clashed in a way that gave Wolf a headache as he turned between them to talk during the soup course. Miss Prescott, thrilled at the seating arrangements, seemed determined to make as much of her time next to Wolf as possible. Continually touching his arm as she spoke, Wolf also felt her thigh touching his. Attempting to move over subtly on his chair just enough to be too far for her to stretch, he noticed the determined woman shift by a similar amount and again felt her thigh warm against his. Nothing about her was subtle.

Apparently, Miss Prescott had multiple aspirations in life, including being a published author. Miss Prescott felt sure that as soon as she found time to write her novel, she would be as popular as Mr Dickens. For want of anything else to say, Wolf asked what her novel was to be about. "Why, it is a fictionalised autobiography," she replied with a laugh that was supposed to be light and flirtatious but, to Wolf's ear, sounded shrill and jarring.

"An autobiography? Has your life been that sensational so far?" Wolf asked, almost immediately regretting the question.

Miss Prescott laid a land on his arm again and said, "Oh, I believe the best is yet to come."

It seemed that, in addition to her plans to write a bestselling novel, Miss Prescott considered herself a landscape artist to rival Turner. She also played the piano so divinely that she swore that she often brought her audience to tears. Wolf could only imagine and hoped there wouldn't be an opportunity for her to prove such a claim that evening.

From what the Pembroke estate's steward had written about the Prescotts, it seemed the father had made a fortune in trade, and that his only child, Maureen Prescott, was his sole heir. Given this, Wolf did wonder why the woman was still unmarried. As he reflected on the question during the fish course, he acknowledged that her brash self-importance likely put off a lot of potential suitors. However, a fortune large enough was usually sufficient for many a man to look past an otherwise undesirable wife. Wolf suspected his title was as much a cause for Miss Prescott's flirtations as any of his personal charms. Yet even then, there were more than enough hard-on-their-luck nobles who would be happy enough to marry beneath them for sufficient coin. The number of American heiresses who had married into the aristocracy was proof enough of that. Despite this, Miss Prescott remained unwed. Why?

Vocalising the question before almost immediately realising he had fallen into a trap of his own making, Wolf asked, "Is there no suitor wooing you, Miss Prescott?"

The woman's eyes lit up greedily, and she answered in what she clearly thought was a seductive tone, "Why, Lord Pembroke, are you hoping to win me for yourself?"

Desperate to claw his way out of the fiery pit he had thrown himself into, Wolf stammered, "Ah, um, I would never presume… I certainly didn't intend… I merely wondered why…"

Miss Prescott finished his thought for him, all flirtation gone from her tone as she said in a clipped, business-like voice, "You wondered why no man has made me an offer given the size of my fortune. Is that not it?"

This was precisely what Wolf meant. However, hearing it spewed forth in bitterness from Miss Prescott's lips, he suddenly felt incredibly foolish for ever raising the topic. Apparently, needing no confirmation from him, Miss Prescott continued, "You make the assumption that I have not been chosen rather than allowing for another possibility: that I chose not to be taken. I am a diamond of the first water, Lord Pembroke, and I do not need high society to pronounce me as such. I have yet to meet a man worthy of me." As she said this, Miss Prescott's tone turned again, and she purred softly, "Until tonight, perhaps." It was all Wolf could do not to shudder visibly.

For her part, Tabitha was busy listening to Reverend Marshall on her right explain his fascination with butterflies while trying not to laugh as Uncle Duncan attempted to engage one of the Miss Edgars in conversation. The sisters had seemed uneasy at being separated during dinner. Whichever Miss Edgar was next to the already rather drunken Uncle Duncan kept throwing nervous glances across the table to where her sister was seated to the right of the vicar.

Looking over the table, Tabitha felt an evil satisfaction in seeing Sir Jerome getting his comeuppance from the dowager who did not attempt to disguise her distaste for the man. On her other side, it seemed the squire was not faring much better. Unbeknownst to Tabitha, after one too many glasses of claret, the man had made the mistake of raising the topic of his friendship and frequent carousing with the dowager's deceased husband. It was hard to imagine that anything he could have said would have endeared him to her less.

Glancing down the table towards Wolf, Tabitha had to bite her lip to quell the giggle that threatened to erupt at the sight of Wolf attempting to stand his ground against Miss Prescott's less-than-subtle machinations. Tabitha was more than secure enough in his love and did not find there to be anything even remotely threatening about Miss Prescott's advances.

All in all, both Tabitha and Wolf found dinner stressful and were glad when dessert was served and the party all rose to take coffee and liqueurs in the drawing room. For once, Tabitha was glad that the dowager refused to allow the men to stay behind for port and cigars; the last thing she wanted was a more intimate encounter with Miss Prescott. However, it seemed that Miss Prescott had other ideas. Leaving the dining room, Maureen Prescott made a beeline for Tabitha.

A DISCERNING WOMAN

Talbot was busy pouring cups of tea and coffee and liqueurs for those who wanted them. Tabitha stood near him, waiting for a small glass of Grand Marnier. The meal had been heavy, and she needed a digestif. Talbot handed her the small glass. Tabitha then turned away and saw Miss Prescott coming towards her. Given the other woman's rude dismissal earlier, Tabitha couldn't imagine why she was making such a clear effort to seek her out now.

"What is that you are drinking, Lady Pembroke?" Miss Prescott asked in a far more polite tone than the one she had used earlier. "I will have the same," she said imperiously to Talbot before Tabitha even had a chance to answer.

Tabitha wanted nothing more than to use this brief pause to escape, but she was far too gracious a hostess to be rude to a guest, even an obnoxious one. Instead, searching for something to talk about, Tabitha said, "That is quite a unique dress, Miss Prescott." While such a statement could have been made sardonically, Tabitha ensured her tone was neutral and friendly.

Miss Prescott smiled and ran her hand down the front of her bodice, exclaiming proudly, "Isn't it! Fashion is my life, you know. Of course, the women who flock to buy gowns from Worth are just sheep. I don't follow trends; I set them."

Tabitha was unsure how much trendsetting could be done from a small village in the middle of Wales, but she kept these questions to herself. As if intuiting Tabitha's thoughts, Miss Prescott continued, "We do visit London regularly. It is there that I have found a modiste who is willing to design dresses to my exact specifications. I pay her handsomely to ensure that she doesn't use my designs for any of her other patrons." Tabitha doubted this was a real risk but controlled her face, masking her thoughts.

The woman continued, "I am a devoted reader of Vogue magazine, you know. It is where I get so many of my ideas. The Americans are so much more daring than the British." As she said this, Maureen Prescott looked Tabitha up and down and gave as little sniff as if Tabitha exemplified all that was wrong with the British Isles."

Tabitha hadn't heard of the magazine, and so had no opinion of whether Miss Prescott's dress did its fashion plates a service or not. She had certainly heard the dowager decry the style and taste of Americans in the past, as well as their speech, manners, and attempts to claw their way into the British nobility.

Hoping that now these bland pleasantries were out of the way, Miss Prescott would be as eager to move on to conversing with others as she was, Tabitha said, "I do hope you have enjoyed your evening, Miss Prescott," and gave a little nod of her head that she hoped would be taken as a polite dismissal.

If Tabitha hoped that Maureen Prescott would take her overly subtle hint, she was wrong. Instead, the woman drew a little closer and said, "I have enjoyed it. Very much, in fact. It is so delightful to have other people of high standing in the neighbourhood." Glancing over at the Miss Edgars, who were back on the sofa giggling, Miss Prescott said conspiratorially, "You can see the standard of society I am forced to endure normally. I have no idea why Father insists on us spending so much time in Wales. If it were up to me, we would give up the estate here and spend all of our time in London. So much more genteel."

Tabitha had no intention of joining Miss Prescott in slandering the other guests, so made no reply except for a weak smile. Even so, Miss Prescott seemed to take from that a shared abhorrence of the social possibilities Pembrokeshire had to offer and moved even closer. "Those of us with taste, style and sophistication must stick together. Don't you agree, Lady Pembroke?"

Where was this heading? Tabitha had an awful feeling she had somehow let herself be led down a very worrisome path. Indeed, not waiting for Tabitha's agreement, Miss Prescott continued, "Let us begin with tea tomorrow. I would love to host you and Lady Lily." Tabitha noticed that the dowager was not included in this invitation. "I hear that Lady Lily is a great lover of all things plants, as is my father. He has some species in his conservatory that I'm sure she would be interested in viewing." Tabitha knew this was a true statement and found she had no choice but to accept the invitation as graciously as possible.

Miss Prescott seemed delighted that her ploy had worked. She smiled brightly, though it did not reach her eyes, and clapped her hands. "Excellent. Then we have a plan—or at least the beginnings of a plan. What fun we will have during your visit, and then we can continue our association when we all return to London."

Was this the awful woman's endgame? Did she hope to use their association in Wales to elevate herself in London well beyond any social circles she might normally aspire to? Tabitha had to admire the woman's sheer audacity. Tabitha did not know how to respond, so she inclined her head and said, "We will see you tomorrow." Turning, she made a quick retreat.

CHAPTER 14

The following morning, everyone gathered at the breakfast table. Even the dowager had left her bedchamber at an unusually early hour. The party had ended late enough that everyone was ready for their beds by the time the last guest departed, and there had been no opportunity to discuss the party and judge their neighbours, something the dowager was clearly eager to do. Uncle Duncan was the only person not to join the morning conversation, being still abed after sampling one too many glasses of Wolf's brandy on top of a copious overindulgence of claret over dinner.

The dowager was the last to enter the breakfast room. She went and inspected the various dishes on offer and stopped short at the last chaffing dish. "What on earth is this?" she asked Talbot, who was busy refreshing the tea and coffee on the table. "It looks like a pile of disgusting seaweed has been served to us this morning."

Talbot put down a carafe of coffee next to Tabitha and said, "It is laverbread, milady. A Welsh delicacy that Mrs Budgers thought his lordship might have fond memories of from his time here as a child. It is indeed made using seaweed."

Wolf admitted, "Laverbread is an acquired taste. But I took rather a liking to it as a child. It's wonderful on toast with bacon and eggs."

The dowager peered at the dark, blackish-green gelatinous puree and said, "I will take your word for it, Jeremy. I thought that the foodstuff we were offered in Scotland was bad, but I see the Welsh partake of even more revolting items. I will not grace this pile of sludge with the title food."

Despite the dowager's customary aversion to any food that couldn't be purchased readily in Fortnum and Mason, the truth was that, Wolf aside, no one else had ventured to try the laverbread either. Wolf had assured Tabitha that once she got used to the slight iodine flavour, it was quite delicious. Tabitha felt that any food that needed the proviso, "Once you get past the flavour of..." was likely not something she would enjoy.

While there had been little opportunity to discuss their various impressions of their neighbours the night before, Wolf had told Tabitha that Squire Partridge had agreed to return that morning to discuss the details of Glynnie's murder. He had mentioned the squire's visit in a low voice the night before, not wanting the dowager to get wind of it. He did not doubt that she would insist on joining them if she found out.

The dowager filled her plate with some eggs and toast and sat down at the table next to Viscount Tobias. Talbot poured her some coffee and added the milk and sugar she always took. She had a bite of egg and a sip of coffee, then launched into her expected denigration of their evening's guests. "I must say Lily, after the horrendous party your mother threw in an attempt to welcome us to Scotland, I thought that your parents associated with some shocking people. But that cast of characters seems positively laudable compared to the parade of misfits, ne'er do wells and parvenus we were forced to endure last night."

She took another sip of coffee and continued, "Those batty old sisters are so in their dotage that they are not fit for polite society. The best I can say about the vicar is that he's a crashing bore with his endless prattle about butterflies. Squire Partridge is what I would expect of a man who considered my husband his closest friend: a lewd, drunken sot who will likely meet the same fate as Philip one day. As for that Miss Prescott, I really have no words to describe my particular aversion to such a gauche upstart."

While the dowager's words were harsh, it was difficult for anyone to argue with their underlying sentiments. Tabitha had been thinking all morning about Miss Prescott's very forceful invitation to join her for tea that afternoon. It had been clear that she had hoped to exclude the dowager, but Tabitha saw no reason to facilitate such a wish. As infuriating as the dowager countess could be on occasion, well, most of the time, there were occasions when she could be useful. Assuming it was possible to tactically aim her at a target with great precision, her special brand of caustic snobbery could be highly effective. Tabitha suspected this was one of those occasions.

Tabitha knew that her erstwhile mother-in-law was never inclined to be of service to her if she could help it. It was an almost knee-jerk reaction to refuse Tabitha aid when she needed it. However, Tabitha had learned a thing or two about dealing with the old woman over the last six months. Turning to Lady Lily, Tabitha said casually, "Lily, this talk of Miss Prescott reminds me, she invited you and me," Tabitha paused momentarily, then making an exaggerated move to look at the dowager, then back to Lily, continued, "and only you and me, to tea this afternoon."

Lily rolled her eyes and replied, "Why do I have to come and spend time with that awful woman?"

"Well, she says that her father has a conservatory full of interesting plants that you might be interested in viewing." That was all that Lily had to hear to be far more enthusiastic about the afternoon's trip. While under the dowager's stern influence, Lily no longer habitually appeared with twigs and other foliage in her thick, dark, curly auburn hair, the young woman's love of all things botanical had not waned.

Having secured Lily's reasonably eager agreement to accompany her, Tabitha took a sip of her coffee and said, "Wonderful, then you and I will take the carriage there this afternoon."

Tabitha could feel the dowager's agitation during this exchange. Finally, unable to contain her aggravation, the woman asked, "So, that vulgarian spinster made a point of precluding me from the invitation, did she?"

Considering how best to bait the woman without showing her hand, Tabitha replied, "I am sure she meant no disrespect. Perhaps she merely thought you would not desire to be one of the party after your rather tense initial interactions."

"You are sure she meant no disrespect, are you, Tabitha? I cannot imagine what could assure you of that. I cannot remember when I last encountered such an impertinent, hubristic parvenu. I refuse to allow that woman the upper hand. I will be joining you this afternoon and will enjoy her horror at my inclusion in the party." Tabitha acknowledged the dowager's insistence with a slight incline of her head while trying hard to suppress a smile.

Having thwarted Miss Prescott's attempts to exclude her, the dowager settled back to eating her breakfast. After her conversation the day before with Rat, the dowager hoped to visit her retired lady's maid, Elinor that morning. She assumed that one of the local men Madison had engaged to help with the horses and carriages during their stay would know where to find the Hughes farm. The dowager considered how she might request that one of these servants drive her without alerting anyone to her plans.

Finally, she decided that attempts at subterfuge would be more suspicious than merely telling a half-truth. So, she said casually, "Talbot, please tell Madison that I will need one of the locals he has hired to drive me out after breakfast." She paused, considering what reason to give. "There is a retainer from many years ago I wish to visit."

The dowager saw Tabitha and Wolf exchange looks, and she could well imagine why; she was not known for her attachment to servants. Perhaps the only exception was her butler, Manning. Even then, her concern when he was arrested had more to do with the disruption of her comfort than with fear for the man's sake at a possible conviction for murder. However, neither said anything, and the dowager was content with doing no more than raising some mild curiosity on their part.

Breakfast was a brisk affair for most at the table. Langley

had to meet Rat to continue the boy's lessons. Lily wanted to make the most of a reasonably nice morning to explore the gardens. Tobias was happy to be dragged along on whatever excursion Lily had in mind and to be her willing assistant as she investigated the local flora. Wolf and Tabitha had their imminent visit from Squire Partridge, and, of course, the dowager had her visit to make. Wolf was too glad that the dowager was otherwise occupied that morning, and so would not insist on being included in the meeting with the squire, to press any further on her outing.

As everyone drifted away from the breakfast table, Wolf leaned over to Tabitha and said in a low voice, "The squire will be here at eleven. I will ask Talbot to bring him through to the study just in case anyone else is still around." While saying this last sentence, he looked meaningfully at the dowager's retreating back. Tabitha nodded in agreement. Even if the dowager was safely out of the house by then, there was still Uncle Duncan to contend with. Neither Tabitha nor Wolf wanted their conversation with the squire to be interrupted by the hellion Scotsman.

Talbot had informed the dowager that the carriage would be waiting for her with a local driver who would be able to find whatever local residence she wanted to visit. She felt that there was no time like the present and informed him she would be ready to leave within fifteen minutes. The dowager considered whether to take Withers with her. She continued to vacillate between there being some possible safety in numbers and a desire to hold her deepest secret as close to her chest as possible. Finally, she decided that the carriage driver would be sufficient security; after all, what real protection could Withers provide?

Settling into the carriage, the dowager considered her upcoming visit. Elinor had been her lady's maid for just a few years. The lady's maid she had brought into her marriage had become unexpectedly sick during a visit to Glanwyddan Hall, and Elinor, a young, local maid, had stepped in just for a couple of days, or so they had thought. When the lady's maid's illness suddenly escalated, she was sent back home to her family, and Elinor suddenly became the lady's maid to a countess.

The dowager thought about the young Elinor. Not normally one to bother herself overly with the lives and the needs of her servants, nevertheless, there had been something about the young Welsh woman that the dowager had found quite comforting. The woman had a soft, almost musical voice and a gentle hand. While she had never performed the services of a lady's maid before, she had proved to be a quick learner. Elinor had learned to sew as a young child and had an almost magical ability with a needle and thread. To that day, the dowager had never seen a stitch so neat and nearly invisible.

Elinor had told the dowager that her grandmother and mother were, what was known locally, as dynion hysbys, or cunning folk. They were believed to have almost supernatural powers to reveal the unknown. The women were also herbalists whose concoctions were believed to do everything from heal a head cold to act as a love potion. Elinor had first confided this information when the dowager was suffering from a bout of illness that the local doctor seemed neither to be able to diagnose correctly nor remedy. Finally, realising in frustration that she had nothing to lose by indulging her maid's beliefs, the dowager had done as she had suggested. She allowed Elinor to take a clipped fingernail and an old piece of mostly worthless jewellery to her grandmother's cottage. The dowager had no idea what supernatural tomfoolery the old crone had performed, but Elinor had returned with a brew that her grandmother claimed was made especially for what ailed the countess.

The dowager hadn't believed any of the hocus pocus, but the brew hadn't been unpleasant tasting and so she had indulged the young Welsh woman and sipped on it. Within the hour, she had fallen into a deep sleep, the first she had enjoyed for days, and woken the following morning entirely well. Even so, the dowager's scepticism that it was the witch's brew that had cured her rather than a good night's sleep remained. However, when she next had a thorny issue that seemed to be beyond earthly powers to fix, she turned to Elinor again. However, the assistance that her maid had provided that day had been the beginning of the unravelling of their relationship and was the reason the dowager felt compelled to visit her more than forty years later.

CHAPTER 15

The carriage ride to the Hughes farm didn't take long, barely leaving the dowager any time to reflect on what she wanted to ask Elinor. Within a few minutes, they pulled up outside of what might have been called a picturesque cottage by someone other than the dowager, who despised any so-called rustic charm. Made of whitewashed bricks with a thatched roof, it had a bright blue front door with ivy climbing up around it. The cottage had a neat garden out front that probably was a delightful riot of colours in the spring. All of this was lost upon the dowager. The driver helped her down and the dowager steeled herself for the conversation ahead of her and knocked briskly on the blue door.

It had never occurred to the dowager that Elinor might not be at home. She was so accustomed to servants doing her bidding that she'd made an automatic assumption that even an ex-servant would accommodate the surprise visit in some way. The dowager was sure that Elinor knew that the family was again in residence at Glanwyddan Hall and must have been anticipating this visit. The possibility of any alternative scenario had never occurred to her until her first knocks went unanswered. Knocking again, this time more aggressively, she considered what her next move would be if no one answered the door. Luckily, before she had to consider that for too long, she heard shuffling, and a voice said, "I'm coming, dal dy geffylau."

The dowager had no time for regional languages and had no idea why the people of the British Isles should not all speak the Queen's English. Over the years of her visits to Wales, she had observed that this language so many of the locals spoke to each other was particularly ridiculous; far too many unnecessary letters and awkward sounds as far as she was concerned. Philip had always claimed he found it beautiful to listen to, but the dowager had never held much stock in what her husband thought.

A few moments after the voice had called out, the door opened. For a moment, the dowager had no idea about the identity of the withered old woman, dressed from head to toe in black, with dull grey hair and sightless eyes. When she had first become the dowager's maid, Elinor had been quite young, perhaps no more than nineteen. The dowager hadn't seen the woman for forty years, so she couldn't be much more than sixty, more than a decade younger than the dowager. Yet, the difference between the two women could not be more stark: time had not been gentle with Elinor Hughes.

It was quite evident that Elinor was blind, and yet she said almost immediately, "Your ladyship? I did not expect a visit from you."

"Is that a fact?" the dowager asked sceptically.

Stepping aside, Elinor asked timidly, "Would you like to come in?"

As much as the dowager had no desire to see the inside of one of these cramped, ugly cottages, she had even less desire to conduct this conversation on the doorstep and so she swept inside. Elinor had a stick in her hand, but she didn't seem to need it to navigate her home. As disinclined to approve of the house as the dowager was, she had to admit it looked spotlessly clean and neat. A fire roared in the fireplace, and a pair of armchairs that looked upholstered well enough stood before it. Elinor indicated to the most comfortable-looking of the two chairs and said pleasantly, "I will make us a pot of tea."

The dowager was not inclined to treat this as a social call. However, she was quite parched and so didn't object. She did wonder how the other woman managed a task such as making a pot of tea without the use of her sight. The small kitchen was off the main room, so the dowager was unable to witness Elinor's ability to manage household tasks on her own. She went and sat in the armchair and decided to use the time to consider further her approach to the upcoming conversation. The five minutes she waited did not help to illuminate the dowager in any way.

When Elinor walked into the room carrying a tea tray with a pot of tea, cups, and a plate of biscuits on it, the dowager experienced the most unusual sensation. It was one she had never felt in her life, and she wasn't sure what to make of it. She stood and said to the woman who had previously waited on her, "Let me take that from you."

If Elinor was surprised at her former mistress' offer, she didn't show it. She shook her head and replied, "That is very kind of you, m'lady, but I am very comfortable making do for myself within my own home." As if to prove the truth of that statement, she walked over to the little table between the two armchairs and placed the tray down as if her sight were no more reduced than the dowager's.

The dowager was fascinated by this and couldn't help but ask, "How long ago did you lose your sight, Elinor, and how do you manage so well?"

As she poured out two perfectly filled cups of tea, Elinor explained, "I began to lose it not long after my marriage. My mother and grandmother had both begun to lose their sight at a similar age, and so I knew immediately what my fate was. I had observed both women learn to live with their condition and understood the new skills I would have to learn in order to live with some independence. I went completely blind almost twenty years ago. Over time, my other senses have become sensitive. For example, I can hear when the cup is full when I'm pouring tea."

The dowager wasn't sure she understood fully what the other woman was saying; how on earth could one hear when a cup is full? However, she'd seen the evidence for herself and didn't question Elinor's words.

Finally, when they were both settled with cups of tea and

the biscuits had been offered and refused, Elinor sat back in the armchair, and asked, "Why have you come, m'lady?"

The dowager never believed in beating around the bush, and answered bluntly, "You know why I have come."

Elinor's face indicated genuine confusion, but the dowager knew the notes could only have come from her. She continued, "I have received notes recently, including one thrown through a window at Glanwyddan Hall the other night. All the notes said a version of, 'I know what you did.' As far as I know, the only living person with any knowledge of my secret is you. Unless that is, you have shared it with anyone else."

"M'lady, I told you I would take that to my grave, and I have been as good as my word. What would I have to gain by exposing you now?"

The question was fair and something the dowager had spent much time pondering. To date, none of the notes had any conditions attached to them. They didn't even threaten to expose the secret—at least, they hadn't so far. "Perhaps for monetary gain," the dowager suggested.

"Have any of the notes asked for money?" Elinor asked with genuine curiosity.

"Not as yet," the dowager admitted. "However, I have been expecting some sort of escalation. Why else send them? The first note, sent to me in London, demanded that I return here and, I quote, 'Pay for my sins.' That suggests that a monetary demand is coming."

Finally, noticing the draped black cloth over a mirror at the side of the room, the stopped clocks, and Elinor's black dress, the dowager asked, "Have you suffered a loss recently?"

"My daughter, Glynda. She was murdered a couple of weeks ago. They say by her husband." Elinor said this in a calm voice, but there was a shakiness underlying her words, and the dowager could see her sightless eyes fill with tears.

"I am sorry for your loss," the dowager replied sincerely.

"I can assure you, m'lady, I have been in no state to begin a campaign of poison pen letters for no good reason," Elinor stated dryly. "I was so consumed by grief that I could barely rise from my bed. If it hadn't been for the kindness of neighbours, I might have withered there and never recovered. It is only within the last few days that I find myself able to go some hours without weeping for my dear girl."

The dowager was not entirely devoid of compassion, and she felt for the grieving mother. She had not felt a similar sense of loss when her son had died, but Jonathan had been an unpleasant child who had grown into a monstrous man. It was hard to mourn the death of such a man, even when he was one's offspring.

Composing herself, Elinor asked, "Is it possible that the notes refer to something other than the secret I hold for you?"

Such an idea hadn't occurred to the dowager, particularly when the notes had only been directed towards her in London. Once they followed her to Wales, she had put aside any doubt. "I have only one dark secret that is in any way connected to this godforsaken area. If you did not send those notes, then someone else has discovered what happened all those years ago and means to put me on notice. Think hard, Elinor. Even if you did not disclose it intentionally, might you have let something drop? Perhaps to your husband?"

"M'lady, David died ten years ago, and I had never breathed a word to him for our entire marriage. As far as he knew, our situation was due to nothing more than your generosity."

"Indeed, that was not a lie. My munificence was pivotal, even if it was not entirely voluntary," the dowager said with a sniff.

"M'lady, I believe we both benefited from the resolution of the situation. I will not apologise for my actions. As to whether someone else might have found out, I will say again, I have not said a word to a single soul since that day forty years ago."

There seemed nothing left to say, and the dowager quickly took her leave, no wiser than she had been as to the identity of her tormentor.

CHAPTER 16

After breakfast, Tabitha and Wolf had retired to the study to await Squire Partridge. They discussed the few details they knew about Glynda's murder. It was not much. It was evident to Tabitha that something about his childhood friend's death haunted Wolf for some reason. They were sitting at the desk in the study, he behind it and she in front. Tabitha reached across the desk to take his hand, "Wolf, none of this is your fault. You must know that. You hadn't seen Glynnie for many years."

"Exactly," he replied. "I had neither seen nor thought of her in more than fifteen years. She had been my dearest companion for many years, making otherwise unbearable visits tolerable. Yet, no sooner had my grandfather died, I never gave her another thought."

"Tell me what was happening in your life at that time," Tabitha asked with genuine interest. Wolf rarely opened up about his earlier life, and she was always intrigued by the nuggets he sometimes threw out.

Wolf thought about the question. It was a lifetime ago; that very young man almost unrecognisable to the Wolf of today. What had been happening? "Well, as much as my grandfather had fallen out with my father and refused to see or acknowledge him, he had provided a small living, primarily to ensure that I was raised sufficiently well to be the earldom's insurance policy and to provide my sisters with some kind of dowry. With Grandfather dead, my Uncle Philip, my father's brother, immediately cut off all funds that he wasn't legally bound to by the will. Basically, nothing more than sufficient monies to ensure my education. Somehow, my father had not anticipated this possibility and had laid no money aside for such an eventuality.

"From that point onwards, I am unsure how we survived. Probably, debts were incurred, and local tradesmen were made poorer for their service to our family. It was not long after this that I escaped to Oxford. As you know, I supported myself during those years with my talents at the gaming tables. I have no idea how my father supported himself. My mother was dead by that time, and my sisters had married well enough. Somehow, he managed to scrape and scrounge enough to keep his old bones together for a few more years. I returned home just once after Oxford. That was when we had our final iteration of the same argument we had been having for years: that I should enter the legal profession."

Wolf paused, deep in thought. "I probably should have returned home on his death and tried to handle whatever debts his estate had racked up. But honestly, I had no money at the time, and I didn't even hear of his death immediately." He paused again, "Though now, I have money. When we return to London, I will ask my solicitor to investigate and see if there are outstanding debts I might make good on."

There was something Wolf had said that caught Tabitha's attention: his sisters. He had never mentioned them before, and she had been nervous about prying. Tentatively asking them about them now, she said, "Have you considered writing to them?"

Wolf considered the question. His sisters, Eliza and Henrietta, were both older than he was and, throughout their childhood, had treated Wolf as the annoying baby brother he probably was. They had been born barely a year apart, shortly after their parents wed. Wolf hadn't been born for another four years. That age difference had been enough to ensure Wolf and his sisters were never close. Comely enough to mitigate their lack of substantial dowry somewhat, they both married at a young age, the last just before their Grandfather's death. "They moved away immediately, and, after Mother's death, rarely wrote and never visited."

Tabitha didn't want to suggest that his sisters might be more open to a relationship with their brother now he was an earl because she knew Wolf had no interest in such sycophants. Instead, going back to the original topic of conversation, she observed, "It seems there was a lot to occupy your thoughts after your grandfather's death. You were living alone with your father and had to deal with the change in your family's financial situation. Perhaps, you should not be so hard on yourself for losing track of Glynda."

Wolf shook his head in vigorous denial of her words. "You are too easy on me, Tabitha. I was a fourteen-year-old boy. Do you think I bothered myself with whether the butcher was paid? Whatever worries lay on my father's shoulders, I never tried to ease his burden. To be honest, I believe I was oblivious to the fact there was a burden. Eliza and Henrietta were no longer at home, and my father decided there was no longer a need for formal family dinners. He ate in his study, and I ate in the kitchen with the cook. Looking back, it was probably easier to pretend that we ate as well as we once had if we were not sitting together in the dining room."

Wolf shook his head at the further placations he expected, "No, Tabitha. I will not accept your excuses on my behalf. I left that summer and never looked back. I had recently become aware of the delights of the fairer sex and I was too taken with attempting to woo a neighbour's daughter to think of the friend I had left behind."

"Wolf, would you have even known how to contact Glynda?"

He shook his head again. "I could have written to Budgie, she would have known. But no, I didn't even bother to stay in touch with Budgie, the woman who loved and nurtured me all those summers. I am almost ashamed to look her in the eye now, knowing how negligent I was."

"You were not more than a child."

"I was a callow, selfish youth."

"You are too hard on yourself. That is something I love about you; you hold yourself to high standards, even higher than you hold others." Tabitha blushed as she said this. They were not yet so comfortable using the word love, and her casual insertion of it in conversation hadn't been premeditated.

In reply, Wolf squeezed the hand he was still holding and said, "And I love your compassion. I love you." Tabitha blushed even more. Wolf continued, "Tabitha, when we return to London, perhaps it is time to…"

Whatever Wolf was about to say was cut off by a knock at the door. Talbot entered and announced Squire Partridge. While the squire was more sober than he had been the night before, he was no less florid and jocular. "Lady Pembroke, Lord Pembroke, thank you again for a delightful evening. Not much in the way of variety within the social circles, if you know what I mean. So always nice to see some new faces. Particularly when some of them are so charming," he ended with, looking meaningfully at Tabitha. She hadn't thought much of the man on first meeting him, and her impressions of him were not improving with time.

Wolf indicated that the squire should take the chair next to Tabitha. Suspecting the man would have no interest in tea and cake, he stood and went to the decanters on a side table. "What can I offer you, Squire?" he asked. "I am not entirely sure what my cousin and uncle enjoyed, but I believe at least one of these is brandy."

"Brandy is just what the doctor ordered," he said and guffawed. As it happened, brandy was exactly what the doctor had told him not to drink if he didn't want to exacerbate his gout. Wolf looked at Tabitha, but she shook her head. It was far too early in the day for her to imbibe. Wolf poured a liberal serving of brandy for the squire and a far more moderate one for himself, then returned to take his seat at the desk.

Wolf knew men like Squire Partridge. He had experienced them growing up, and he saw them around him too often now that he'd ascended to the earldom. These were men who enjoyed the power and prestige a title such as magistrate endowed but had no real interest in using their position to advance the common good. He did not doubt that the squire was far too much of a bon vivant to concern himself with whether an innocent man had been accused or not. There was nothing to be gained by attempting to appeal to his sense of justice. However, Wolf was equally sure the man's sense of self-preservation and, more importantly, self-aggrandisement could always be appealed to.

Thinking how best to achieve this, Wolf looked at the man before him and considered that he had been his degenerate uncle's bosom friend. That did not speak highly of Squire Partridge. "Squire, thank you for coming this morning and indulging me. I asked you here so I might learn more about the murder of Glynda Thomas."

Wolf always preferred to provide as little information as possible during an interview and instead get an unvarnished response. Whatever Squire Partridge had thought he'd been summoned to discuss, he clearly hadn't expected this, and his surprise was evident. "The blacksmith's wife? Surely, that is not something your lordship wants to trouble himself with."

The man's words enraged Wolf. Why did so many people in the upper circles of society consider that lower-class lives had less value? He saw this all the time; a duke is killed, and it is a heinous crime that must be avenged immediately. A beggar or a prostitute is killed, and they are disposable and unworthy of justice. If there was any argument that might persuade him to be more open to taking on occasional investigations, it was this one: ensuring justice for the lowly and indigent who had no one else to advocate for them.

Steeling himself, Wolf answered, "I consider everyone who lives on my estate or is in any way associated with it to be worth my trouble. As far as I'm concerned, all this," he gestured around the room, intending to speak of the estate, "and all the wealth, status, and other entitlements that the earldom brings, impose on me a duty of care to those encompassed by my power, no matter how lowly."

Squire Partridge's first instinct was to chuckle. He knew for a fact that Philip Chesterton, the last but one earl, had felt no such scruples. From what he'd heard of Jonathan, he had been even less inclined to care for the welfare of the people within his dominion. While Squire Partridge's holdings were far less significant than the earldom's, he nevertheless prided himself on caring as little for his servants and tenants as if he had a mighty estate. He respected Wolf far less for his compassion and sense of obligation.

Trying not to make his judgement obvious, the squire asked, "And what do you want to know about the Thomas murder?"

"I knew the victim, Glynda Hughes then, in my much younger days. We played together as children during my summer visits to the estate."

Judging by Squire Partridge's face, his respect for Wolf had not increased with the knowledge that he had associated with a child from a local, working-class family. Wolf continued, "So, as you can see, I have a personal interest in understanding more about her murder and the arrest of her husband."

Squire Partridge had eaten a good breakfast, but that had been hours ago and he was ready for luncheon. He half wondered if he might be invited to sup at the earl's table but decided that Mrs Budgers' cooking, while excellent, was not sufficient to warrant another meal spent with this stiff, dour new earl. Last night's claret had been superb. However, the squire suspected that, unlike his uncle, Wolf did not let it flow freely in the middle of the day. The squire wanted to finish up this conversation as quickly as possible and be on his way. Perhaps there was still time to catch that young filly of a maid making up his bedchamber.

"What is there to tell, your lordship? Mr Thomas was discovered lying over his wife's bloodied and battered body, a hammer covered in her blood by his side. The constable was called for. Mr Thomas did not put up a fight, but he denied he had killed his wife. Constable Evans saw no reason to believe Mr

Thomas as anything other than guilty, and I concurred. Rarely is a case as easy to decide as this one."

"And what do you believe his motive was in killing his wife?" Tabitha asked.

"Why does a man ever strike a woman?" the squire asked as if it were the stupidest question in the world. "She nagged him, she bothered him, she questioned him? For my own part, I do not dispute the man's right to keep his wife in check; his crime is taking it too far. I am sure that she came upon him while he had the hammer in his hand, nagged him to a fever pitch of temper, and he struck out without thinking. I am holding him over for the assize court on the charge of manslaughter rather than murder." Squire Partridge said this last part as if he were doing the blacksmith the greatest favour borne out of a feeling of great sympathy for a man who might want to beat his wife to death.

Tabitha felt bile rise in her throat at the man's words. He spoke with more compassion for the husband he believed killed Glynda than for the victim herself. She did not doubt that if the squire had the authority to pardon the man for the very understandable crime of killing an annoying wife, he would have. Tabitha thought about all the times Jonathan had struck her. She knew that, were he to one day have gone too far and killed her, men like the squire would likely have excused her husband's behaviour much as the squire was now.

Wolf could see the tightness around Tabitha's eyes and guessed how close to home this conversation felt. He wanted to wrap up the interview as quickly as possible. "I would like to speak with Mr Thomas this afternoon." Wolf said this as a demand rather than a request. He had no time to playact any social niceties around this awful man.

For his part, while his sense of his own importance was offended by the earl's tone, the squire's desire to be gone from Glanwyddan Hall and return home to seek out his new maid was stronger. Answering curtly, he said, "He is being kept in the lock-up in Pembroke Dock. We do not have resources sufficient in Lamphey to hold a man for a prolonged period. I'm sure

Constable Evans can assist you in getting access, if you insist."

With each party eager for its conclusion, the interview was wrapped up quickly.

CHAPTER 17

Once Squire Partridge was shown out, Tabitha and Wolf discussed a possible visit to Pembroke Dock to see the accused man. While Tabitha was always loath to be left out of investigations, it was clear that the visit needed to be made as soon as possible. That afternoon, she had the planned visit to Miss Prescott, and the trip to Pembroke Dock and back was too far for her to do both.

"Will you take Langley with you?" Tabitha asked. In one of their prior investigations, Lord Langley's ability to drop the home secretary's name had come in handy when trying to get access to a prisoner.

Wolf considered the question. He was the Earl of Pembroke and would expect his title to open even more doors in Wales than it did elsewhere. Nevertheless, it was always helpful to have Langley's ability to get the home secretary to telegraph him back immediately in reserve. "Yes, I will ask him to accompany me. After all, if one earl is imposing, two must always be better," he said with a rueful smile. Wolf was still uncomfortable with the obsequious kowtowing that his title tended to engender.

Tabitha was no longer concerned that Wolf would intentionally exclude her from investigations out of a misguided protectiveness or worse, a lack of belief in her abilities. She did not doubt that he valued her intellect, bravery, and ability to help solve cases. She also knew that, even when his first instinct was to protect her, he accepted that such urges were his problem to overcome, not something to impose on her. It was a large part of why she loved him: he trusted her to be a full partner in any investigation. He didn't always like it, but he didn't fight it.

Just as he had to accept her full involvement in a case, she had to accept that didn't mean that she needed to be part of every conversation. As Tabitha grew to feel more comfortable with Wolf's trust in her, she felt less need to force her way into every interview. Langley was a far more sensible partner for a visit to the prison in Pembroke Dock. Perhaps, in turn, she might even find out some useful information from Miss Prescott. After all, the woman had spent her entire life in the area; presumably, she had at least a passing acquaintance with Glynda and her husband.

Each comfortable with their tasks for the afternoon, Tabitha and Wolf removed to the dining room for luncheon. Entering the dining room, they found Bear, Langley, and Rat. The young boy was listening intently as Lord Langley explained a mathematical principle it seemed they had been working on that morning. As he listened, Rat was tucking into a raised game pie with gusto. Even though the boy hadn't been living on the harsh streets of Whitechapel for more than six months, he still attacked each meal as if he didn't know when the next one might be. Tabitha happily observed how the boy had filled out and no longer was the painfully thin, undernourished child she had taken in. He had also had a growth spurt recently, and she made a mental note to suggest to Lord Langley that the boy needed new trousers. Tabitha suspected this was the kind of thing Langley would neither notice nor care about without prompting.

Bear still wasn't entirely comfortable eating meals in the dining room rather than the kitchen, so Tabitha was happy to see him choose to eat with them that day. As Tabitha and Wolf sat, the dowager swept into the room with Lady Lily and Viscount Tobias in tow. "I see no reason why Tobias may not join us, if he wishes," the dowager said.

Tobias turned pleading eyes on Lily, reminding Tabitha very much of Dodo begging for a treat, and said, "Please say I can come, Lily."

Tabitha wondered why he was so keen to accompany them on their visit to Miss Prescott that afternoon. The young man normally tried to stay out of his godmother, the dowager's, way as much as possible. Despite his improved behaviour of recent, she was still far too prone to acerbic condemnation for Tobias to go out of his way to be in her company. At least part of this was answered when the young man continued eagerly, "Mr Prescott was telling me about a translation of Herodotus' Histories that he has."

Tabitha smiled. It hadn't been that long ago that they had discovered Viscount Tobias in a Brighton gaming hell after having been sent down from Cambridge. When they had first met, he was a sulky rake of a young man, only interested in gambling, drinking, and chasing thoroughly inappropriate women. The transformation of recent weeks was almost unbelievable. It seemed that all those visits to the British Library and British Museum with Lily may have awakened some latent academic interests in the young man. As she saw Lily bestow a look of pride such that a mother might on a toddler's first steps, Tabitha wondered how heartfelt Tobias' sudden interest in ancient history was. However, she decided to give Tobias the benefit of the doubt and believe that Lily's seriousness about academia had somehow unlocked something in the besotted young man.

Lily smiled indulgently at Tobias and patted his arm, "Then you may accompany us."

The dowager watched the exchange and also smiled. Her granddaughter continued to rise in her estimation. She wasn't sure how much of the young woman's gentle manipulation of Viscount Tobias was calculated and how much was the girl's intuitive grasp of the opportunity ahead to settle herself comfortably with someone so entirely malleable. Either way, the dowager approved.

Just as everyone had sat and begun eating, Uncle Duncan stumbled in, looking worse for wear. Tabitha wondered how long the man had stayed up drinking the night before when they had all retired. Looking around the table, he said cheerfully, "Aren't ye all lookin' bonnie and braw this mornin' at ye breakfast."

The dowager sniffed and said caustically, "It is afternoon, Mr MacAlister, and it has been for quite some time, and you are sitting down to luncheon."

It was unclear to Tabitha if Uncle Duncan didn't hear the contempt in the dowager's voice whenever she spoke to him or if he didn't care. He always seemed to laugh off her words, no matter how dripping in scorn they were. This time was no exception, "As far as ah'm concerned, breakfast is the first meal ah eat in a day, nae matter when ah eat it."

Shaking her head in exasperation, the dowager turned to Tabitha and said, "I told Talbot to have the carriage waiting for two o'clock. We will be keeping this visit to the minimum required by etiquette, and I expect to be home well before three."

"As I told you at breakfast, you do not have to join us if you do not wish to."

"And let that social climber hoodwink you into being another rung on her ladder? I do not think so."

Tabitha should have been insulted at the implication that she was unable to defend herself against Miss Prescott's social machinations alone, and coming from anyone else, she might have been. However, coming from the dowager, it was so expected that she barely noticed the slight. Instead, turning to Wolf, Tabitha said, "Miss Prescott must be around the same age as you. Did you ever interact when you used to visit?"

Wolf shook his head. "I'm sure I would remember someone like that. I did not interact very much with anyone off the estate, except Glynda, of course."

The dowager looked up. "Glynda? Who was that?" Wolf realised what he'd done; he'd had no intention of mentioning his childhood friend or her murder in front of the dowager. She must have seen the panic in his eyes, and smelling blood, she narrowed her eyes and asked, "What is this now? I have heard nothing of a Glynda."

While there hadn't been anything particularly noteworthy, even less suspicious in Wolf's words, the old woman had the nose of a bloodhound for when things were being kept from her. Wolf knew that he would only get himself and Tabitha in deeper trouble by trying to cover up his slip. Instead, he said in an attempt at a nonchalant tone, "Oh, just a childhood friend. I asked Mrs Budgers about her yesterday and learned of her tragic death recently."

Was this merely a terrible coincidence? The dowager found that hard to believe. Only that morning, she had been talking to Elinor about her daughter Glynda's death, the same Elinor who was privy to her deepest, darkest secret. And now it appeared that this Glynda was Wolf's childhood friend. Was there some kind of connection? If there was, the dowager couldn't imagine what it might be. Under normal circumstances, she might have taken this opportunity to share her thoughts with the others. These were not normal circumstances, and she kept her suspicions to herself. However, she did ask, "Are you planning to investigate the murder, Jeremy?"

It was now Wolf and Tabitha's turn to look suspiciously at the dowager; they hadn't mentioned that Glynda had been murdered. A tragic death might have encompassed a host of different possibilities. Why had the dowager immediately jumped to the conclusion that Glynda had been murdered? Did she know something that she wasn't sharing? Tabitha and Wolf exchanged looks; what was going on?

As if by unspoken agreement, Wolf acknowledged his interest in exploring Glynda's death further. "After speaking with Squire Partridge," Wolf tried to say this casually enough that it could have meant that they talked the previous evening, "I have decided to visit Glynda's husband in the Pembroke Dock lock-up this afternoon."

Turning to Langley, Wolf asked, "Would you join me?" Wolf didn't need to explain to Langley the help he might expect him to be able to provide. Given that neither Lily nor Tobias, to say nothing of Uncle Duncan, had any idea about Langley's role in

British Intelligence, it seemed best not to go into great detail. Langley expressed his willingness to join Wolf.

Now, the dowager was torn; she wanted to go to Pembroke Dock to learn more about the murder of Elinor's daughter and to try to understand what connection there might be to whoever was threatening her. However, she would not give Miss Prescott the satisfaction of her absence from the afternoon visit. That she was torn was quite evident, and Tabitha wondered at the dowager's surprising interest in the dead woman. Finally, realising that she would be able to get all the details out of Wolf on their return, the dowager made her decision to keep her afternoon plans as they were.

Within thirty minutes, the party had broken up, and arrangements for the various afternoon activities were finalised. Wolf and Langley would leave immediately for Pembroke in one carriage. The dowager, Tabitha, Lily, and Tobias would take the other carriage to take tea with Miss Prescott. Rat would go and find Melody and Dodo in the nursery. Uncle Duncan would retire to the library, ostensibly to read the newspaper but with every intention of having a large brandy and taking an afternoon nap before the fire.

CHAPTER 18

Tabitha thought long and hard about what to wear for their afternoon visit. While she should have ignored Miss Prescott's slight against her outfit the previous evening, it had stung. She was determined not to be caught on the fashion back foot again. During her marriage, Tabitha's dresses had been designed and sewn by a conservative modiste of Jonathan's choosing. Since his death, she had been branching out over the last few months and had been daring enough recently to order some gowns from the haute couture House of Worth.

Of course, she knew what Miss Prescott claimed to feel about Worth gowns; she had been quite plain-spoken the evening before. Yet, Tabitha wondered whether that was merely the sour grapes of someone unable to order gowns from the exclusive atelier. From what Tabitha had heard, Mr Prescott was certainly well-off by Pembrokeshire standards, but that was a far cry from the wealth that an account at Worth demanded. Tabitha suspected that her Worth rose, watered-silk gown, with its daringly modern cut and sleeves, would throw Miss Prescott into a frenzy of envy. While Tabitha was normally above such petty rivalries, there was something about the woman that brought out the very worst in her.

Tabitha had no secrets from Ginny and rather shamefacedly confessed her desire to one-up Miss Prescott. Ginny laughed and replied, "M'lady, that is nothing to be ashamed about. It is the most natural emotion given the insults you told me were lobbed at you last night. And the woman's blatant flirtations with his lordship alone are reason enough. I will make sure that she never again doubts where his lordship's heart lies."

Ginny's words caused Tabitha to blush deeply. She had never spoken openly to her maid about the acknowledged love between her and Wolf, yet somehow, her maid had intuited everything. If only Tabitha had known the truth: that most of the household staff had been rooting for their pairing for some months and that some of the less scrupulous may have even made small wagers on when an engagement would be announced.

The Worth gown had been very expensive, but looking at herself in the mirror, Tabitha believed it money well spent. At Ginny's suggestion, she accessorised the dress with a very simple yet stunningly beautiful necklace of filigreed gold studded with pink tourmaline and matching drop earrings. The entire ensemble was of understated sophistication. For a moment, Tabitha wondered if it was too understated. It was clear that Miss Prescott's taste ran more to showy and loud. Then, shaking her head at her worries, Tabitha scolded herself for caring so much about what the other woman thought.

The truth was a little harder to shake off: while she did not doubt the sincerity of Wolf's love, their mutual declarations were still quite recent and not yet public. A little, insecure voice in her head worried that Miss Prescott could so easily dismiss her as being married to Wolf. Then, a more rational voice reminded her of Miss Prescott's rudeness and clear desire to make cow eyes at Wolf. The woman's dismissal of Tabitha obviously had ulterior motives. Even so, Tabitha couldn't deny that she had a petty desire to outshine Miss Prescott that afternoon. She wasn't proud of how she felt, but she acknowledged it.

Finally, satisfied that Ginny's hair styling and very subtle use of rouge and powder ensured that she looked her very best, Tabitha made her way downstairs. She thought that Wolf and Langley had already left, but she found Wolf in the drawing room waiting for the other earl. Taking in her outfit, he raised his eyebrows.

"What? Is it too much?" Tabitha asked anxiously.

"You look beautiful—quite stunning," he promised her. "Yet that is not the outfit I might have imagined you wearing for an afternoon visit to a social connection in Lamphey."

"It is too much, isn't it? I knew it was."

Wolf came over and took her hands in his, raised them to his lips, and kissed her knuckles. "From what I observed of Miss Prescott yesterday evening, I can see why you might want to make clear your social dominance."

That was even worse! Wolf must have seen the effect his words had and hastily said, "I didn't put that well. Let me try again. You are the Countess of Pembroke." He lowered his voice, and said a little haltingly, "And I hope will be that twice over soon enough." Tabitha blushed at his words. This was the first time he had alluded to marriage. She wasn't sure how to reply, but luckily, Wolf continued, "It is only fitting that it be made very clear to Miss Maureen Prescott that there is only one woman deserving of that title."

Tabitha smiled, "Thank you, Wolf."

Whatever else may have been said was interrupted by the sharp rapping of the dowager's cane on the floor. "How many times do I have to walk in on such scenes?" the dowager asked irritably.

Neither Tabitha nor Wolf knew how to reply to such a statement. However, as with so many of the dowager's questions, it was rhetorical. She looked Tabitha up and down and said in a tone of surprising approval, "That will show the upstart, will it not! I did not credit you with sufficient backbone to indulge in such an exquisitely vengeful thrust and parry. Brava!".

Tabitha wasn't sure that she didn't find the dowager's approbation more disturbing than her condemnation. Lily and Tobias soon joined them. Everyone donned their outerwear and made their way out to the carriage.

Prescott Manor was no more than a ten-minute carriage ride

and Tabitha suspected it was even closer to walk to over the fields. Again, she wondered how Wolf and Miss Prescott had never crossed paths. As they drove towards the house, Tabitha considered if Mr Prescott had inherited or had bought it. She couldn't put her finger on exactly what made the house so unappealing; it looked like a hodgepodge of styles from different eras but was hardly the first grand house to be added to thus over the years. It was more that each new build seemed almost intended to be as much in conflict with the ones that went before it as possible. There had been no attempt to create a cohesive whole out of the varying architectural styles.

The dowager took one look at the house and announced, "I did not believe anything could be in worse taste than Miss Prescott's outfit last night. However, it seems I was wrong and that her home is even more ugly and garish." Tobias laughed; he found his godmother quite amusing when she wasn't aiming her scathing wit in his direction.

Lily gently slapped Tobias' arm and said, "Toby! Behave."

Toby, was it now? That was interesting, thought Tabitha.

"Well, it is jolly ugly, isn't it?" Tobias whined. "Why is it alright when godmother says that it is and not when all I do is laugh? It isn't fair." Sounding more like a five-year-old than a grown man, Tobias folded his arms and sulked until the carriage pulled up outside of the house.

The large, oak door was opened by a butler who even the dowager wouldn't be able to find fault with. The butler led them through a hallway overly packed with suits of armour and marble busts. Walking into the drawing room, Tabitha felt as if her senses had just been assaulted; it seemed that Miss Prescott's love of loud colours and bold fabrics extended beyond her wardrobe. Just as with the woman's outfit the previous evening, any one of the items in the room in and of itself might not have been considered gauche. Together it was all such a chaotic jumble of colours and shapes that the room almost immediately gave Tabitha a headache.

The dowager took one look at the room and said, "Are we

expected to sit in here? Is there no room less discordant we might be greeted in?"

Whatever the butler might have thought about such a request, he maintained the usual inscrutability that was in the job description of every butler and said, "Miss Prescott will be down in a moment."

The dowager seated herself on what might be considered the least awfully upholstered chair in the room and remarked, "A hostess not waiting to greet her guests? I have never heard of such a thing. Clearly, they do things very differently in the country than in the best houses in London."

Miss Prescott entered the room at that moment, evidently catching the dowager's words, and blushed deeply. "I am so sorry for keeping you waiting, Lady Pembroke. I had no idea you would be in attendance," she stuttered, caught off guard by the dowager's inclusion in the group.

"So, you thought it acceptable to keep Lady Lily and the other Lady Pembroke waiting?" the dowager asked acerbically. As it was obvious that was exactly what Miss Prescott thought, she didn't bother to answer. What game was the woman playing? Tabitha was very glad that the dowager had been manipulated into insisting on joining them.

Having thought she had successfully excluded the horrible old woman from her invitation, Maureen Prescott found herself on her back foot, not a feeling she was used to or enjoyed. She had planned exactly how she wanted the social visit to unfold, with her performance at its centre. If she wasn't careful, this woman would derail all her plans.

Miss Prescott had known from the first moment that she had laid eyes on Tabitha that she had nothing to worry about from the so-called countess. Yes, she had a certain prettiness, if you liked that kind of thing, but she had no backbone. The only evidence Maureen needed of this was Tabitha's easy acceptance of the invitation to tea despite 'her rudeness earlier the previous evening. However, this dowager countess was another matter; there was a part of Miss Prescott that respected a worthy adversary, or would if her plans weren't being thrown into disarray.

Luckily, the maid had followed her mistress into the room with a tea tray and the soothing reassurance of the social ritual of offering and pouring tea gave Miss Prescott time to gather her thoughts. She knew that she was meant for great things. She knew that even if it was not evident to her at any one moment, her timing would reveal itself later to have been perfect and moreover necessary for her future to unfold as it was meant to. Miss Prescott had known from a young age that she had been chosen, was special, and that all she needed to do was to follow the path laid out for her. Even if she didn't understand now why this dowager countess had been thrown into that path as an obstacle, the truth would be revealed to her in the fullness of time.

As tea was being poured, the dowager watched Maureen Prescott. While the dowager was never one to underestimate her own abilities, she recognised that, on occasion, she did not give others the credit she should; this might be one of those occasions. Yes, Miss Prescott was gauche and her taste headache-inducing, but there was a cunning there that the dowager was almost tempted to admire. It was evident to her that Miss Prescott had invited Tabitha and Lily and purposefully excluded the dowager herself with a plan in mind. Was it merely simple social climbing? That certainly was the most obvious answer.

The dowager was sure that Miss Prescott had immediately recognised in Tabitha's spineless niceness an opportunity for manipulation, so unwilling was she to cause pain to others. Whereas, in the dowager herself Miss Prescott must see a sharp and cynical mind that could not be moulded to her ends. Except, Miss Prescott had underestimated who she was up against. This was exactly what the dowager most enjoyed: a semi-worthy adversary whose defeat, while ultimately beyond doubt, nevertheless was hard-won enough to provide entertainment. She took a sip of her tea and settled back in her chair, determined to wring every ounce of pleasure out of this matching of wits.

"Lady Pembroke," Miss Prescott began, addressing Tabitha, "how is that you never visited Glanwyddan Hall during your brief marriage?"

"As you say, my marriage to the previous earl was brief and during that time he chose not to visit the estate. He preferred to remain in London." While it wasn't obvious to Tabitha what point Miss Prescott was attempting to score with this first shot across the bow, she had no doubt the woman was setting the stage for something.

"And how do you find our sleepy, little village?" Miss Prescott continued.

"This is a beautiful part of the country and, while I have not seen much of Lamphey and its environs yet, I have no doubt I will be delighted."

"Indeed, I am sure you will be. Certainly, it would be good for you to take in as much as you can during this trip, given that it is unlikely you will return."

Tabitha's eyes flicked up at this, and she observed her hostess. What answer was she looking for? The implication was clear enough: Wolf would marry, and she, Tabitha, would no longer be welcome at the estate. There was no doubt in Tabitha's mind that if she questioned why Miss Prescott assumed such a thing, she would be playing into her hands. Instead, she took a sip of tea and used the time to consider how she might pivot.

Tabitha decided to ask the question that had been niggling at her, "How is it, Miss Prescott, that you and the current Lord Pembroke never met as children? You must be of an age, after all, if you are not even older than he is."

The dowager almost spat out her tea; perhaps Tabitha had more guile than she gave her credit for. Did she really just call her hostess old? Miss Prescott seemed similarly aware of the allusion to her age. A sour look crossed her face, but when she spoke, she managed to maintain a cool detachment, "Perhaps we are of similar years. As my father's only child, he insisted on providing me with the education he would have a son. So, I did not spend my days running aimlessly in fields and climbing trees to sit in treehouses. Instead, I learned Latin and mathematics. I continue to devote time to the improvement of my mind and can speak to the value of an education beyond what is considered necessary to snag an earl at eighteen."

Ignoring this very clear return of fire, Tabitha gestured to Lily and said, "Lady Lily hopes to continue her botanical studies. Perhaps even attend university."

Lily blushed and said, "That would certainly be my dream. To study under some of the great botanical minds of the time is what I want more than anything."

"Why would you wish to emulate the gardener?" Miss Prescott asked dismissively.

"The study of botany has, and will continue, to reveal secrets that will help propel mankind into the next century," Lily explained patiently, not realising the intended slight. "Uncovering plants that will deliver new medicines, resilient crops, and more—that is the great promise botany holds out." As always when she discussed her passion, Lily's eyes shone at the dream of a future she could only hope to somehow participate in.

As much as Miss Prescott enjoyed playing with her prey, she was aware that the dowager countess would only allow this visit to last for the bare minimum of socially acceptable time; she couldn't waste those precious minutes in such a pointless salvo. Instead, she pivoted back to her originally planned topic, and asked, "Do you ride, Lady Pembroke? If you do wish to see more of the local countryside, there is no better way than on horseback."

Tabitha hadn't ridden since her marriage to Jonathan but was an able horsewoman and had always loved the freedom that galloping over the fields afforded her. She had briefly hoped that she might be able to ride in Wales, but after his father's death, Jonathan had sold off all the thoroughbreds and all there were now in the stable were carriage and farm horses.

Seeing the gleam in her guest's eyes, Miss Prescott offered, "My father keeps an excellent stable, and, of course, I am an outstanding rider. You must join me tomorrow morning. There is a wonderful trail through the woods up to a peak, from which you get a breathtaking view of the valley."

This was an enticing offer, and yet, Tabitha had a niggling worry; why was Miss Prescott suddenly so eager for her company? It was also interesting that the offer had not been extended to Lily, who seemed unbothered to be excluded. Tabitha was so undecided that she glanced over at the dowager and caught the woman's eye. The look on her mother-in-law's face portrayed all the scepticism that Tabitha felt, yet she found herself replying, "I would love to, Miss Prescott."

Immediately on saying these words, Tabitha realised that she did not have a riding habit or boots with her. As if reading her thoughts, Miss Prescott said, "Do you have need of the loan of an outfit? I could send one over later this afternoon."

Mentally scanning the many outfits Ginny had packed for their trip, Tabitha knew she had nothing that could even be quickly adapted, and she definitely had no riding boots. However, the thought of borrowing clothes from Miss Prescott, her flamboyant taste aside, did not sit comfortably with her. What was worse, turning down the offer or taking her chances with whatever garish outfit the woman saw fit to make available? Finally, Tabitha's innate politeness won out, and she said she would be very grateful for the loan of appropriate clothes and boots. She did not miss the grin on the dowager's face; it was clear the woman was enjoying both her current discomfort and eagerly anticipating the outfit she would find herself wearing the following day.

Luckily, the minimum allotted time for their visit was almost at an end, and the dowager wasted no time standing and making it clear she felt they had fulfilled all the obligations of etiquette. Lily looked disappointed at not having had a chance to see Mr Prescott's conservatory, but one look at her grandmother's face and she knew better than to suggest that they prolong their visit.

CHAPTER 19

During the carriage ride to Pembroke Dock, Wolf, Langley, and Bear, who had decided to tag along, discussed what little they knew of Glynda's murder. "My observations so far are that Constable Evans is more interested in filling his belly than doing his job ably and that Squire Partridge is all too ready to clamp the most immediate suspect in irons so he can get back to the comfort of his fireplace with a glass of brandy in hand."

Langley hadn't met the constable, but having sat opposite the squire at dinner the previous evening and heard his intoxicated attempts to charm the dowager, he did not doubt the accuracy of Wolf's observation. "Of course, that doesn't mean that Mr Thomas isn't guilty, even if it was not premeditated. Perhaps his wife came to visit him at the forge, they argued, maybe he raised his hand to her in anger and she fell and hit her head on an anvil."

"That is quite a fanciful and detailed tale," Wolf teased. "Have you been reading the penny dreadfuls again?"

Langley smiled at the gentle ribbing. It was as surprising to him as it was to Wolf that they had formed such a trusted and friendly bond. Maxwell Sandworth, the Earl of Langley, had never found it easy to make friends as a child or as a young man. As an adult, he had been gravely disappointed in love and had spent some time travelling the continent alone. Returning home after the death of his brothers, he accepted the duties of the earldom but anticipated living out his days as a lonely bachelor, even if that meant the title came to an end.

The last thing Langley ever imagined was that he would find himself suddenly part of this almost extended family group – particularly one that included the dowager – having formed genuine and meaningful friendships with Tabitha, Wolf, and Bear. He certainly would never have predicted that he would be the guardian and mentor to a young boy and utterly in thrall to a four-year-old girl. While there was nothing about his current situation that fit the picture of the life he had imagined for himself, he acknowledged that these people brought companionship, intellectual challenge, and joy to his life, filling a void he hadn't even realised existed.

In particular, his relationship with Wolf, as part mentor, part older brother, was growing into a friendship that Langley cherished. Given how they had started, it was quite astounding where they found themselves just a few months later.

The ride to Pembroke Dock took under an hour, and they soon entered the bustling marine town that had quickly grown from a small village after the Royal Navy Dockyards were built there in 1814. Sailors, merchants, and shipbuilders thronged the narrow streets, and the entire town echoed with the clangs of busy shipyard work. They passed the bustling harbour filled with ships, their passengers, and crews. Just past the harbour stood the solid, stone buildings of Pembroke Dock"'s police station and lock-up.

Ports were notorious for their mix of greedy merchants, shifty opportunists, drunken sailors and the occasional criminal eager to escape Great Britain. Wolf could imagine it was no easy task to keep order in such a town. Pulling up outside of the police station, they descended from the carriage, and Bear suggested he explore the town while Langley and Wolf exert their aristocratic authority.

When Wolf had inherited the earldom and had first made use of the average person's defence to the aristocracy, he had done so begrudgingly and with great discomfort at the necessary assumption of airs. He had found then, and on subsequent such outings, that the most effective manner in which to achieve his intended goals was to mimic his grandfather. Adopting the old earl's manner, walk and even tone of voice, Wolf had managed to slip on the mantle of arrogant nobility with an ease that had caused him some discomfort. However, he had made his peace with this charade's effectiveness and, entering the police station, he straightened his shoulders and felt his mouth pull into his grandfather's condescending moue almost without thinking.

Wolf had long come to realise that what most people, including he and Tabitha initially, took for cold arrogance in Langley was actually some social awkwardness and shyness. Whatever the reason, Langley had the benefit of many years of approaching minions with aristocratic disdain. Between the pair of them, they must have been a terrifying sight for a poor country police constable who thought the hardest part of his day would be dealing with drunken, brawling sailors.

The unfortunate constable, who had swapped with a colleague for the afternoon shift at the last minute and was suddenly regretting that decision, was a PC Timothy Timmons. PC Timmons was a young man who had only been part of the Pembrokeshire Constabulary for six months and felt very unprepared to handle whatever the two fearsome-looking toffs were going to demand.

Wolf took the lead, approaching the lanky, spotty young constable and saying, in a growling baritone, "We are seeking a prisoner you may have in custody, a Mr Rhys Thomas."

Whatever PC Timmons had been expecting the aristocrats to say, that wasn't it. Rhys Thomas was well-known in the police station; there weren't so many murders in Pembrokeshire that such a violent one would go unnoticed by any policeman. Unsure of what these men might ask next, PC Timmons was relieved that he could answer this initial question easily enough, "We do. He is awaiting the assize in our lock-up." Then PC Timmons paused. That these men were toffs was evident, but what kind of toff was unclear. Just to be on the safe side, he added, "M'lord."

"I am the Earl of Pembroke, and this is the Earl of Langley. We wish to talk with Mr Thomas."

PC Timmons' first reaction was relief that he had appended the m'lord as an afterthought. He had never met an earl, let alone two. He had met a baron once who had been caught up in a tavern brawl, but that man had been a drunken sot with none of the noble gravitas of the two men before him.

PC Timmons wasn't sure what the protocol was for giving aristocrats, let alone ones with local titles, access to prisoners, and he didn't want to be responsible whatever it was. "Let me go and fetch the sarge." Without waiting for the two earls to reply, PC Timmons hurried off to interrupt Sergeant Edwards' tea break. While Sergeant Edwards would not be happy at the interruption, in truth, his tea breaks were long and frequent. It was often more likely that one of those – or lunch – was interrupted than his work was.

As PC Timmons had anticipated, Sergeant Edwards was sitting in the break room, reading the newspaper and nursing a cup of tea. The Chief Constable of Pembrokeshire had his office in the town of Haverfordwest, far enough away that Sergeant Edwards was not concerned about unannounced visits. Sergeant Edwards was a rotund man with a prominent nose and somewhat bulbous, dull blue eyes. He had a particular fondness for digestive biscuits. Mrs Edwards ensured he always had a supply, which he kept in a tin box that the constables breached at their peril. He had just taken his third one of these biscuits and was dunking it in his tea when PC Timmons entered the room.

"What are you doing in here, Timmons?" Sergeant Edwards demanded. "You're supposed to man that desk at all times. Unless the Queen herself comes in, you stay at that desk." PC Timmons stood in the doorway, almost visibly shaking with nerves. "Is the Queen here?" his superior demanded facetiously.

"Not the Q-q-q-queen, but t-t-t-there are two earls," the young man stuttered.

Sergeant Edwards narrowed his eyes; was the young constable mocking him? He had always found Timmons so nervous and unassuming that he had nicknamed him Timorous

Timmons. He didn't seem the sort to be lippy, but you never knew.

Seeing his superior's scepticism writ large on his face, PC Timmons hastened to assure him, "Honestly, sarge, two earls. One of them is the Earl of Pembroke, even."

Like most people in Pembrokeshire, the sergeant knew that their most recent overlord had died recently and had been replaced by his cousin. He'd also heard word that the earl would be spending his Christmas at the estate. Given this, it was not totally ludicrous to hear that the man himself was now waiting in the police station. Maybe it was unlikely he was actually in the station, but not that he was in the town. Leaving his half-dunked biscuit on his saucer, Sergeant Edwards pushed himself up with a sigh, moved past his constable, and made his way to the front desk, where he found two toffs, much as he had been warned.

Wishing he hadn't spilt some tea on his shirt earlier, Sergeant Edwards approached the two men and introduced himself, "Your lordships. I am Sergeant Edwards. How can I help you today?"

Sergeant Edwards hadn't extended his hand, which saved Wolf the effort of disdainfully rebuffing it. Instead, he replied, "Sergeant Edwards, we would like to talk with Rhys Thomas."

Wolf didn't say why they needed to talk to the imprisoned man, and he suspected Sergeant Edwards would not ask. This suspicion was confirmed when the sergeant said, "Follow me, your lordships." He turned and made his way down a corridor and then down a narrow staircase to an ill-lit subterranean level. The police station's lock-up seemed to have multiple cells, and a few faces appeared at the cell bars, eager for something to break up the monotony of their days.

Sergeant Edwards led them down to the end of the cells, where they saw a man sitting forlornly on a narrow bed, staring at the walls. The man didn't even acknowledge their presence until the sergeant put the key in the lock and said, "Thomas, you've got company." Suddenly unsure how such a visit should be handled, the sergeant asked, "Should I bring you chairs, m'lords?"

Wolf shook his head, but then considered how they might best put Rhys Thomas at his ease and said, "Actually, that would be appreciated, Sergeant." This left the sergeant with a new dilemma: Should he leave the toffs alone with the prisoner? Rhys Thomas had been very compliant since they had arrested him, and there was no reason to believe he would become violent. However, he was an accused murderer, so who knew what he was capable of?

As if intuiting the man's dilemma, Langley said, "You may leave us here with Mr Thomas. We are not concerned."

What did this mean? Could he lock two peers of the realm in one of his jails with a murderer? On the other hand, he couldn't really leave the cell door unlocked while he got chairs; what if the prisoner overpowered them and escaped?

Again, realising the man's concern, Langley said, "You may lock the door behind you. His lordship and I are more than capable of minding ourselves." Not one to question the commands of his betters, Sergeant Edwards nodded, left the cell, locking it after him, and went to find chairs.

Once the sergeant was safely out of the way, Wolf looked at the broken man, who was sitting glassy-eyed before him, and said, "Mr Thomas, I knew your wife, Glynda, as a child. I am so sorry for your loss."

At this, Rhys Thomas looked up with curiosity, noticed how the men were dressed, and asked, "You're Wolf? I mean, Lord Pembroke, the new earl?" Wolf nodded, and Rhys continued, "You said my loss. So you don't believe I killed Glynda?"

"Did you?" Wolf asked.

The man shook his head vehemently and said, "Glynda was the love of my life. I would never have hurt a hair on her head. As if it's not bad enough to lose her, being accused of her murder is more than I can take."

Langley, who did not have the personal connection to the victim that Wolf did, pointed out, "You would not be the first husband who loved his wife but beat her in a moment of rage."

Something flashed in Rhys' eyes, but he replied, "Maybe. But I didn't. Ask anyone who knows us."

Wolf intended to do just that, but it led to the inevitable question, "So, why were you arrested if it is so beyond belief?"

Before he had a chance to answer, PC Timmons, who had been tasked with finding and delivering the chairs, appeared at the cell. He unlocked the door, brought the chairs in, and then left, locking up behind him. Wolf and Langley sat, and Wolf asked the question again.

"Because I was found at the scene, covered in Glynda's blood," the prisoner acknowledged. "But I had just arrived back at the forge, found her body and had bent down to see if she was still alive. Then I was found like that."

"Who found you at the scene?" Langley asked.

"A Miss Maureen Prescott. I'm not sure if you know her. She came to get her horse reshoed. She had sent a note that morning saying she would be by that afternoon. She found me like that and had one of her grooms hold me down while the other went for PC Evans."

Miss Prescott? Wolf thought. That was convenient. If only he'd known this before Tabitha went for tea, she could have questioned Miss Prescott about her discovery. No matter, he would call on the woman, perhaps even later that afternoon. He asked, "Why don't you tell us everything that happened that day, Mr Thomas."

Rhys Thomas looked so relieved to have someone ask him these details finally without assuming the worst that he brightened up noticeably. "Well, the day started out as normal. I went home for lunch at noon, as I always do. Glynda had some leftover stew from the night before, and I had that. We talked about this and that. Her sister just had twins, and she was telling me that she'd gone over that morning and that both babies are colicky, and her sister was beside herself. We've twins ourselves, our middle two, and so she felt for her."

"Was there anything out of the ordinary at that point?" Wolf asked.

"Well, Glynda was baking some bara brith. It's one of my favourites, and it's not something she would normally make for no reason."

"So, why was she making it?" Wolf asked. He didn't believe that Glynda's baking was a piece of material evidence in her murder, but he'd learned not to leave any stone unturned in interviews.

"Well, it was our Pauly's birthday the next day, and it's also his favourite. I teased her that I never got any on my last birthday and she gave me a playful slap on the arm and said that I was a grown man, wasn't I now?" As he said these words, the burly man's eyes filled with tears. He wiped his eyes with the back of his hand and continued, "So I ate my stew and went back to work. About two hours later, Billy Morris, the baker's lad, comes by and said they were having problems with the hinges on one of the ovens at the bakery and could I go and look. It didn't take me long to fix; not much of an issue in all honesty. I was in and out in maybe thirty minutes. Then I went back to the forge."

As he said this, tears started to fill the man's eyes again. "I'd closed the doors to the forge when I left, and they were open when I got back, but I didn't think much of it. I went in, and that's when I saw Glynda lying near the anvil, covered in blood. One of my hammers was next to her, also covered in blood. I fell onto my knees in the hope that she was just hurt. But it was clear she was dead. I must have dropped onto her body in the shock of the moment. I know I was calling out her name and crying. Then, the next thing I knew, Miss Prescott's groom had pulled me up and had my arms behind my back. Then old Ian Evans turns up and says I'm under arrest. I don't even remember everything that happened after that. And here I am now."

Wolf had heard a great many men, and even some women, proclaim their innocence in his time. It was the rare instance where the proclamations were founded on truth; he believed this was one of those times. The man was genuinely distraught and did not fill his narrative with the unnecessary details that the guilty often incorrectly believed made their stories more credible.

"Do you have any ideas on who might have killed your wife?" Langley asked, beating Wolf to the punch by a few seconds.

"Glynda was a wonderful woman; everyone loved her. You remember, m'lord," he said, turning to Wolf, who nodded his agreement. "As she was as a child, so she was as a grown woman: kind, generous, loving. I've been wracking my head to think of anyone who might have had a grievance against her, and I just can't."

Wolf thought about the man's story and added, "And more to the point, surely anyone wanting to hurt Glynda would be more likely to go to your house. They wouldn't expect to find her at the forge, would they? Why was she even there?"

"You're absolutely right, m'lord. I have no idea why she came to see me. She hadn't mentioned anything earlier, and it wasn't a usual thing for her to do. So there's no reason for someone to expect her to be there. This is what I've been thinking: that someone was in there to do some thieving. She came upon them, and they attacked her."

It wasn't the craziest theory Wolf had ever heard. "Have you had problems with thieves in the past, Mr Thomas?" More to the point, he thought, what was there to steal at a blacksmith's forge? He supposed the man's tools of the trade had some value, but most of them were heavy. They didn't seem to be the easiest items to steal and then sell on. Did Lamphey and its environs really have a problem with that sort of crime? He could more believe it of London, where everything had a price, and there were always criminals like Mickey D and his boys ready to take advantage of whatever situation presented itself.

Rhys Thomas considered the question, "Well, no, we haven't had problems like that as a rule. But since all the foreigners have been coming in to work the quarries and then losing those jobs, we've certainly had more strangers roaming, even being a nuisance at times. But it's normally stuff like stealing eggs, sometimes even a sheep. What's a vagrant going to do with my old, sooty chisels and files?"

What indeed? Wolf thought to himself. The mention of vagrants reminded him of the pranks being played on the Hall. He asked Rhys whether he'd heard of them, and the man admitted word had got back to the village, particularly about the dead ravens, which had started some talk of curses and black magic.

"Why, m'lord, do you think there's a connection with Glynda's death?" Rhys asked.

"Honestly, I am not sure," Wolf confessed. "But I mean to find out."

CHAPTER 20

Neither Wolf nor Langley spoke much on the carriage ride home. Bear, taciturn at the best of times, knew better than to interrupt Wolf's ponderings. Finally, just as Lamphey was coming into view, Wolf looked up from staring at his clasped hands and asked Langley, "What do you think is going on?"

Langley considered the question. He was a logical man and rarely indulged in flights of fancy. His worldview was formed on the belief that rationally explained patterns underlay most of what otherwise might be deemed 'magical' or 'heaven-sent'. "I think that there have been a string of events, what we're calling pranks, that have been clearly aimed at your family, if not you. And then there has been a murder where the victim just happens to be your childhood friend. These all happen within days of each other and were around your first announced visit to the estate as earl. To my mind, that all seems unlikely to be coincidental."

Wolf agreed, and this very thought had been the subject of his ponderings since they left Pembroke Dock. "But why? What has my visit triggered, and why murder Glynda?" Whatever guilt Wolf had felt about his neglect of his childhood friend for so many years paled into insignificance against the realisation that he may have indirectly been the cause of her death.

"Perhaps the grudge isn't against you but against the estate?" Bear suggested.

"Then why Glynda? Why not one of the servants? Not that I wish any harm on any of them, but they are far more tied to the estate than a woman I played with as a child," Wolf said, running his hands through his hair in frustration at the conundrum. Then a thought struck him, "The universe of people who even know that Glynda and I were friends as children is a small one. Mrs Budgers, in whom I have absolute faith, maybe the other servants at the time, most of whom are not even still on staff. I suppose it is possible that some of them still live in and around Lamphey, but again, what grudge might they hold?"

"Of course," Langley pointed out, "you are forgetting anyone Glynda might have told over the years. Did her parents know of the friendship? It is hard to imagine they did not, given how many years it spanned."

"I think I will visit her mother. In fact, you can drop me off in Lamphey on your way back to the Hall. Just send the carriage back for me. I would happily walk back, but I can only imagine what the dowager countess would say about the new earl being seen walking down the road." Wolf had considered whether to have Langley join him. However, he did not want to overwhelm the grieving mother; it was enough that he would be imposing on her when her sorrow was so fresh.

Wolf's opinion of the Hughes cottage could not have been further from the dowager's the previous day; he found it charming. In truth, he would happily swap all the finery and trappings of the earldom to live peacefully with Tabitha in such a cottage. He paused before the door, considering what he wanted to ask Glynda's mother. He had no idea if she had known about their friendship as children, and even if she had, what did that really indicate? It had all been a long time ago. Finally, realising he could only loiter on the doorstep for so long, he knocked on the door.

Wolf heard some shuffling and then a voice calling, "I'm coming, dal dy geffylau."

Again, unlike the dowager, Wolf had always found the Welsh language to be beautiful and had even tried to get Glynda to teach him how to say a few things. Combing back through his memory, he thought he remembered how to say hello. When an old woman opened the door, he said, "Shwmae."

The old woman, who was clearly blind, replied, "Shwmae to you as well, stranger. What can I do for you?"

Hello had been the extent of the Welsh he remembered. Wolf asked, "Am I speaking to Mrs Hughes?"

"You are. And am I speaking with the new Earl of Pembroke?" Wolf was amazed. How could this blind woman possibly know such a thing? Intuiting his surprise, Elinor Hughes said, "We do not get many English aristocrats around these parts. And certainly, there are not many who might come knocking on my door." The woman's logic was faultless. Of course, Wolf had no idea that another English aristocrat had come knocking on this same door just the day before.

"I am the new Lord Pembroke. May I have a few minutes of your time, Mrs Hughes?"

"Of course, m'lord. It would be an honour." Elinor led the way into the cosy living room the dowager had sat in the day before. Yet again, Elinor offered tea, and like the dowager, Wolf marvelled at how the blind woman navigated her home and maintained her independence.

Finally, settled in the armchairs, each with a cup of tea, Wolf began, "Mrs Hughes, I must tell you how very sorry I was to hear of your loss." He paused, considering how to phrase his next sentence. "I am not sure if you ever knew, but Glynda and I were good friends as children."

Mrs Hughes put her teacup back in its saucer, turned her sightless eyes towards him, and answered, "Yes, I knew. Of course, she didn't tell me at first. But Glynda had chores to do and was away far too often and for too long for me not to notice. That first summer, young as you both were, that she was away every day for hours at a time made me worried. Honestly, of all the things she could have told me about where she was, the last I'd expected was that she was up at the Hall and had befriended you."

"I was so grateful for that friendship, Mrs Hughes. I am not sure what you know, or what you knew, of my circumstances, but I was hardly a welcome guest those summers. My grandfather barely tolerated me and only insisted I visit as an insurance policy for the earldom; a prescient move, as it turns out. As for my uncle, he made his dislike of his brother's son very evident. If it had not been for Mrs Budgers and then Glynnie, I am not sure how I would have survived those long weeks each year."

"Ie, I knew," Mrs Hughes said, which luckily sounded enough like yeah that Wolf understood. "At first, when I confronted Glynda, Glynnie as she was then, she didn't want to tell me. But I threatened to send her to her great-grandmother's cottage. My mother and grandmother were what we called dynion hysbys, cunning folk. Maybe you English call them wise women or even witches. Either way, my grandmother was held in great respect by everyone in the village, but also feared, including by her great-grandchildren. That was all it took for Glynnie to confess everything."

Wolf nodded his head but didn't interrupt Elinor's narrative. She continued, "That evening, her father and I discussed what was to be done. The old earl was well respected in the village. He took care of his tenants and was known to be a fair landlord. But to be respected was not the same as to be loved. He was a stern man, and all the village children knew better than to wander onto the grounds of the Hall. Well, all the village children except my daughter, it seemed. My first instinct was to forbid her from doing so again. But as David and I talked, we discussed what you've said, that you were a young boy, likely unwelcomed in your grandfather's home."

"Did you know the story of my father's banishment?" Wolf asked.

"It's a small village, and most of the servants at the Hall were born here; word got about. Your father was always thought highly of," she paused, "more so than your uncle, if I might say. Because of that, I felt for your plight. Eventually, we told Glynda that she was to stay well away from the Hall and should be sure never to find herself around the old earl. As far as I know, she followed those rules."

"Thank you, Mrs Hughes. That you allowed Glynnie to continue coming had more of an impact than you could possibly have realised at the time. She was my only friend in those days. When Mrs Budgers told me of her death, I was devastated. I cannot imagine your grief."

"It means a lot, m'lord, that you bothered to come by to express your condolences."

At Elinor's Hughes words, Wolf was wracked by guilt. He hadn't really come by to express his condolences but rather to discuss her daughter's murder and its possible connection to him. As guilty as he felt, he was sure that Glynda's mother was as concerned as he was to find her daughter's killer.

"Mrs Hughes, I must confess, that is not my only reason for visiting you today," Wolf admitted.

The old woman smiled, "Is it not, m'lord? What can an old, blind woman do for an earl?"

"I went to visit your son-in-law, Rhys Thomas in Pembroke Dock lock-up today." Whatever she'd been expecting Wolf to say, this clearly wasn't it. Elinor could not have looked more surprised at his words. Before she could ask the obvious question, Wolf explained, "For many years, I have acted as a private inquiry agent of sorts. I have continued to help with select investigations even after inheriting the earldom." This explanation put a high gloss on Tabitha and Wolf's investigative work over the past six months, but it seemed the simplest explanation to give.

"So, you are investigating Glynda's murder?" the grieving mother asked with a hitch in her voice.

"I am. While Glynda and I lost touch after my grandfather died, I have nothing but the fondest memories of my dear friend. I had hoped to reconnect with her on my return to Lamphey. Instead, on learning of her murder, I felt that the least I could do was to ensure that justice was done."

Elinor cocked her head to the side and considered his words. "And you don't think that justice has been done with Rhys' arrest?" she asked.

"Do you?" Wolf replied. "Do you think your son-in-law capable of killing his wife?"

Wolf observed the woman's face as she considered his question. In the short time he had spent with Elinor Hughes sitting in front of her fireplace, he had determined that she was a strong, intelligent woman—just the kind of woman he could imagine Glynnie had grown up to be. He was genuinely interested in Elinor's gut reaction to his question.

"No, I don't think Rhys killed Glynda. I know PC Evans said that Rhys was found by her body, covered in her blood." As she said this, Elinor's eyes filled with tears, but even as they rolled down her face, her voice remained composed. "But even then, I don't believe he's guilty. Theirs was a love match if ever I saw one. Rhys was a couple of years older than Glynda. I think she'd had her eye on him for some time, but it wasn't until her fifteenth birthday that she suddenly blossomed into a beautiful young woman from the gangly child she'd been. Suddenly, Rhys took notice of her. He was always respectful. Immediately came and asked my David if he could court her. They were married within a year, and you never saw a couple happier."

Elinor paused and wiped the tears on her cheeks. "I loved my David with all my heart, but there was something between those two that was special. Do you know he still picked her flowers, spring through autumn. Twice a week, he'd bring her bluebells and daffodils. Then wild roses. Whatever was growing about, he'd pick and bring to my daughter and present her with the posy like he was still courting her. In all those years he never so much as raised his voice to her, let alone his hand. I cannot imagine anything that would have caused him to hurt my Elinor, let alone kill her."

"After speaking with Mr Thomas today, I also do not believe he killed her. I would like to find out who did." Wolf paused again, then continued, "Mrs Hughes, I am not sure if news of the various pranks aimed at the Hall have made their way to your ears." Elinor nodded. "Those pranks seemed to have begun around the time of your daughter's murder. That was also the approximate time when we sent word that we would be spending Christmas at Glanwyddan Hall."

"You think Glynda's death has something to do with the dead raven and the like?" Elinor asked.

"I think it is possible the same person perpetrated both and that perhaps I am what links the two," Wolf admitted. Now, he asked the question that he had really come to the cottage to answer, "Who else knew of my friendship with Glynda?"

The old woman thought about the question, taking a sip of her tea as she did so. "Well, her father knew, of course. Glynda wasn't my oldest; I have another daughter, Ruth. They were very tight as children, so I'd be shocked if Ruth didn't know. It wasn't something we aimed to keep secret, and we didn't tell Glynda not to tell anyone. But we also didn't go out of our way to spread word of it about. I doubt the old earl would have taken kindly to his grandson mingling with a village girl, and we didn't want word to get back to him. Glynda was a sharp girl and I think she realised that it wasn't something to let get around more than necessary. But it's a small village, people talk. I can't say for sure that it wasn't known, only that no one ever said anything to me or my husband. I assume word didn't get back to the earl?" she asked.

"Not that I know of," Wolf answered. "As you pointed out, if it had, he surely would have forbidden the friendship."

Wolf did not need to ask Elinor Hughes much more. However, sensing the woman might not get many visitors, he stayed for another cup of tea and was happy to reminisce about his dear friend Glynda with her grieving mother.

CHAPTER 21

During the carriage ride home from the Prescott residence, the dowager indulged in a thoroughly enjoyable and, to her mind, well-deserved disparagement of everything about Miss Prescott, from her home to her clothes to the apparently inferior quality of tea they had been served. Lily didn't bother to pay attention and looked out of the window. Tabitha nodded her head occasionally but felt no need to join in the backbiting. She did not like Miss Prescott and was sure the woman's desire for her company had some ulterior motive. Nonetheless, she also was sure the dowager's dislike had as much to do with the Prescott's' lack' of a title and the origins of their wealth in trade as it did with the woman herself.

Luckily, the carriage ride was brief, and upon arriving back at the Hall, the dowager pronounced herself in need of a nap before dinner. Lily and Tobias disappeared into the garden, and Tabitha was glad of some free time to visit Melody in the nursery.

After a delightful two hours reading to Melody and participating in a dolls' tea party, Tabitha returned to her bedchamber to find Ginny eyeing an outfit laid out on the bed. "This came for you earlier with a note," she said.

Tabitha wasn't sure what she expected Miss Prescott to send over. While she feared the riding habit would be as tasteless as the rest of Miss Prescott's clothes, she also realised that the woman clearly considered her outfits to be in the height of fashion. Would she really send such a dress for Tabitha? It seemed Tabitha's thought process was accurate. Instead of some loudly patterned or garishly coloured outfit, the riding habit on the bed was a dull olive colour. The style was at least twenty years out of date and probably wouldn't have been considered fashionable even then.

Ginny handed Tabitha the note that had accompanied the outfit. "My dear Lady Pembroke. This riding habit belonged to my dear Mama, whose height and lack of figure were similar to your own." Had her physique just been disparaged by Miss Prescott? Tabitha continued reading out loud, "Moreover, based on your clothes, I believe you will be more comfortable in something more muted than perhaps I wear." Well, she wasn't wrong there, though not for the reasons Miss Prescott imagined. "You should not feel obliged to return the outfit or boots to me."

"Was I just insulted multiple times?" Tabitha asked Ginny.

"I believe so, m'lady. However, I do think that I can make something of this. I have my sewing basket with me, and I have a lovely piece of ribbon that will beautifully match this fabric."

"Ginny, you are a treasure. I am to ride tomorrow morning. That will not leave you much time."

"It's more than enough time, m'lady. I would rather sew my fingers to a bloody mess than allow this Miss Prescott the satisfaction of believing she has one over on you." Tabitha assured her maid she did not need to endure any such injury and that she would appreciate anything that could be done in the few hours available."

It was almost time for dinner, and Ginny had already selected an evening gown. She helped Tabitha into it before working her magic on her mistress' hair. Leaving her room, Tabitha encountered Lily in the hallway. The young woman smiled shyly and asked, "Could I talk to you before we go down, Aunt Tabitha?" She indicated her room, and on Tabitha's assent, Lily opened the door and led the way in.

Lily's maid was nowhere to be seen, and Tabitha suspected Lily had been waiting in the hallway for her to exit her room so she could get her alone. What on earth was this going to be about?

Tabitha and Lily sat on two of the armchairs arranged around the fireplace. Tabitha said nothing, waiting for the young woman to explain herself. Whatever she wanted to talk about, Lily was clearly nervous, biting her lip and twisting her hands. Finally, unable to bear the awkward silence and conscious that they would be missed if they didn't descend to the drawing room soon, Tabitha asked, "Is this about Viscount Tobias?" It was just a guess, but she couldn't imagine what else Lily would be so anxious to talk to her about.

Lily nodded, then said, "He has asked me to marry him."

It had been evident for some time that the young man was quite smitten, and so this was not a total surprise. However, it had never been clear whether Lily returned his feelings. Looking at her now, Tabitha thought that perhaps she did after all.

"And what did you say?" Tabitha asked. She realised it was most inappropriate for Tobias to ask Lady Lily before asking her father's permission. However, the laird was many hundreds of miles away in Scotland, so perhaps Tobias' lapse in etiquette could be excused.

Lily looked up, suddenly seeming much older than her eighteen years. "I do not love him. However…"

What on earth could come after 'however'? Tabitha wondered.

"However, I like him very much."

Only four years separated Tabitha from Lily, but sometimes, it felt like an eternity. This was one of those times. Adopting the world-weary tone of a much older woman, Tabitha said, "In my experience, that may not be a strong enough foundation for marriage, Lily." She wasn't sure what Lily knew of Tabitha's horrific marriage to Jonathan, but she suspected that his sister, Jane, Lily's mother, had realised what a brute her brother was.

"I have no desire to get married," Lily admitted. "However, as you know, it is the dearest wish of my parents and grandmother. Moreover, they want me to marry well and are willing to force me to endure who knows how many seasons in order to make that happen."

Tabitha sighed. "You should not marry Viscount Tobias just because doing so will please your parents. Trust me, I know all about the folly of doing so. Nor should you agree to spend your life with a man merely to avoid the London Season. In the grand scheme of things, a few months of polite parties and balls is nothing compared to a lifetime shackled to a man where there is no genuine affection and mutual respect."

At this, Lily looked up, her eyes shining, "But that is just it; he loves and respects me. He has no desire to curb my scientific studies. Quite the opposite. He has promised to support me in every way he can, from setting up a laboratory for me in a marital home, to accompanying me to as many Royal Society lectures as I please. He has even offered to allow me to attend university lectures. I will never meet another man willing to be so indulgent and it is quite clear to me that my father, however loving and generous he is, will not allow me such academic freedom unmarried."

Tabitha sighed again. "So, you are willing to marry Viscount Tobias merely to continue your botanical studies? That seems a hard price to pay."

"Does it? All I have ever wanted was to study. To be allowed to read and learn all day. To be in the conservatory investigating plants. All of this is closed off to me as a single woman of my class. Ironically, I would be better off if my family was less wealthy and distinguished. As it is, my parents will hound me until I agree to marry. In Viscount Tobias they will have a son-in-law more titled than they had reason to hope for. Whatever trouble Toby has caused in the past, he is still the grandson of Grandmama's dearest friend, and her godson."

Tabitha wasn't sure how to phrase her real concern. Finally, she decided there was no delicate way to put it and came out and said, "Lily, how can you be sure that Tobias will live up to all his promises once you are married? He is young and, until very recently, quite feckless. As he matures, he will become more serious about the title and estate he will inherit one day. When he is earl, do you think he will still be inclined to indulge you?

I am sure that he says he will, but that is a very different thing than being a sitting member of the House of Lords and risking the censure and mockery of other peers."

Lily gave her a pitying look and said, "Aunt Tabitha, the world is changing. Perhaps not quickly enough to save me from marriage, but still, it is changing. We will see a new century soon, and it will be one where women can be more than wives, mothers, or prostitutes."

When Tabitha and Wolf had first met Lily, she had been an ardent believer in women's suffrage and many of the causes promoted by the Scottish Labour Party. Tabitha admired the girl for her passionate support for women's rights and better labour practices. Nevertheless, she was not as confident as Lily that a few years would bring the radical reforms she desired.

Tabitha had debated Lily enough times to realise that merely throwing cold water on the young woman's dreams would not dampen her righteous enthusiasm. Instead, she leaned forward and put her hand on the other woman's, saying, "Lily, I pray that you are correct, but what if you are not? What if the world does not change fast enough, but Viscount Tobias does change?"

"That is a risk I am prepared to take. In fact, it is one I have to take because there is no better alternative. Yes, Toby may turn into a tyrant, but he is not one today. If, by marrying him, I can pursue my studies and advance botanical studies even for a few years, it will be more than I will achieve by any other means. I know he can be absurd on occasion, but Toby is a good man at heart, and I believe he truly loves me. That is enough."

Tabitha tipped her head in acceptance of Lily's wishes. "I believe you need something from me," she observed astutely.

"I would like you to talk to Grandmama for me."

At this, Tabitha couldn't help but laugh out loud. "You cannot possibly believe that I am the best messenger to deliver this news to the dowager countess? In fact, I cannot imagine anyone she is less inclined to take notice of."

"She doesn't think as badly of you as you believe, you know," Lily observed.

"We can agree to disagree on that. However, even if you are right – and you are not – why not have Viscount Tobias tell her himself? She is your nearest relative within a few hundred miles. I am merely an aunt through marriage. As it happens, Wolf is your nearest male relative. It would not be an utter lapse of social etiquette for Tobias to apply to your cousin, who is also the highest-ranking family member, for your hand in marriage."

"Yes, yes. Toby can do that. However, we both know that whatever Mama and Papa think, the person who most desires for me to have my season and be presented to the Queen is Grandmama."

Tabitha was astounded that the truth hadn't dawned on Lily weeks before. "Lily, the dowager countess lost all interest in your Season quite a while ago. Have you not noticed?" Tabitha wasn't sure what Lily and Tobias realised about the dowager's solo investigation that had been the cause of her going missing for days only a few weeks before. At the time, Tabitha and Wolf had decided that Lily was too happy to be relieved of dance lessons or endless lectures on the details of the Queen's extended family to wonder about the reason for her reprieve. Was it possible they still had no idea what had been going on under their noses?

Lily looked genuinely surprised to hear that her grandmother had become almost as bored of preparing Lily for the Season as Lily herself. "Truly, Aunt Tabitha? You think she will not be unhappy?"

"Unhappy? I think she will be thrilled. After all, your Season was to be in the service of snaring an eligible husband. If you have managed to do that all on your own, then I am sure all you will get is her approbation. Lily, if you are truly intent on this path, then I believe that Viscount Tobias should ask Wolf for his permission, if only so we can assure your parents that all the necessary formalities were taken care of. You should talk to your grandmother."

Tabitha didn't bother to mention that she doubted the news would be the surprise to the dowager that Lily believed it would be. She'd seen the glint in the canny old woman's eye when she looked at her godson and granddaughter. Tobias was an extremely eligible catch for Lily, and to have achieved it without having to endure the endless circus that was the social season would only add to the dowager's delight.

CHAPTER 22

Uncle Duncan had surfaced in time for dinner and seemed even more intent than ever on torturing the dowager with his flirtations. Despite the woman's stated preference otherwise, he insisted on taking her into dinner and then sitting next to her.

"Ah've heard there are some bonnie wee lanes around here that a couple could easily lose themselves in," he said, leering at her over his soup course.

"While I wholeheartedly approve of the notion of you getting lost, I can assure you that it will not be in my company," the dowager said haughtily, throwing in a sniff for good measure.

"Ah've a fondness for a lass who likes a good chase," he said in an even more lecherous tone.

It was astounding to Tabitha that the dowager, who was not normally slow on the uptake, didn't realise that she was only encouraging the rogue rather than deterring him. Eager to distract Uncle Duncan and the dowager, Tabitha asked Wolf, "So what of Mr Thomas? Do you believe him guilty?"

Wolf hadn't mentioned his conversation with Elinor Hughes to anyone on his return. Still, looking around the table, he saw no reason for anything less than a full disclosure of his afternoon. However, mindful that most of the servants were local, he told the footmen they could leave until after the soup course when they returned with the fish. Whatever the men thought about so obviously being dismissed from the discussion, they did as they were bid and left the room, closing the dining room door behind them. Talbot remained to pour wine. Not only were Tabitha and

Wolf sure of his discretion, but he had no ties to Lamphey.

Satisfied with their privacy, Wolf described the visit to Pembroke Dock and his instinct that Rhys Thomas was innocent. Langley backed this up with his own views on the topic. Wolf then explained the theory they had formulated in the carriage: that Wolf was the common denominator across the pranks and the murder and that perhaps there was one perpetrator.

"But why?" Tabitha asked.

"That is the question we cannot answer," Wolf admitted. "Why and who? Though perhaps if we knew one, the other would be more obvious. How many people knew about my childhood friendship with Glynda? Anyway, that question sparked an idea, and on the way back, I went to visit Glynda's mother."

At this news, the dowager dropped her soup spoon, which fell onto her plate with a clanging that caused all heads to turn in her direction. The woman had gone a deathly shade of white; it was as if all the blood had drained from her face in a moment.

"Mama, are you alright?" Tabitha asked in a concerned voice.

"I am perfectly fine," the dowager snapped. Then she turned to Wolf and, in a rather strangled voice, "And what did Elinor Hughes have to say to you?"

At this, Wolf narrowed his eyes suspiciously and asked, "Lady Pembroke, how do you know Glynda's mother's name?"

The dowager realised her mistake too late. She searched for an excuse, but there was none except the truth: "Elinor was my lady's maid many years ago. She left to marry one of the footmen."

"How is this the first we are hearing of it?" Wolf asked.

The dowager had recovered her composure enough to snap, "I cannot imagine why you believe this was something I needed to share. If you remember, I did say that I was going to visit an old retainer."

"Mama, when we mentioned Glynda Thomas yesterday, you failed to disclose your connection to her mother," Tabitha chided.

"I do not appreciate you taking that tone with me, Tabitha," the dowager disdainfully informed her. She had always believed that the best defence was to go on the offensive—the more self-righteously chagrined one could be, the better. "When you mentioned Mrs Thomas yesterday, I had no idea that Elinor was her mother. I have not heard from or spoken with Elinor in over forty years. When I discovered this fact yesterday afternoon, I saw no reason to mention it."

Tabitha considered their earlier conversation and remembered something that had bothered her then. "Mama, was that how you knew that Glynda had been murdered?"

"How else would I have known?" the dowager snapped again.

"Why did you not mention this when we were talking about it at luncheon and were discussing her death?"

Adopting her most arrogant and condescending tone, the dowager looked at Tabitha and asked, "Since when do I owe you any explanation of my comings and goings and the conversations I have, Tabitha?"

Tabitha and Wolf exchanged glances; there was definitely more to this story. However, it was obvious the dowager would not be pressed any further, at least here and now. Instead, the conversation turned to the afternoon social call with Miss Prescott.

"An appalling woman in every way," the dowager pronounced. "No doubt she will be capitalising on our acquaintance for a long while to come. I have no idea why you agreed to visit the woman and deliver to her the social acceptability that our presence in her drawing room will convey to society."

"Mama, what choice did I have? She was a guest in this house. I could not very well decline to accept a reciprocal invitation. And, let me remind you that your presence there was entirely by choice," Tabitha said with perhaps more exasperation in her voice than she intended.

Ignoring this observation, the dowager replied, "I cannot

imagine what possessed you to accept a second invitation from her. An unfortunate decision was made to invite her for dinner," at this, she glared at Wolf, "and then a second poor choice compounded the first when you could not find some good reason to decline her invitation to tea. However, once we entered her drawing room and sipped on that inferior Darjeeling and those tasteless biscuits, any perceived scorecard of social etiquette was tallied as equal. Our obligations were at an end. Now, by agreeing to ride with her, on her horses, nonetheless, not only do you put yourself under a new obligation, but you have dragged us all along with you: she will now expect yet another invitation back to Glanwyddan Hall."

Focusing less on the dowager's grievance and more on an element of her complaint, Wolf asked, "You are going to ride with Miss Prescott? Do you even have a riding habit and boots with you?" He couldn't put his finger on why, but something about this proposed outing made him uncomfortable. Perhaps it was nothing more than that he wasn't a particularly good horseman himself. His father never had the funds to stable horses other than ones for the carriage or the home farm. He might have ridden when he visited his grandfather as a boy, but his Uncle Philip had no interest in teaching his nephew, and his grandfather was far too old to get on horseback.

Tabitha quickly told the story of the riding habit and boots that had been sent over, and Ginny's plan to make the outfit far more flattering than Miss Prescott had intended for it to be. Wolf chuckled and said, "I will come with you tomorrow. I want to ask Miss Prescott a few questions." Tabitha cocked an eyebrow questioningly, and Wolf continued, "It seems that she was the person who found Glynda's body." He then told them what Rhys Thomas had said about Miss Prescott arriving just as he was leaning over his wife's body.

Tabitha could only imagine what Maureen Prescott would make of Wolf accompanying her the following day. She was sure to take it as a very personal compliment. Nevertheless, Tabitha also realised that Miss Prescott would be far more open to discussing what she saw at the blacksmith's forge with Wolf than with her, and so a plan was made.

When Tabitha returned to her bedchamber after dinner, she found Ginny still hard at work on the riding habit. Miss Prescott had sent over a very drab hat as part of the outfit, and it was on the dressing table, already looking much smarter with a ribbon tied around it and a red feather attached.

"Ginny, you must have eyestrain if you have been working on this all evening. I am sure that whatever you have done is a great improvement over what was sent. I do not want you to stay up half the night continuing to work on it."

The maid smiled at her always thoughtful mistress. "Don't you worry yourself on my account, m'lady. I'm almost finished." Standing up and holding the jacket in front of her, Tabitha could see that it had been taken in for a more flattering fit and that it was now edged in a lovely red ribbon. "I've only taken the skirt in a tad, but I think that with the jacket and hat looking so much better and the boots shined up to look like new, you will shock that Miss Prescott with how fine you appear." Tabitha doubted that Miss Prescott would consider any outfit that wasn't garishly coloured or patterned fine. Still, at least Tabitha would have the satisfaction of knowing she presented an elegant figure.

The following morning, when Tabitha entered wearing her riding habit, the breakfast room was surprisingly empty. The only person sitting at the table was Wolf, who was nursing a cup of coffee and seemed lost in thought. Putting some eggs and toast on her plate, she joined him.

"You seem far away," she observed.

"I had an interesting morning," Wolf admitted. "I was in my study going over some of the estate accounts. The estate manager is coming by later, and we are going to review all his proposed maintenance work. Anyway, I was sitting there when there was a knock at the door, and you will never guess who wanted to talk with me."

"Viscount Tobias?" Tabitha asked, hazarding a guess that her conversation with Lily the previous evening had put a plan into motion.

"You know?" Wolf said in surprise. "How?"

"Lily ambushed me last night to ask for my help. I suggested that Tobias ask your permission and that she then be the one to talk to Mama. She was under, what I believe is a false impression, that the dowager countess will be unhappy at the match. I explained that her grandmother lost any interest she may have ever had in preparing Lily for the Season weeks ago. Tobias is a very eligible match and saves everyone a lot of time and trouble."

Tabitha paused, wondering how much of her conversation with Lily to reveal. Finally, she admitted, "While it may be a love match on his side, it is not on hers. Or so it seems. I do not know what he understands of her feelings, but he has assured her that he will support her academic studies in any way he can. I questioned whether she could be sure he would always be inclined to keep that promise, but she is determined. She said that however long he supports her will be longer than she is able to further her botanical studies otherwise. It was hard to argue with that logic, even though I still have my doubts. What did you tell him?"

"Well, once I got over the initial surprise, I told him that I could see no reason why he could not formally make an offer to Lady Lily. Honestly," he admitted, "I have no idea what the correct protocol is here. Do I send a telegram to Hamish?"

"I do not doubt that Hamish and Jane will be ecstatic about the match. A future earl is far higher than they had likely ever hoped for. I believe that if the dowager approves, then everyone else will be happy to bless the union. And why would she not approve?"

"Well, when we first met Tobias, he had been sent down from Cambridge and then banished from his father's house for his gambling debts. He was imposing on a friend's generosity while racking up new debts, so one might question his eligibility."

"All that is true. However, you must admit he has been on his best behaviour since our return from Brighton. Love has made a new man of him. Even the dowager has been impressed with his reformation. And at the end of the day, he is from a highly-ranked, very respectable and wealthy family. While his father may be holding the purse strings very tightly at the moment, I am sure that once Tobias is settled, the earl will be appropriately generous with his allowance. Let us not forget that the viscount is the dowager's godson and the grandson of her dearest friend. One could hardly imagine a match she'd be more likely to smile upon."

"Let us hope," Wolf replied. "So what happens next? Now he has my consent, he proposes, Lily tells her grandmother, and then I send a telegram to Scotland?" Wolf had trouble viewing himself as the head of the family and as someone with the authority to handle such matters.

"I think that is a reasonable plan. Given that Lily has already told me about it, I assume the proposal is a mere formality and that she will try to find time with the dowager as soon as possible. Perhaps, she should be the one to write to her parents."

No sooner had Tabitha spoken these words than Lily and Tobias entered the breakfast room together. The young man had a soppy, lovestruck look on his face, and Lily seemed earnestly happy. Tabitha was still worried at the bargain the young woman was making. In many ways, Lily's calculus was not all that different from Tabitha's own when she accepted Jonathan's proposal. Her reasons for accepting had been very different, and perhaps Tabitha had been more romantically inclined and imagined herself a little in love with Jonathan. However, in hindsight and with the benefit of her new understanding of what true love was, Tabitha could imagine the quagmire Lily might find herself in at some point. What if she eventually fell in love with someone else? What if Tobias became frustrated with the lack of reciprocation? What if...?

With these concerns in mind, Tabitha looked carefully at Lily's face. She looked happy enough, but was that merely because she felt she had found a way around her parents' strictures? Perhaps sensing her aunt's concern, Lily flashed her a warm smile.

Lily and Tobias filled their plates and then sat down. "I assume congratulations are in order?" Wolf asked.

"Yes, Toby has asked me to marry him, and I have accepted," Lily said shyly. As his affianced said this, Toby watched her with the sweetest, silliest grin on his face.

"When will you talk to your grandmother?" Wolf asked, cognisant that the dowager needed to hear this news as soon as possible and from Lily herself.

"Talk to me about what?" the dowager demanded, entering the room at that very moment.

Lily and Tobias' eyes both went wide, and they looked anxiously at Tabitha and Wolf for rescue. Watching this play out, the dowager came and sat at the table and asked, "So, the deed is done, is it Tobias? It's about time too!"

"What are you talking about, godmother?" Tobias stammered.

"It's all been quite pusillanimous if you ask me." Seeing the looks of stupefaction on the faces of everyone, the dowager asked, "Did you think I did not realise what was happening? I have eyes you know. Tobias' infatuation with my granddaughter has been obvious for quite a while. Of course, I have alerted your Mama and Papa, and it goes without saying, I assume, that they are thrilled. Jane promised not to say anything until Tobias finally plucked up the courage to offer for you. You better write to her immediately and put her out of her agony."

Lily rose, went over to her grandmother, and kissed her on the cheek. The dowager, unused to such shows of affection, blushed slightly. As she waved her away, she said, "Pish posh. There is no need for such sentimentality. Did you believe any of us would not approve, child?"

"Well, I know that Mama and Papa were very keen for me to have my Season. And I thought that you were, too," Lily admitted.

"Your parents want to see you well married. The Season is merely the mechanism to ensure that happens. For my part, if your engagement saves me from weeks of balls and soirees filled with some of the most crashing bores in England, then all the better." Then, addressing her godson, the dowager said, while wagging a finger, "Tobias, if you do anything to make my granddaughter unhappy, and I mean anything, I will personally horsewhip you. Do you understand me?" Tobias nodded his head, too scared to say anything.

"Good," the dowager continued. "Then I believe we understand each other. You should go down to the village and send a telegram to your parents, Tobias. It is about time they received some good news from you for a change."

CHAPTER 23

After breakfast, Tabitha and Wolf called for the carriage and made their way the short distance to Prescott Manor. Tabitha warned Wolf about the hideous architecture and, even worse, decorating. "Do you think he inherited the house?" she asked.

"My understand is that Mr Prescott is a self-made man, and so I assume he bought it."

"Why would anyone buy such a monstrosity?" Tabitha wondered out loud.

"Surely, it can't be that bad?" Wolf said.

"Just wait. You make your own mind up."

Not long after this, the house came into view. "Oh my goodness," Wolf exclaimed, lost for words.

"Exactly!" Tabitha said triumphantly.

On being admitted to the house by the butler, Tabitha could see from the expression Wolf was trying but failing to control that his judgement of the house's interior matched her own. "Just wait until you see the drawing room," she whispered.

Yet again, Miss Prescott was not waiting for her guest. They were shown into the over-decorated drawing room, and a few minutes later, their hostess swanned into the room wearing a fuchsia riding habit and a matching hat with a large peacock feather in it. Seeing Wolf, she came up short, smiled wolfishly, and exclaimed, "Lord Pembroke, what a delight. I see you could not keep away. But you are not dressed for riding. I hope you intend to join us."

At this, Maureen Prescott turned her attention to Tabitha, and her expression indicated that she was unhappy with Ginny's alterations to the riding habit. Attempting to school her face, Miss Prescott said, "I see you altered my mother's outfit."

"Yes, my maid works miracles with a needle. You did say there was no need to return it, and so I took the liberty of making a few alterations."

Unable to hide her displeasure, Miss Prescott noted, "It looks as if more than a few alterations were made. I hardly recognise the outfit."

Unsure what reply to make to this, Tabitha pivoted the conversation and said, "Lord Pembroke will not be joining us for our ride, but he has a few questions for you before we head out."

Miss Prescott took a seat and said, "Questions? About what?"

"About the murder of a local woman, Glynda Thomas," Wolf answered.

"What of it?"

"I was told by Mr Thomas that you discovered him leaning over his wife's body, covered in blood, had your footmen restrain him and then called for PC Evans. Is that correct?"

Maureen Prescott had her leather riding gloves in her lap and spent a moment staring down at them before answering, "Indeed. I was happy to do my civic duty and apprehend a murderer." She stopped and considered Wolf's words. "You spoke with Mr Thomas, Lord Pembroke? Why?"

"Glynda Thomas was a dear childhood friend of mine, actually the only friend I ever had when I visited here."

Tabitha thought that Miss Prescott winced slightly at these words, but she recovered quickly, if indeed that had been her reaction, and asked, "And so you felt compelled to visit with her killer?"

Wolf answered, "I was something of a private inquiry agent before I inherited the earldom." Tabitha had never heard him refer to his thief-taking in such a way and found it an interesting choice of words. Wolf continued, "Over the last few months, Lady Pembroke and I have continued to take on the occasional case." As he said this, he indicated to Tabitha and smiled warmly at her. Maureen Prescott wrinkled her nose at this, and her mouth puckered as if she were eating a lemon drop.

"So, you are investigating Glynda Thomas' murder? What is there to investigate? I witnessed her husband moments after killing her. There can be no doubt that he is the perpetrator."

"That is what I want to ask you about," Wolf explained. "I spoke to Mr Thomas and I believe he is innocent."

At these words, Maureen Prescott stiffened her spine slightly and said in an aggrieved tone, "Do you question my narrative? I know what I saw with my own eyes, and my footmen can also testify to the truth of my story."

"I have no doubt you believe what you saw to be true, but I think there is a good chance it is not. For Glynda's sake, I feel that I need to make sure that justice is done and that her children are not left orphans. Mr Thomas said that you had sent a note earlier that day telling him you needed to get your horse reshoed."

"That is correct. As if anticipating his next question, she said, "You may wonder why I did not send one of my grooms down with the horse. The animal has very high spirits and responds best to my voice and touch. He does not like being reshoed, and I felt I should be with him to keep him calm."

That was a reasonable enough answer, and Wolf nodded, then continued, "According to the timetable Mr Thomas laid out, he went home for lunch then returned to the forge at one o'clock. Two hours later, he got called out to fix an oven hinge for the baker. That took thirty minutes and then he returned to the forge where he found the doors open and his wife dead on the floor. So, by my calculations, that was about four o'clock. Does that seem about right to you, Miss Prescott?"

All her flirtatiousness long gone, Miss Prescott said coldly, "If that is what you say, I have no reason to dispute it."

"So, you turned up at the forge and did what next?" Wolf asked.

"Normally, when Mr Thomas was working, he had the doors to the forge flung open. That afternoon, one of the doors was ajar, but it was unclear if the blacksmith was there. I sent a footman in to see, and the next thing I knew, he was yelling. The other footman ran in to join him and I followed. I found Mr Thomas lying over his wife's bloodied body, with his hands held behind his back by my footman. I quickly instructed the other footman to find some rope and tie the man's hands, and then to go and fetch the constable."

"How did Mr Thomas seem during all this?" Tabitha asked.

Turning a cold, hard stare at Tabitha, Miss Prescott answered, "At that time, my thoughts were on restraining the man and turning him over to the police. I did not take time to assess his mental state."

"Might I talk with your footmen to get their perspective?" Wolf asked.

Miss Prescott looked as if she would love to find a way to deny the request, but instead, she answered, "Given that my word seems to be insufficient, I will call them so they may also be interrogated." Turning to Tabitha, she said, "I find myself quite out of sorts with all this talk of murder and unable to take that ride after all."

Tabitha was relieved to hear this. As much as she missed horse riding, the idea of spending hours in Miss Prescott's company and dealing with the woman's barely veiled insults negated any excitement she might have had about being on horseback again.

Miss Prescott rang the bell, and after barely a minute, her butler entered the room. "Richardson, please fetch Shandley and Hectors. Lord Pembroke has some questions for them."

With that, she settled back in her chair. Wolf looked at Tabitha; he wasn't sure how best to phrase what needed to be said. Realising there was no good way to relay the request, he said, "Miss Prescott, if you don't mind, I would like to interview each of the footmen separately and without you in the room."

Miss Prescott's eyebrows shot up, and her mood seemed to sour even further, "These are my employees, and this is my father's house."

Adopting the most conciliatory tone he could, Wolf

explained, "I have conducted many such interviews of servants over the years, and it is my experience that they are normally very hesitant to speak when their employer is in the room." This didn't seem to mollify Miss Prescott at all, and so Wolf added, "I cannot tell you how much I appreciate your assistance, Miss Prescott. It is extremely gracious of you."

Finally, these words seemed to warm the woman up a bit, and an almost flirtatious look came over her face again, "As if I could deny you anything, Lord Pembroke."

A few minutes later, Richardson was back in the room. "Shandley and Hectors are waiting outside, miss. Should I send them in?"

Casting one more look at Wolf, Miss Prescott said, "I will be leaving. I am returning to my bedchamber to change. You may tell the grooms that we are not riding after all. Once I am gone, send Shandley in." The butler nodded and left. Miss Prescott then rose and said, "I will bid you both farewell. Lord Pembroke, I look forward to meeting again under more propitious circumstances." With that, she left the room without saying a word to Tabitha.

As soon as Miss Prescott had gone, a tall, good-looking young man entered. Tabitha and Wolf assumed this was the footman. "Mr Shandley, I assume?" Wolf asked. The footman nodded but didn't say anything. Wolf had learned not to try to get servants to take a seat in their master's drawing rooms. Instead, he left the young man standing, nervously playing with his fingers.

"Do you know why I want to talk to you?" Wolf asked. Shandley shook his head. "I hear that you and another footman were with Miss Prescott a few weeks ago and came upon Mr Thomas, the blacksmith, and the body of his dead wife." Shandley nodded his head but said nothing.

Realising this was not getting them very far, Tabitha said gently, "Mr Shandley, you may speak freely in front of Lord Pembroke and myself. You are not in trouble, we merely wish to hear, in your own words, what happened that day. Are you able to do that?"

"Yes, m'lady," the man said. "I'll try."

"Wonderful. Then, let us start at the beginning. Tell us about the trip down to Lamphey."

"Well, normally, it wouldn't need two footmen to go with, but the groom, Roberts, had to tend to a poorly mare, and so Miss Prescott asked me and Hectors to accompany her. Rainbow, that's the horse's name, can be a bit of a handful. Beautiful animal, but very high spirits. Hectors grew up around horses and is particularly good at handling them. Miss Prescott was worried that Rainbow might be hard to control while the blacksmith was reshoeing him and so wanted us to hold him firm."

That all made perfect sense, and so Wolf jumped ahead, "You arrived in Lamphey at the forge. What happened next?"

"Well, the doors weren't fully open like they normally are when Hughes is working. Just one door was open a bit, and Miss Prescott told me to go in and make sure the blacksmith was around. I did that and almost as soon as I walked in, I could hear sobbing. I went towards it, and it was an awful sight, I can tell you."

Now that the young man had warmed up to his subject, he was quite enthusiastic in the telling of it. "Mrs Thomas, she that was the blacksmith's wife, was laid on the ground with all this blood around her head. And Mr Thomas was laying across her body crying like a baby."

"Was he saying anything?" Tabitha asked.

The footman thought for a moment, then replied, "He was repeating fy nghariad, over and over." Realising that Tabitha and Wolf wouldn't understand the Welsh, the footman explained, "It means my love."

"Was there a likely murder weapon nearby?"

"Yes, m'lord. There was a hammer, covered in blood."

"What did you do next?" Wolf asked.

"Well, I ran over and grabbed Mr Thomas, and held his hands behind his back, then called for Hectors."

"Did Mr Thomas struggle?"

"Not a bit. The man just kept sobbing and saying my love, my love, over and over. Then, Hectors ran in, followed by Miss Prescott. She was ever so brave; didn't bat an eye at all that blood, just calmly told Hectors to find some rope to bind the blacksmith and then, when that was done, told me to go and fetch old Evans. I mean PC Evans."

"Thank you, Mr Shandley, that will be all. Please send in Mr Hectors on your way out."

The other footman told the same story. Wolf was always suspicious when stories were too alike; it sometimes indicated that witnesses had been coached. However, the two footmen had the expected differences in minor details but told overall similar stories. Once Hectors had been dismissed, Tabitha and Wolf let themselves out.

In the carriage, Tabitha said, "While I am grateful to be spared an afternoon with that woman, the sudden change of plans seemed out of proportion to the conversation. She even seemed irritated with you for a while there."

Wolf agreed and observed, "I have met people like Miss Prescott before. She believes herself to have a superior intellect and to be playing a game of chess where the rest of us are merely pawns."

"Not unlike someone else we know," Tabitha pointed out.

"Indeed. And just like the dowager countess, she is not happy when she feels she is losing control of a situation. From the moment she walked into that room and saw that I was there and that you were looking far more stylish than she had planned, I believe her mood began to sour."

"Well, I do not believe that your presence upset her. In fact, she seemed very happy to see you."

"Perhaps not as much as you believe. She had a plan for this afternoon. I will not claim to know what she hoped to achieve by taking you out riding, but whatever it was, the board was not set as she had expected it to be, and that threw her off. Then, we began to ask questions about Glynda's murder and to press her for details. Finally, we insisted on talking to her footmen and essentially dismissed her from her own drawing room. Just imagine how the dowager would have taken such events." When he put it like that, Tabitha understood better Miss Prescott's petulance.

CHAPTER 24

With Tabitha and Wolf on their way to Prescott Manor, Lily and Tobias in the study composing a letter to her parents, and Langley busy with Rat, the dowager removed herself to the Green Room to contemplate what was going on around her. Wolf believed that the connecting tissue between the happenings at the Hall and Glynda's death was him, but what if it were her instead? What if the secret that she had thought buried for so long had somehow resurfaced, and an innocent woman had died because of it? The dowager had no idea why Glynda Thomas might have been sacrificed for her sins. Whatever the reason, it seemed too great a coincidence to the dowager that she had received a note showing knowledge of her secret and then the daughter of the only other person who knew that secret was killed.

The dowager wasn't sure what she feared most, that the murderer was biding their time and that she might be attacked next, or that Tabitha and Wolf would keep digging and would eventually uncover her secret. Either way, she knew that she could not just sit back and hope that nothing more would happen. She thought about her conversation with Elinor. The dowager believed that the woman had not told anyone intentionally, but what about unintentionally?

Then, she thought about all those years ago. Did it really matter anymore? Philip, Jonathan, and Colin were all dead. There might be some scandal, but she would weather it as she did everything: with her head held high, daring anyone to say anything to her face. She felt some twinge of something perhaps akin to guilt at the idea that Glynda Thomas' husband might hang for a crime he didn't commit, but in truth, that was at most a secondary concern, perhaps even tertiary.

The dowager sat in the Green Room, remembering the past and wondering what she should do. Her musings were interrupted by Wolf, who had returned from Prescott Manor.

"How was that awful woman?" the dowager asked. "Did she tell you anything illuminating?"

"Not particularly. We also spoke with the footmen who were with her, and everything the three of them said confirmed that the evidence against Rhys Thomas is purely circumstantial. There is no reason to believe that the situation was not precisely what he claims: that he came back to the forge, found his wife dead, and in his grief and shock, threw himself on top of the body."

"When you spoke with Mr Thomas, did he indicate why his wife had visited the forge?" the dowager asked.

Wolf shook his head, "He had no idea. He had gone home for lunch, and his wife had been busy baking. He said that it was not at all usual for her to visit him at work."

The dowager thought about the investigation they seemed to be in the middle of and wondered aloud, "Do we need a board? I know we don't have the corkboard with us, but perhaps Ginny could help us make the kind of makeshift one using a painting and a sheet that you and Tabitha first used."

Wolf had been thinking along much the same lines. A board and notecards had first been Tabitha's idea as a way to keep track of clues and also to group them and even create timelines. Jumping up, he said, "You are absolutely right. I will ask Bear to help Ginny find the necessary materials and we will all regroup after lunch and start writing up what we know." With that, he rushed out of the room.

The dowager stared after him. Had she just made a rod for her own back? She had suggested that they record clues and try to find connections between them, yet she was holding back what was likely the biggest clue of them all. Was it possible to reveal that she had a secret without saying what it actually was? Perhaps that was the only solution to her dilemma.

On returning to Glanwyddan Hall, Tabitha had retired to her bedchamber to change out of the riding habit back into a day dress. Ginny had been in the room busy tidying and had looked up in surprise at her mistress' return. "That was a quick ride, m'lady."

"Ha! There was no ride. Lord Pembroke and I asked Miss Prescott some questions and she became out of sorts and declined to ride anymore."

"And what did she make of your riding habit?" Ginny asked with glee.

Tabitha sat at the dressing table, and Ginny helped her remove the hat and jacket. "Well, I believe that my outfit put her in something of a bad mood before we even started questioning her. So, well done, Ginny!" The maid glowed with pride.

Unsure of what to do with the rest of her morning, Tabitha decided to visit Melody in the nursery. There, she spent a wonderful hour and a half helping the little girl with her letters. Finally, descending downstairs, she made her way to the dining room, where everyone else was already gathered. Tabitha was interested to see that Rat had joined them. Neither Tabitha nor Wolf had any problem with the boy joining them for family meals. Quite the opposite, they both felt he needed more practice honing his table manners. Even though they had both assured him that he was more than welcome to eat with them when there were no guests, the boy still chose to eat his meals either in the kitchen or in the nursery with his sister. Making eye contact with Langley as she walked in, Tabitha gestured with her chin towards Rat and lifted her shoulders in query slightly.

Understanding the question, Langley explained, "I have suggested to Rat that a vital part of the career I am training for will be the ability to mingle with people of all walks of life. As such, he needs to be as comfortable eating with a king as he is with a pauper. Because of this, he will now join us regularly for meals." Rat looked less than enthusiastic about this news.

"Welcome, Rat," Wolf said, clapping the boy on the back as he moved to take an empty chair beside Langley.

With Tabitha supposed to be out riding and Wolf's time of return uncertain, Talbot had arranged for a cold collation for lunch. The advantage of this was that there were no servants except for the butler in the room. Looking over at Bear, Wolf asked, "Were you able to locate and assemble the necessary materials?" Bear indicated that he was. "Good," Wolf said. "We will all be removing to the library after lunch, where we will discuss the investigation so far using a board that Bear and Ginny have managed to improvise for us."

Wolf caught Lily and Tobias rolling their eyes at each other and said, "This is not a mandatory exercise; only those who wish to need to join."

"Can I join, m'lord Wolf?" Rat asked.

Wolf looked at Langley. After all, he was the boy's mentor and guardian. Langley wiped his mouth and said, "I think that this would be very educational for Rat and that his very logical brain could be of great use." The young boy beamed with pride at this praise.

The meal was over quickly. No one felt the urge to linger. Lily and Tobias wanted to escape before the upcoming discussion suddenly was no longer voluntary, and everyone else was eager to start discussing the investigation.

The library at Glanwyddan Hall was huge. Tabitha had thought that the one at her family's estate was impressive, but this one put that to shame. As she looked around the large, oak-panelled room, lined with books from floor to its very high ceilings, the dowager commented, "These books have been collected over many generations of Chesterton men. Of course, such erudition was entirely lost on my husband."

There were many comfortable-looking leather armchairs in the library, and propped up against a sideboard was a board that looked much like the very first one Tabitha and Ginny had constructed out of a painting covered in a taut piece of fabric. Next to it, Bear had arranged a stack of notecards, some thread, hat pins, and pens. Everyone took a seat, and Tabitha sat down with the notecards in her lap.

"So, let us start with the pranks. We believe they started just over two weeks ago, not long before we decided to come here for Christmas, in fact. These began harmlessly enough and then escalated to arson and dead animals being left outside the doors." Wolf had not sat, and as he spoke, he paced up and down in front of the fireplace. "Then, two weeks ago, Glynda Thomas, my childhood friend, was brutally murdered. I believe that all these incidents are connected."

As he paced, Wolf noticed Rat squirming in his seat and looking very uncomfortable. The boy hadn't told anyone about his interaction with Billy Morris because he hadn't wanted to break the dowager's confidence. However, now that it seemed the pranks might be connected to a woman's death, Rat felt guilty about not having shared what he knew.

"Rat, do you have something you'd like to share?" Wolf asked.

"Um, well, sort of. It's just that the day after we arrived, I went down to the village to take Dodo for a walk. On my way there, I could feel I was being followed. I thought some boys were waiting to jump me if I'd taken the shortcut through the woods, so I stayed on the main road."

Tabitha looked very concerned, but Wolf caught her eye and indicated that she shouldn't interrupt the boy's story. Rat continued, "I went and looked in the bakery window. There were some nice-looking iced buns. So, I went in and talked to the baker's wife." At this, Rat glanced at the dowager, who opened her eyes at him just enough to indicate she expected to keep her part in his outing a secret. "Anyway, while I was in there, the baker's son, Billy Morris, came in. From the way he was eyeing me, I just knew that he was one of the boys waiting to jump me. Nasty piece of work he is."

Rat sensed that no one would be happy to hear how he lured Billy Morris into the graveyard and then threatened him with a knife. Instead, he told a sanitised version of the story, "When I left the bakery, he came out after me, and we had words."

Finally, Tabitha could not hold back anymore and interrupted, "Did he hurt you, Rat?"

"Nah! A girly country boy like that hurt a Whitechapel lad like me? But the entire thing made me believe that he could have been responsible for the pranks. I'd heard some of the servants suggest that he might be responsible. But here's the thing: I used to know boys like that on the streets. They'd do anything for money and nothing just for the fun of it. Honestly, if m'lady Tabby Cat and m'lord Wolf hadn't taken me in, I would have been one of those boys soon enough. I think that if Billy did those things, someone paid him to do them."

After Rat announced this, there was silence. Then Wolf said, "Let us put Billy Morris on a notecard, and when we finish here, Bear and I will pay the boy a visit." It was not hard to imagine why Wolf wanted Bear to accompany him; if the man's size and visage didn't scare the boy into telling the truth, nothing would.

Wolf continued, "Now, let us turn to the murder itself. Here is what we know," Wolf held up one finger, "Rhys Thomas went home for lunch daily. He says that there was nothing unusual about this particular day." Wolf held up a second finger, and Tabitha started a new notecard, "He returns to the forge and a couple of hours later, Billy Morris comes by and asks him to come and look at one of father's ovens." Wolf paused, "Billy Morris again. Can that possibly be a coincidence?"

"When we speak to Billy, I think we need to confirm this story with the baker himself," Langley observed. Wolf nodded his agreement.

Holding up a third finger, Wolf said, "Let us assume that it is true that he was called out because it is too easily verified to be a good lie. Mr Thomas seems like a sharp enough man; I doubt he would include something like that in his story if it were not the truth. So, next, and this needs to go on as a question, Tabitha: why did Glynda visit the forge? It seems it was not a common occurrence."

"Perhaps someone sent her a note telling her to go, m'lord Wolf."

"A very astute observation, Rat," Wolf told the boy. "But who? It is unlikely it was her husband. Surely, she would know his handwriting."

Tabitha felt awful asking the question, but it had to be said, "Could Glynda read?"

"Yes," Wolf said definitively. "Her grandmother had taught her, and I would sometimes take a book from the library here and we would read together. However, whether her husband could read and write is another matter, and as I said, surely, she would know his handwriting."

"Perhaps someone came and told her to go. Maybe they told her there was a problem or something," Rat offered.

"Another fine point."

During all this, Langley was sitting beaming with pride at the logical suggestions made by his protégé. Tabitha noticed this, and it made her heart sing. Finding a suitable place for Rat in their lives had not been as simple as it had been with his sister. Lord Langley turned out to be the perfect guardian and mentor for the boy, and it seemed as if a more personal relationship was developing between the two.

Now Wolf held up a fourth finger, "We know that someone opened up the forge before Glynda arrived. If it wasn't Rhys Thomas, who was it? Then, one of two things happened: either Rhys Thomas was lying and he was there when his wife arrived, they fought perhaps, and he killed her. Or, he is telling the truth, and whoever picked the lock at the forge lay in wait for Glynda and killed her."

Tabitha interjected, "We got confirmation from Miss Prescott as to the time she arrived at the forge. So, if Mr Thomas killed his wife, there was not a lot of time between when he returned from the bakery to when she turned up during which the murder could have taken place."

"True, but how long does it take? Though, why would Glynda's husband send her a note asking her to come to the forge and then leave to fix the baker's oven?" Langley pointed out. "That makes no sense. So, it must have been someone or something else that caused her to visit. Perhaps she had a key to the forge, found it locked and let herself in. She waited for her husband, and as soon as he returned, they argued, and he struck her."

"That is certainly possible," Wolf allowed. "It's a tight timeframe, but possible." He held up a fifth finger and continued, "Finally, Miss Prescott and her footmen arrive at the forge and find Mr Thomas prostate over his wife's body. We know that Miss Prescott had sent a note earlier that day saying she would come by later that day, and she has explained why she had gone with her horse rather than sending the groom. Her footmen corroborated everything she told us."

Tabitha took the notecards she had written up and pinned them to the makeshift board with the hatpins, then took some of the red threads and made some connections between them, such as there were. "It is interesting that the pranks seem to have stopped since that rock was thrown through the window on our first night here."

"Well, to be fair, we have not been in residence very long," Wolf observed. "However, your point is valid, and we should write up a notecard with that as a question: have the pranks stopped and, if so, why?"

They all sat in silence for a few minutes, looking at the notecards on the board, each lost in their contemplations. Wolf continued to feel very guilty at the thought that, somehow, he might have set this all in motion. The dowager felt anxious at the part her secret might have played and the thought that she might have to reveal it at some point, and Rat just felt very proud at how many of his contributions were written up..

Finally, Wolf interrupted the silence and said, "I do not believe there is anything else to add now, and so Bear, why don't you and I go and have a talk with Mr Morris and his son?"

"While you are gone, I must sit with Mrs Budgers and Mrs Jenkins and go through the plans for the Christmas Eve party." Turning to the dowager, she asked, "Mama, would you be so kind as to join us? You must have been at some of those parties over the years and can provide vital insights."

The dowager harumphed, "I did attend one or two of those follies. I have no idea why my father-in-law felt compelled to keep that tradition going. Just send everyone a few coins and be done with it. Certainly, for all his faults, Philip was wise enough to put a stop to this party the year his father died."

Perhaps the dowager wasn't the best person to ask for help after all, Tabitha thought. However, the ask had been made and so both women rose to go and meet the housekeeper and cook.

CHAPTER 25

Mrs Morris had just finished serving the doctor's housekeeper when the bell to the bakery rang. Looking up, she couldn't have been more surprised to see a handsome toff, who could only be the new earl, accompanied by a very large man with a rather terrifying-looking face. The baker's wife immediately dropped into a curtsey and said, "M'lord, what an honour. How can I help you today?"

Wolf could see that there was no need to use the full force of the aristocracy against Mrs Morris; she was overawed enough already. Instead, he approached the counter and said kindly enough, "We have not been introduced yet. I believe you are Mrs Morris?"

The woman blushed to the roots of her hair when she realised the earl knew her name. "Indeed I am, m'lord," she said, still in her curtsey.

"Please, do get up, Mrs Morris. I am not the Queen." The baker's wife did as commanded and then waited for further instructions. Had the earl come to buy a loaf of bread? That was highly unlikely. While there had certainly been some eccentrics in the family over the years, none had stooped to doing their own shopping.

"Mrs Morris, I would like to talk with your husband and your son if they are available," Wolf explained.

"Our Billy? What has he done now?"

Wolf found it telling that the boy's mother immediately assumed her son's guilt. Clearly, the rumours about the boy had merit. "I am not sure, Mrs Morris. At the moment, I merely have a few questions. Do you have a parlour in which I might talk with them?"

At this request, Mrs Morris began a frenzied mental inventory of the state of her small parlour. She knew that Mr Morris had been reading the newspaper there last night. She was almost certain she had folded it and put it away. Of course, she had been working in the shop most of the day. Who knew what chaos Billy and the other children might have caused? It crossed her mind to ask the earl and his giant to wait for a few moments while she went and tidied up. However, on reflection, she decided that leaving a toff to cool his heels in her shop was likely an even greater blunder than letting him enter a parlour that might have a newspaper laid out on the table.

"Please follow me, m'lord, to our parlour. Then I'll go and fetch Mr Morris. I believe he has Billy helping him this afternoon, so you're in luck." The baker's wife bobbed a curtsey again and hurried out of the room. A few minutes later, she returned with an ordinary-looking man with the beefy shoulders, neck and arms of someone who spent his days punching dough and pulling heavy trays out of ovens. By his side was a boy, probably a few years older than Rat, with a very sullen look on his face.

Mr Morris entered the room, still wiping flour off his hands and onto his apron. Seeing the two men in his parlour, he bowed his head and said, "M'lord, Polly here, I mean Mrs Morris, says I can help you with something. And that you want to talk to our Billy as well. Let me just say, whatever he's done, poaching, stealing apples, other mischief, I'll pay for, and he'll never do it again. Right lad?" As he said this, Mr Morris clipped his son round his head.

"Why do you always think I've done some wrong?" the boy asked in a whiny voice.

"Because you usually have," his father answered. Then, turning to Wolf and Bear, he asked, "Can the missus get you anything? Tea, maybe?"

"No, we need nothing," Wolf assured him. "Merely to ask you

and your son a few questions. Why don't we all sit?"

The parlour was small, with one sofa and two armchairs. Wolf and Bear each took one of the chairs, and Mr and Mrs Morris perched nervously on the edge of their sofa, with Billy left standing, his arms folded defiantly, his entire face and posture indicating that this interview was not going to be easy.

During the short carriage ride into Lamphey, Wolf and Bear discussed how to conduct the interview. Bear suggested beginning towards the end with the undisputed facts: the baker's oven had a broken hinge, and the blacksmith had been sent to fix it.

Wolf followed Bear's suggestion and stated this information. Mr Morris nodded in acknowledgement of its truth. Wolf then asked, "Is it common for these ovens to suffer such breakages?"

Mr Morris thought for a moment, "Well, I put a lot of wear and tear on them. But the blacksmith had been out only a few weeks before to fix that one. He always does good work, does Rhys Thomas, and so I was surprised it had broken again so soon. There must have been a weakness in the metal."

"And so, you sent Billy to the forge to get the blacksmith?" Wolf asked, assuming that was what happened.

"Yes. Rhys came straight away and fixed it. Didn't take him long. He was surprised it had broken again so quickly. Said he must not have sealed it properly the last time and that he wouldn't charge me for the work. That's the kind of honest man he is. I still can't believe he killed Glynda. And right after he'd been here as well." As her husband said this, Mrs Morris shivered as if the proximity in time of the two events had somehow put her own family at risk.

As the baker spoke, Wolf knew what the next question had to be: "Mr and Mrs Morris, did Billy return with Mr Thomas?" Wolf watched Billy closely as he asked this question, and he could see the boy's face change from sullen to worried. He realised he had asked the right question.

"Now you come to mention it, he didn't. He's supposed to be helping me in the bakery every afternoon, but he's always skiving off. I care more that he helps me in the morning when I'm very busy, so I usually look the other way when he slinks off to meet his friends. He'd noticed the broken hinge and gone to fetch the blacksmith for me. After that, I'm sure he felt that he had helped enough for that day."

"So, Billy was the one who saw the broken hinge?" Wolf asked. "Where were you during this time, Mr Morris?"

"That's usually the time I'm in the storeroom taking inventory of supplies. It's no good finding myself out of flour the next morning. We've been particularly busy in the shop of recent, and I was worried that my usual order wouldn't come soon enough."

"Thank you, Mr Morris, for that clarification. Let me recap," Wolf said. "Billy was alone in the bakehouse. He alerted you to the broken hinge. You then sent him to fetch Mr Thomas, but he didn't return with the blacksmith? Is that correct?" The baker nodded his head in assent.

Then, turning to Billy, who had been looking increasingly uncomfortable as the timeline had been laid out, Wolf said, "Now, Billy, let's see if I have this right. You knew your father would be in the storeroom and went and smashed the oven's hinge. Then you fetched the blacksmith, but instead of returning with him, you went and told his wife, Glynda Thomas, that her husband needed her in the forge. Is that about right?"

Billy Morris was so shocked at this accurate recitation of his movements that he dropped his arms to the side of his body and opened his mouth as if to protest. However, no words came out. His parents both turned to look at him suspiciously, "Billy, is what his lordship says true? Did you break the hinge and then send Mrs Thomas to the forge? Why would you do that?"

It was obvious to Wolf and Bear that the baker and his wife hadn't realised the full import of Wolf's words and thought that their son's biggest crime was destroying their property. Billy still didn't reply, but the guilt was written all over his face now.

The boy's eyes flicked from side to side, one moment looking at Wolf, then his parents and then his parents, as if casting about for a way out of his dilemma. Finally, some of the tension seemed to leave his face, and he replied to the second part of his father's question, "When I went and asked the blacksmith to come and fix the hinge, he asked me to go and tell his wife to meet him at the forge in a few minutes. He must have been planning to kill her all along."

It was noteworthy that Billy completely ignored the question about breaking the oven hinge, but Wolf didn't press him on it; the answer had shown itself clearly on the boy's face. Instead, Wolf asked in a very casual tone, "Was Mr Thomas also the person who had you leave dead animals up at the Hall and burn one of my barns?"

Billy's eyes went wide again, and his parent's faces turned stony with anger. At first, Wolf wasn't sure if that anger was directed towards him for daring to ask the question, but it quickly became clear who the real target of their ire was. "Billy Morris, so it was you, after all? You swore up and down you had nothing to do with all of that. I even defended you to Mrs Hawley when she came right out and said that everyone suspected it was you. I've never been more ashamed."

Mrs Morris then turned towards Wolf and said, "We are so sorry, your lordship. Whatever punishment you think is fitting, Mr Morris and I will go along with."

"Why does everyone believe him?" Billy said with a snarl. "Just because he's a toff with a fancy accent and nice clothes? He doesn't know anything." Even as Billy said these self-righteous words, his guilt was evident. Billy Morris was many things: devious, avaricious, quick to see an opportunity, but he wasn't a good actor.

Ignoring the boy's defiant denial, Wolf repeated, "Was Mr Thomas the person who paid you to play those pranks on the Hall?" Wolf paused, "Or was it someone else?"

Wolf had been lied to enough times in his thief-taking career that he could often tell when someone was about to tell a falsehood, even before the words left their mouth. While he had no doubt that Billy Morris was a proficient enough liar to deceive his parents easily enough, he wasn't yet a hardened enough criminal to convince Wolf. As expected, Billy's next words were an almost grateful affirmation that, indeed, it was Mr Thomas who put him up to everything. Then the boy added, as if he'd suddenly had an epiphany, "He said that Mrs Thomas had always carried a torch for your lordship from when you were children. Knowing you were coming, he wanted to warn you off from approaching his wife. He must have killed her out of jealousy." Wolf didn't point out that the rock had been thrown through the window at the Hall after Glynda had been killed and Rhys Thomas arrested.

As Billy told his story, Wolf thought he looked almost relieved to have been handed that ready-made falsehood. As soon as he had finished, he recrossed his arms and reassumed his sullen pose. Wolf suspected they would not get much more out of Billy Morris that day. Feeling they had learned all they would for now, Wolf stood, followed by Bear, and said, "Thank you for your time, Mr and Mrs Morris. I will leave it to you to decide how best to punish your son."

With a great profusion of gratitude mixed with many beginnings of pardon, Mr and Mrs Morris saw their illustrious guests out.

Back in the carriage, Bear asked, "Do you agree that the boy was lying throughout?"

"Of course. I do not believe for a moment that Rhys Thomas felt that I was any threat to his marriage. There was not one thing about our interaction with the man in the lock-up to suggest that. It was evident that the boy was lying about everything."

Wolf stopped, thinking for a moment, "However, what I find interesting about his lie is that a boy his age knew about my childhood friendship with Glynda. Elinor Hughes acknowledged that it wasn't a secret but said that she and her husband encouraged Glynda not to talk about the friendship, so I doubt it was known generally. It is possible that Mr and Mrs Morris knew, and that Billy had overheard something and seized on that nugget to bolster his story. However, it is equally possible that whoever did pay him to do those things up at the hall was the person who told him."

"What is our next move?" Bear asked. "We could certainly press the boy further."

"We could, and it may come to that. But for now, let us leave him to stew and see what happens next."

CHAPTER 26

Rat watched the Pembroke carriage leave the bakery and drive out of the village. He had used the shortcut through the woods to follow it down and had hidden when it stopped. Wolf and Bear had descended and then entered the shop. He wasn't entirely sure why he had shadowed the men. Perhaps if he'd asked to accompany them, they might have even agreed, though probably not.

Rat felt that he hadn't fully conveyed how much he recognised in Billy Morris a thuggish similarity to the older boys in Whitechapel, who had bullied the young boy and stolen his coin and food whenever they had a chance. While Rat acknowledged that he might have followed in those boys' footsteps and joined a gang if he had been living on the streets much longer, he didn't believe he would have turned into a tormentor of younger children. At least, he hoped he wouldn't have. There was a meanness to Billy Morris that went beyond a bored child being mischievous on occasion.

As soon as Wolf and Bear had said that they would go and talk to the baker and his son, there had been no doubt in Rat's mind that the boy would lie through his teeth. He had every faith in Wolf. However, he didn't think Wolf understood what he was dealing with in Billy Morris in the way that he did. He certainly knew what Billy would do as soon as Wolf and Bear left: he'd run to whoever had paid him to do the pranks and send Mrs Thomas to the forge in the hope of some coin for the warning. Rat just had to wait and then follow him.

What Rat hadn't factored in was the tongue-lashing that Mr

and Mrs Morris gave Billy once their visitors had left. It was a reprimand that went on for quite some time and ended with the punishment of full days in the bakery with no time allowed for slouching off with his friends. They promised there would be more to the punishment but that they had to discuss what other penalty they might bring down on Billy's head. Meanwhile, they sent him down to the storeroom to sweep up around the bags of flour.

Billy knew that his parents would spend at least some time in debate, with his mother wringing her hands and bemoaning her fate in having such a child, and his father silently fuming as his wife chewed his ear off. If there was any moment when he might slip away to deliver the warning, it was then. He'd have to be quick. It only took so long to sweep the storeroom and his father would expect him back up in the bakehouse for his next chores, but he thought he'd have time if he went now.

Rat had almost given up waiting and had started to think that he might have misjudged the next moves of his nemesis when he saw Billy slip out of the bakery's back door and hurry up the alleyway. Rat was quick and light on his feet, but he had to be particularly careful following Billy Morris; this was not London, with its dark alleys all around and enough people on the streets that it was easy to follow someone discreetly. This was a country village with very few people out and about and few places to hide. Nevertheless, after leaving a decent amount of space between him and his prey, Rat followed the older boy.

Billy Morris was trying to be almost as careful about not being seen as Rat. He didn't want to be spotted by a nosy neighbour or even by a friend. He had a mission to perform, and he needed to fulfil it quickly and cautiously. Billy had been causing trouble in Lamphey from almost the moment he could walk and so he knew every nook and cranny of the village and all the best hiding spots. He moved quickly from one shadowy hideaway to another, moving quickly and quietly between each. Once Rat realised that the other boy's plan was to move unseen through the village, he copied his movements, always one hiding spot behind Billy. Rat had the advantage that it had never crossed Billy's mind that his intention to slip away stealthily to warn his benefactor might be anticipated. So, he didn't pay any attention to noises behind him, too concerned about not being seen himself.

It was easy enough to follow Billy through the village, but once he left it behind and struck out across the fields, it was much too hard to trail him incognito. Rat decided that the best course of action was to leave as much space between him and Billy as possible without losing sight of the other boy. Luckily, after crossing one field, Billy went into some woods, and Rat was able to hurry to catch him up using the trees as cover. At some point, Rat stepped into a pile of leaves, causing them to rustle loudly enough that Billy turned his head. Pausing for a moment, he then decided it must have been a squirrel and continued.

He walked through the woods for a good fifteen minutes before exiting out onto a long driveway. Rat could see a house up ahead, but Billy was making for the stables over to the right. There was not much cover between the stables and the woods, and Rat thought that his best bet was to wait and confirm that Billy was going into the stables and then, once he had disappeared inside, make his way there quickly. He saw Billy run down the driveway, using the trees lining it as some kind of cover, and then quickly cut across in front of the house to the first and largest of the stables.

As soon as Billy entered the stable, Rat followed his path, making his own use of the trees as cover. The house seemed quiet enough, Rat thought, as he dashed across to the stable, unsure what his move might be once he got there. He wanted to see who Billy met with, listen to their conversation, and then quickly escape to relay what he'd heard to Wolf.

When Rat had first come to live at Chesterton House, he had lived in the carriage house with the horses and with Madison, Wolf's driver. However, these stables were far larger than the carriage house had been, and he had no idea how such structures might be laid out. Creeping to the open stable door, he peeked around and saw Billy deep in conversation with a man who looked like a groom, but he was too far away to hear what they were saying. Some of the stalls had horses in them, but others were empty with their doors open. Rat slipped into the first one, then, peeking out to make sure that Billy and the groom still had their backs to him, ran to slip into its neighbour.

The next two stalls had horses in them, but Rat still couldn't hear the conversation and knew he had to get closer. Taking a chance, he left the safety of his hiding spot and ran what felt like a very long way to the next empty stall. At least he'd thought it was empty. Instead, he found a donkey in the back corner of the stall, busily eating oats out of a bucket. The donkey's companion was a duck, of all things. As Rat snuck into the stall, the donkey looked up from his food and started braying loudly, which caused the duck to start flapping its wings and quacking.

Rat wasn't sure what to make of these animals, angry at having their home invaded by a stranger, and backed himself up against the wall of the stall, hoping the donkey and duck would lose interest. However, they didn't, at least not quickly enough. Before Rat knew it, a large, angry-looking man was standing at the door to the stall, saying, "Buttercup, Daffodil, quiet yourselves. What on earth has got you so put out?" Rat hoped that if he was very quiet and still, the man might not notice him hiding in the corner, trying to make himself as small as possible.

Just as the man turned to go, he must have noticed Rat out of the corner of his eye and said, "What do we have here? A trespasser? What are you looking to steal, lad?" The man came over and grabbed Rat by his collar as he did so, noticing that Rat's clothes were far finer than he'd expected a local lad to wear.

"Hey, Billy, come over here and see who've I've caught," the man said.

Moments later, Billy Morris was standing in the stall, watching Rat squirm in the large man's grip.

"I know him," Billy announced. "He's the toff who has come to visit up at the Hall. He threatened me the other day with a knife and told me to stay away from him."

Walking up to Rat with a mean scowl on his face, Billy demanded, "What are you doing here, toff?"

Rat thought quickly about what he might say and answered, "I was just exploring the neighbouring fields and woods and came upon these stables. I thought I'd come in and see the horses. I didn't mean any harm."

The man holding him looked inclined to believe the story, but Billy narrowed his eyes and said, "It's a bit dodgy that the grown toffs come and question me, and then this mini toff suddenly is here."

Roberts, the groom, was very good at taking orders, but he was not meant for decision-making. Billy's story had been interrupted by the noise from the donkey and duck. Still, Roberts had heard enough to realise that the situation had spun out of control and that the mistress would need to be told. He knew she wouldn't be happy and hoped that she wouldn't blame him. The mistress was not above using her riding crop as punishment for even minor infractions. He could only imagine what she might resort to in this situation.

"Go into the tack room and get some rope, Roberts said to Billy. We'll tie him up and then you can watch him while I go and fetch the mistress. She'll know what to do and she'll want to talk to you about your visitors anyway."

Billy knew who had hired him, but all communications and payment had come through Roberts. For all his bluster, the boy was terrified to speak directly to the lady of the house. He'd heard too many rumours over the years about what she was capable of when her temper was roused.

CHAPTER 27

Arriving back at Glanwyddan Hall, Wolf went to find Tabitha. After asking Talbot where she might be found, he discovered her in the housekeeper's parlour just off the kitchen. She and the dowager were sitting with Mrs Jenkins and Mrs Budgers going over plans for the Christmas Eve party. As he entered the office, he heard Tabitha say, "We are going to surprise Rat with a birthday cake and presents on Christmas Eve. I doubt he has a preference as to cakes, the boy seems to enjoy every kind of sweet treat, so I am sure he will adore anything that you make, Mrs Budgers."

All the women looked up at Wolf's entrance, Mrs Budgers smiling adoringly at her Wolfie. "Am I interrupting, ladies?" he asked.

"Not at all," Tabitha replied. "I believe that we are finished here." She stood, saying, "Mrs Jenkins and Mrs Budgers, everything you have outlined is wonderful. I will leave the execution in your capable hands but do let me know if there is anything you need, anything at all." The two servants, who had stood when their mistress did, both bobbed curtseys.

Wolf led Tabitha and the dowager back out of the servants' hall towards the library so that they could add to the board what he and Langley had learned from Mr Morris and his son. With everyone settled comfortably, Tabitha with blank notecards in hand, Wolf began to tell them the story he and Bear had heard and what they believed to be false in Billy Morris' telling of it.

As she wrote up a notecard for each being of information, Tabitha asked, "So, Billy claims that this was all Rhys Thomas' doing, purely out of jealousy at his wife's supposed infatuation with you?"

Wolf nodded, "That is what the lad claims."

"And yet you do not believe him?" the dowager asked.

"Neither Bear nor I do. The story just doesn't make sense from a timeline perspective. Billy told us that Rhys Thomas paid him to do those pranks to warn me off from his wife. However, my understanding is that they began before we announced that we were visiting the Pembroke estate for Christmas. I need to check with my steward to confirm that, but I am certain they preceded even our decision to come here for Christmas."

Wolf continued, "Then there is his assertion that he went to fetch Mr Thomas to fix the oven hinge, and it was then that the blacksmith asked him to fetch Glynda and tell her to go to the forge. The boy claimed that this proved that Rhys planned to kill his wife."

"That makes no sense," Tabitha interjected. "If Mr Thomas had gone home for lunch, why then have Glynda come to the forge later to kill her?"

"Indeed. Why have her come to the forge at all? If there was something he wanted to talk to her about, why did he not have that conversation at home? And why send Billy Morris, thereby ensuring a witness to the supposed fact that he was the one to send for Glynda?"

"What about the oven hinge?" the dowager asked.

"Billy never admitted to that, but it was quite clear from his face that he had broken it intentionally. He managed to skip over my accusation, but I have no doubt he was the perpetrator."

"In which case, the notion that the blacksmith somehow intentionally set this chain of events in process makes no sense," Tabitha pointed out. "If Mr Thomas planned to kill his wife by luring her to the forge, are we to believe that having Billy Morris suddenly pop up to be sent as a messenger was a convenience he merely took advantage of?"

"Even beyond that, why did Billy break the hinge? His claim is that Rhys Thomas was the mastermind behind the pranks and that he, Billy, merely did what he was paid to do. By that logic, we must assume that whoever did pay Billy, was also the person to tell him to break the hinge. Why would the blacksmith do that?"

Tabitha considered the question, chewing on her lip as she often did when contemplating a thorny question. "Well, perhaps Rhys Thomas wanted to give himself an alibi. Being called out to the bakery might have seemed like the perfect cover for where he was when his wife was murdered."

"Then why throw himself on the body weeping? Are we to believe that he created an alibi for himself and then returned, murdered his wife and was then prostate with grief?"

"Well, he did not necessarily know when Miss Prescott would be arriving, so it is possible that he returned, murdered his wife, immediately regretted his actions, threw himself on the body and had no reason to believe he would be discovered," Wolf said. "However, the whole thing seems convoluted and quite unlikely. If you squint and do not think about it too deeply, perhaps it is just about possible that it could have happened like that…"

Tabitha finished his sentence, "But it hardly seems like the simplest possible answer."

Wolf smiled. Throughout their previous investigations, he had advocated for the principle of Occam's Razor: the most straightforward solution is probably the correct one. "That's exactly my thoughts on the matter."

Tabitha wrote everything they had discussed on notecards and pinned them to the board, grouping them where appropriate and linking connected thoughts with the thread. When she was done, she stepped back and reviewed all the information they had gathered. Turning back to Wolf, she said, "Are we now confident that whoever paid Billy Morris to burn the barn and leave the dead animals was also the person who murdered Glynda?"

"I do not think there is any doubt that Billy Morris was involved in everything. Based on his scrambling to think of who he might say paid him, I believe that it was one person behind it all but that person was not Rhys Thomas." Wolf paused, reflecting on what Billy Morris said earlier and added, "I do think that it was telling that the motivation Billy gave was Rhys' supposed jealousy of me and that the reason for the pranks was to send me a message. I do not think he could have come up with that out of thin air. I believe it possible that he was telling the truth then and that the lie was who paid him, not why they paid him."

Nodding in agreement, Tabitha asked, "So, what do you think we do next? Question Billy Morris again and try to get him to admit who is really behind this?"

Wolf considered the question. "Perhaps. Though, I get the sense that Billy Morris will not just roll over and give up the name, and there is only so much pressure I can put on a child."

"Give me five minutes with the rascal and he will say whatever we need him to," the dowager pronounced with something akin to pride. Tabitha and Wolf did not doubt that the dowager countess would be able to browbeat almost anyone and bend them to her will, but it seemed like subjecting an eleven-year-old boy to that should be a last resort.

Instead, Tabitha asked, "Is it worth going to Squire Partridge and laying this information in front of him? At the very least, if we can point to the possibility that someone else is behind all this and may be responsible for Glynda's murder, perhaps he can be persuaded to release Rhys Thomas from the lock-up."

Wolf shook his head, "After our last conversation with the squire, I doubt that he will be persuaded by circumstantial evidence that, as even we concede, could still point to Rhys Thomas as the murderer, however unlikely it now seems. I believe that the good squire is far too lazy and self-satisfied to care whether justice is served. As far as he is concerned, he has a culprit behind bars. If he releases Rhys Thomas but we can provide no other suspect, then Squire Partridge is worse off than he was before. There is nothing I have seen of the man that leads me to believe he would willingly put himself in such a situation just to save someone's life on the chance that they may be innocent."

The dowager sat listening to this as uncertain as she was previously about how exactly her dark secret fit into the overall investigation. Now that Tabitha and Wolf seemed convinced that the same person was behind the pranks and murdered Glynda, what did that mean for her role? How did murdering Elinor's daughter achieve the mysterious and nefarious purpose of the sender of her poison pen notes? She felt that she needed to talk to Elinor Hughes again before she made any determination as to what to reveal about her secret.

Looking at the clock on the mantelpiece, the dowager determined that she had more than enough time to summon the carriage and pay an afternoon call. As she stood up, she realised that making two visits to see an old retainer in as many days was bound to cause suspicion. The dowager was self-aware enough to know that excusing the second visit with claims of excessive affection for a woman who had been her maid decades ago would not fool anyone.

"I have an idea, and I will need to take the carriage to visit Elinor Hughes in order to see if it has merit," the dowager proclaimed.

"What is your idea?" Tabitha asked with genuine curiosity.

The dowager paused, "It may be nothing. And so, I believe it is for the best if I test it out by speaking with Elinor first. Alone."

Tabitha and Wolf exchanged glances. There was something suspicious about the dowager's behaviour and tone of voice. She was definitely up to something, but with a shrug of his shoulders and a reply of a quick shake of Tabitha's head, they communicated that neither of them had a clue what it might be. Seeing that, no matter what they thought of her explanation, she would be getting no serious challenge to her plan, the dowager left the room quickly before either Tabitha or Wolf had second thoughts and suggested joining her.

When the dowager had left the room, closing the door behind her, Tabitha asked, "What on earth is all that about, do you think?"

"There has been something off about her behaviour ever since that rock came through the window. I cannot quite put my finger on what it is, but the dowager countess seems on edge for some reason. It is as if she has been waiting to see if something will happen."

Tabitha thought back to that first evening at Glanwyddan Hall. "I remember how quick Mama was to say that the note wrapped around the rock was aimed at one of the servants. The note said, 'I know what you did.' What if that message was for her?"

Wolf considered the suggestion: "We've been assuming that the common denominator in all these events is me, but of course, I am not the only person with a history at Glanwyddan Hall and with Glynda. It turns out that Elinor, the dowager's lady's maid from years ago, is the mother of my childhood friend. Perhaps the dowager countess is the thread running through this all. Do you believe that she suspects that is the case?"

"I do. I really do. Though I cannot imagine how we get her to open up about whatever it might be if she has not told us so far. I suggest that we wait until she returns from talking with Mrs Hughes and then confront her," Tabitha suggested. Wolf had no better plan and so agreed.

Even since the rock had come through the window, and they had been thrown back into an investigation, Tabitha and Wolf had barely had any time alone. Any time they had tried to steal a few precious moments, someone, usually the dowager had interrupted them. Realising that the library door had a key in its lock, Wolf stood, went to the door, and locked it.

Watching him, Tabitha raised her eyebrows and asked saucily, "Why Lord Pembroke, whatever are you doing?"

Wolf approached Tabitha, gave her his hand, raised her, and led her to a chaise longue on the other side of the library. He sat down and pulled her onto his lap. Tabitha put her arms around his neck and looked into his heavily lashed, deep blue eyes. "You know, if anyone were to discover us like this, you would have no choice but to marry me," she said teasingly.

"Then perhaps I should unlock the door and encourage someone to walk in on us," Wolf said in a serious voice that did not match Tabitha's joking tone. She smiled hesitatingly in reply, and he said, "Is that what it will take for you to marry me?" This was the first time they had ever talked about the future and marriage, and Tabitha suddenly felt a deadly serious pall fall over what had been a light and fun moment.

"So far, you have not asked me to marry you," she pointed out.

"Tabitha, I do not believe that you have any doubts as to my desires," Wolf said. He put his hand to her face and gently stroked her cheek. His touch caused Tabitha to shiver with a desire she had never even known she was capable of feeling. "However, if there is any such doubt, let me put that to rest immediately. Tabitha, I want nothing more than to make you my wife."

Leaning towards Wolf, Tabitha lightly brushed her lips against his and replied, "I love you, Wolf."

"I feel there is a but at the end of that sentence," he said with more edge to his voice than he had intended. "If we are not to be man and wife, then what would you have us be?" Before Tabitha could answer, Wolf continued, "I will not make you my mistress."

That was the last thing Tabitha wanted, yet she couldn't find the words to articulate her feelings. Turning her head so she didn't have to answer his fierce, piercing gaze, she said in a small voice, "I love you Wolf more than I ever imagined it possible to love a man and I cannot imagine not spending my life with you, but..."

"I knew there was a but coming," Wolf said with some bitterness in his voice.

"However," Tabitha said, as if that word would be somehow softer, "I still have these fears nagging in the back of my mind that I cannot seem to banish entirely."

"I am not Jonathan," Wolf pointed out. He did not need her to tell him what those fears were. He knew enough of Tabitha's deceased husband's control over every aspect of her life to not understand where her fears came from. Taking her chin in his hand and gently turning her face towards him, Wolf said in a very gentle voice, "The next time I come to you and talk about this, I will address every fear you have and banish them for good. And when I do, you will agree to be my wife."

Tabitha had no idea how he would finally be able to dispel her deepest fears and doubts, but she had more faith in Wolf than any person alive. So, she smiled and said, in a voice filled with love, "I truly hope that comes to pass."

CHAPTER 28

Finding herself back at Elinor Hughes' unappealing cottage door not much more than twenty-four hours after her last visit, the dowager paused before knocking. She considered what she was trying to discover. When Elinor had been her maid and had provided invaluable help that had enabled the then countess to keep her darkest secret, the maid had not known the entire story. Loath as she was to reveal any more than she needed to, the dowager realised that she had to tell someone more than the half-truths that she had been claiming so far. Perhaps it made the most sense for that person to be the one who already knew some of what had happened.

Finally, at peace with what she had to do, the dowager knocked at the door. Almost immediately, she heard the same phrase in Welsh, followed by "I'm coming." A moment or two later, Elinor answered the door. "M'lady," the old, blind woman said, "I thought you might return."

"Why is that, Elinor?" the dowager asked, genuinely curious about what second-sight powers the woman before her might have.

"Because there is unfinished business that has allowed the earth to crack open and the Gwrach y Rhibyn to roam the valley."

"What on earth is that grach, or whatever it is you said?" the dowager said impatiently. She had little time for magic and myth.

"The Gwrach y Rhibyn is a dark spirit that is known to warn of impending death," Elinor explained. "Two days before her death, Glynda was out picking wild herbs and a Gwrach y Rhibyn appeared before her, wailing and shrieking. The last time that Glynda had seen such a spirit had been just before her grandmother, my mother, had died. My daughter ran to me, terrified that it was my death that was being forewarned. Never did she expect it was hers."

The dowager thought it was more likely that Glynda Thomas had encountered some mad hag than a dark spirit, but she wanted Elinor's help and so kept her doubts to herself. "May I come in?" the dowager asked in a tone of unusual deference and politeness. Elinor gestured for her to enter the cottage.

"I was just going to make a pot of tea, m'lady, if you would like to join me."

The dowager did not feel inclined to participate in the social ritual of afternoon tea. Still, she recognised that sipping the restorative brew seemed to encourage conversation, and so she indicated that tea would be most welcome.

Yet again, the dowager marvelled at how Elinor managed to navigate her cottage and the tea-making despite her blindness. Finally, settled in the same armchairs as the day before, teacups in their hands, Elinor said, "Now, why don't you tell me what you didn't yesterday?"

The dowager looked into her teacup for a moment, deeply uncomfortable with the notion that she was about to share her very deepest secret with this woman over whom she no longer held any real sway. However, she could think of no other way in which to glean what she needed to know, and so she began, "I believe you know why I came to you for help all those years ago, Elinor."

"Ie, the sleeping potion that my grandmother made for you to put your husband into a waking sleep such that he woke the next morning convinced that you and he had lain together as man and wife."

Hearing it laid out that bluntly made the dowager wince, but she didn't dispute the description. "Indeed, that was the aid you and your grandmother afforded me. I suspect that you had your suspicions as to why I was in need of such help," the dowager said hesitantly.

"I was your maid, m'lady. I knew the violence that your husband was capable of and believed you wished to avoid any future intimacy while maintaining the illusion that it was happening."

The dowager winced again but nodded at the truth of what the other woman said. "What you do not know is that I lay with a man other than my husband." From the knowing look on Elinor Hughes' face, the dowager suspected that was perhaps not the secret that she had believed at the time. She continued, "It was a moment of madness, born of my deep unhappiness in my marriage. As you may have heard, after bearing my husband two daughters in quick succession, I was then unable to give him a son and heir. I made an effort in the beginning, but lying with my husband was an unpleasant and sometimes quite violent experience, as you have pointed out. I soon found any reason to avoid it. This included putting hundreds of miles between us whenever possible."

The dowager stared into the fire, lost in memories of those difficult, early days of her marriage. "I was surprised to find that Philip cared not a whit about an heir; he quite despised everything about the earldom and the estate, wanting nothing more than to spend his days on horseback with his dogs around him and his nights lying drunkenly in the arms of some whore. However, his father, the old earl, cared a lot, and it was he who had summoned me back to Wales, on pain of cutting my allowance, to perform what he saw as my only reason for living: to bear a son and heir."

The memories became even more painful to bring to mind, but the dowager had nerves of steel and refused to shrink from even the most difficult recollections. "I was forced to stay in Wales for two months, banned from the separate room I had slept in on my few trips down over the years, and instead forced to sleep next to my brute of a husband. Luckily, many nights, he retired late and so inebriated that he almost immediately fell into a drunken stupor. However, one night, I was not so fortunate; I believe his father had prevailed on Philip to control his drinking for that one evening, and my husband used me particularly cruelly, leaving the ugly bruises on my arms that you may remember."

Elinor nodded; she had been quite aware of the violence her mistress had been subjected to and had felt deeply for the young countess. "What you do not know is that my husband was unable to perform his husbandly duties that night, which was one of the reasons for his even more brutal use of me. I swore then that I would do whatever it took in order never to have to lay with the man again."

The dowager paused. Most of what she had said so far had likely not been new information for Elinor. However, the most damning memories were about to be recounted; they had to be recounted. "Philip's brother, Colin, the current earl's father, was nothing like his brother. He was gentle and kind and took pity on his brother's lonely, misused wife. I had long believed that his feelings for me were more than fraternal. The day after that awful night with Philip, I seduced my brother-in-law in one of the hay barns. From the moment he put his seed in me, I knew that I had conceived. I cannot say why I was so certain; perhaps it was merely wishful thinking, but I knew."

Elinor picked up the thread of the story, "And so that is when you came to me and asked if my grandmother could make a sleeping draught that would make your husband believe that he had successfully lain with you."

"Indeed," the dowager acknowledged. "Neither you nor she asked why at the time, though now I believe that you had your suspicions." Whether Elinor had or hadn't, she kept her thoughts at the time to herself. The dowager continued, "Luckily, my husband always kept a decanter of brandy in his bedchamber and, assuming he was sober enough that he did not fall to sleep immediately, would pour himself a glass, which he sipped until he finally fell into a sufficient state of intoxication to sleep. I was able to put your grandmother's brew into the brandy, and as she had promised, he tasted nothing out of the ordinary."

The dowager thought about the words the cunning woman, Elinor's grandmother, had said to her all those years ago, "As she said would happen, he fell into a state that was neither awake nor asleep. I forced myself to sit astride him and mutter some words that he might remember. The following morning, he woke particularly cheerful, with every indication that he believed we had engaged in successful congress the previous night. I repeated this charade every day for two weeks. Finally, the day came for my courses. With my daughters, I had not realised that I was pregnant so early, but it seemed that providence took pity on me that day, and I was able to tell my husband and father-in-law that I had conceived.

"Once I had performed my only useful function, I was allowed to leave Wales and return to London for my confinement. I believe that the old earl was more than aware of his son's predilection for violence and saw the wisdom in not jeopardising the pregnancy by subjecting my body to his aggression. As you know, I gave birth to a son, Jonathan, who inherited the earldom. There was no doubt in my mind that he was not Philip's son but instead sired by his brother, Colin. Jonathan was the current Lord Pembroke's half-brother."

Putting her teacup down on the small table to her side, the dowager realised how relieved she was to finally say these words out loud to another human being, more than forty years after the events she had recalled.

"Did his lordship's brother never suspect?" Elinor couldn't help but ask.

"We never spoke again after I left Wales. The next I heard, he had married some woman his father didn't approve of for some reason. The woman had enough of a dowry that they were able to live in some kind of genteel poverty. After the birth of such a healthy baby boy, I was relieved of the burden of having to provide a spare and kept my distance from Wales and my husband as much as I could." This was the entirety of the dowager's secret and speaking it out loud made her wonder anew at who believed they knew some or all of it besides the woman sitting in the other armchair.

"When you asked your grandmother for her brew, what reason did you give?" the dowager asked.

"I told her that the old earl was forcing you to sleep in the same bed as your violent husband and that you wish for him to sleep but wake sure that congress had taken place. That was all."

"Once I fell pregnant with Jonathan, did she question how that would have been possible given the potion I was giving him?"

"I had told her of that last, violent time and the bruises he had given you. She assumed that you had fallen pregnant then. In all truth, I believed that likely as well, though I knew how regular your courses were and so did have a sliver of doubt."

"When you came and told me of your wish to leave service to marry the footman and your hope that I would apply to the old earl to allow your husband to remain in service here, you were kind enough not to throw that suspicion in my face," the dowager said gratefully. Instead, the young maid had merely asked that the then countess help her in gratitude for the assistance she had provided in her mistress' time of need.

"If you did not say anything even to your grandmother, then who knows and how?" the dowager asked, cutting to the heart of the reason for her visit.

"M'lady, while I do not have the full powers that my mother and grandmother had, I have something of the dynion hysbys in me. In particular, I have some knowledge of reading tea leaves. Would you like me to try to divine what is happening?"

The dowager barely believed in the mysteries of the Bible and had absolutely no time for tarot or any other kind of magic and mysticism. Yet all those years before, she had turned to the cunning women for aid, and, for whatever reason, their help had worked. Recognising that she had few other alternatives for trying to solve the mystery of who sent the notes, she agreed to Elinor's suggestion.

The blind woman rose, took the tea tray back into the kitchen, and returned with it a few minutes later. "Instead of brewing the tea in the pot, I have boiling water and leave the tea leaves loose in the cup," she explained. There was a small dining table and chairs in one corner of the room, and Elinor took the tray there and placed it on the table, then invited the dowager to join her. The dowager couldn't believe that she was indulging such absurdity, but she joined Elinor and sat in one of the chairs. Elinor took the cup and handed it to the dowager. "Hold this cup, close your eyes, and remember all those years ago. Let the tea feel what happened and your pain. Then think about the notes and what has happened since you arrived in Pembrokeshire."

As she held the cup and closed her eyes, feeling more than a little ridiculous, the dowager had a thought. Her eyes snapped open, and she said, "If you are blind, how do you read the tea leaves?" While she didn't know much about such practices, from what she did know, she understood that the tea leaf reader looked at what patterns were left after water was poured in, swirled around, and then deposited out of the cup.

Elinor smiled. "You are correct; usually the tea leaves are looked at with the eyes. But my mother and grandmother, and many generations of women before them, had all lost their sight, so they used their other senses to learn what the tea leaves said."

As far as the dowager was concerned, this was even more absurd than the notion of reading the tea leaves by looking at them, but at that point, she felt she had gone too far to back out now. She said nothing in reply. Instead, she closed her eyes again and let her mind drift back over the story she had just recounted to Elinor Hughes. The dowager had glossed over that one fevered act of love with Colin Chesterton, but now she let her mind dwell on it. While she had used Philip's brother in the hope that his seed would implant and save her from another brutal night with her husband, if she were honest, the experience was seared into her memory. Never before and never again did she experience true passion and the wonder of being held in the arms of a man she desired and who looked at her with love. Remembering that encounter now, she felt something she was unused to: regret.

Finally, the dowager opened her eyes and handed the teacup back to Elinor who then poured hot water into it, swirled it around for a minute or so, and then poured it out. Somehow, even without her sight, she seemed able to dump the water while keeping some, if not all, of the tea leaves in the cup. Elinor then sat very still, her eyes closed, holding the cup in both hands. The dowager watched the other woman's face, hoping she might intuit something of what Elinor believed she was seeing.

Minutes went by, and just as the dowager was about to lose patience and break the silence, Elinor opened her blind eyes, put down the teacup, and said, "Someone saw you that day in the barn. I am not sure who it is, but it was a girl. She kept the secret for a long time, unsure at first the import of what she had seen."

Now, the dowager's impatience was beyond her control, and she said, somewhat snappishly, "What do you mean you are unsure who this girl is?"

Elinor replied gently, "The tea leaves are not a newspaper reporting on every last detail. Instead, they show shadows, wisps of memories, glimpses into the past, that is all."

The dowager was unimpressed by this explanation and asked, "Is there nothing more you can tell me?"

Elinor Hughes picked the teacup up again and repeated the silent contemplation for another few minutes. Eventually, she put the teacup back down and said, "This girl kept her silence for all these years, but within the last year she told it to someone. That person has been sending you the notes."

It had taken a while, but the dowager finally felt that they were getting somewhere. Thinking about what she had talked about with Tabitha and Wolf in the library, the dowager explained, "Lord Pembroke believes that whoever threw that rock and note through the window at the Hall and was responsible for the pranks may have also murdered your daughter." It wasn't until the words were out of her mouth that she realised that Glynda's mother might find this news to be anything other than merely an interesting observation.

The other woman's blind eyes seemed to shine with what

might have been tears, but she said in a composed voice, "Yes, I believe that Lord Pembroke is correct. At the end of the reading, I felt great anger, jealousy, greed, and, more than anything, evil."

Just as the dowager was leaving the cottage, Elinor put a hand on her arm and said, "M'lady, I sensed something else; a child is in great danger. I can't tell if it's a girl or a boy."

"What child?" the dowager said, irritated at the vagueness of the supposed premonition.

"I did not see who. I only felt how great the threat was."

It seemed that the tea leaves had given up all the secrets they were going to, and the dowager took her leave from Elinor Hughes. In the carriage ride back to the Hall, she realised that the visit to her maid, rather than having resolved her dilemma, had instead made it thornier. If Elinor and the tea leaves were to be believed – and the dowager's scepticism was far from gone – then it was indeed her own, darkest secret which had somehow precipitated the chain of events that had led to Glynda's murder. How long would she be able to keep her secret safe, and was it perhaps better in the long run if Tabitha and Wolf heard the truth from her lips?

CHAPTER 29

Billy Morris and the groom, Roberts, had tied Rat up and stuffed some disgusting, dirty material in his mouth. Rat had not been living a life of aristocratic luxury so long that he had lost his Whitechapel street smarts. He did not doubt that he could take on Billy Morris and win if he needed to. Despite the violence of the streets of Whitechapel, Rat had managed to steer clear of a lot of the trouble that some of the boys his age managed to find. Nevertheless, he and Melody had been orphaned for over a year before they moved into Chesterton House. Not only had he been responsible for food and shelter for himself, but for his very young sister. He hadn't had the time to pick fights with other street urchins, but sometimes he'd had to in order to protect Melody. He could take care of himself if it came to it.

Then there was the fact that he had his knife in his boot, something that had never occurred to the baker's boy, who hadn't seen where the weapon had come from when they first met. If only he could loosen the ropes around his hands, he could free himself and would stand a chance. However, it wasn't just Billy he'd have to face; the groom was a large man, and Rat wasn't as certain about his odds against him. However, he was fast and nimble and, perhaps with the advantage of surprise and the knife, he might stand a chance and be able to escape.

The boy tried to wiggle his hands again, but if the groom knew nothing else, he knew how to tie ropes so that they held. At that moment, what Rat wanted more than anything was to get the rag out of his mouth, but that had also been tied quite firmly about his face.

Rat hadn't been tied up long in the barn when he heard voices, including a woman. There was no doubt that she was the mistress Billy and the groom had been talking about; everything from her snooty accent to her domineering tone conveyed authority. He had a hard time hearing the conversation, no matter how he strained to catch the words. Finally, Rat managed to scoot over towards the barn door and could more clearly make out the words.

"So, let me see if I understand this correctly, Billy. Lord Pembroke and another man came and questioned you and your father about Glynda Thomas' murder?" the woman asked.

"Yes, that's right, miss. They knew an awful lot about what had happened, and I didn't know what to say. And then, I had this brilliant idea, like. I told them that Blackie Hughes had made me do it all. The dead animals and calling Mrs Hughes to the forge. I said that it was all his idea." Billy said this very proudly. He believed that his spur-of-the-moment finger-pointing was a stroke of genius. After all, the blacksmith was already in the lock-up, accused of his wife's murder. "Only makes sense that the same person paid me to do it all," Billy said, looking very pleased with himself.

This was Billy's first direct interaction with the person who had paid him to cause mischief. While he'd been in no doubt who his paymaster was, all communications had gone through the groom, who had known immediately who to hire to get the job done. Billy's reputation for being a troublemaker was well-established in the village. As Roberts had told his mistress, if anyone saw Billy burning the barn or leaving the dead animals, they wouldn't question his motives; the boy was well known for raising hell for no good reason. The promise of coin was sufficient to encourage the lad to take the risk.

Maureen Prescott looked at the freckled boy scornfully. Did all her hopes and dreams really rest on the chubby shoulders of this child? She believed firmly that she had been given a heavenly mission to pursue, not because someone else could not be found to do it, but rather because she had been specifically created for such a purpose. Having suffered some disappointments and setbacks as a younger woman, any one of which might have diminished a lesser mortal, Maureen did not doubt that the universe had great plans for her. All she needed was to wait patiently for those divine plans to be revealed fully.

Miss Prescott had seen many of the young women she had grown up around water down their dreams, make compromises, marry the first man who offered for them, and become nothing more than wives and mothers. Instead, Maureen had always been special and had known, from a very young age, that providence had great things in store for her if only she stuck to the plan and didn't waver from her vision. With the title of countess almost within her grasp, now was not the time to let insignificant insects like Billy Morris get in her way.

Trying to control her anger, Maureen Prescott said, "And then, as soon as Lord Pembroke left, you immediately made your way here to tell Roberts what had happened?"

Billy beamed with pride, "Yep! Straight away. Ran right over, I did."

If Billy Morris had been a more intelligent or even observant boy, he would have seen the tightness around Miss Prescott's mouth and heard the growing tension in her tone. "And by coming here immediately, you then led this other boy, who is somehow connected to Lord Pembroke, right to my door." This wasn't phrased as a question but rather as a terse statement of fact.

When it was laid out quite so bluntly, even Billy could see that perhaps his plan hadn't been as brilliant as he'd first thought. "Well, I didn't know I was being watched. Did I miss?"

"Well, I think that what we can say with certainty is that it never occurred to you that you might be walking into a trap. Whether it would have been obvious to someone of greater intelligence is another matter."

Billy thought he was being insulted, but Miss Prescott used big words, saying them in such a terrifyingly calm yet menacing voice, that Billy didn't know which way was up as she continued to glare at him.

"I need time to think," Miss Prescott said to no one in particular.

"If you don't mind, miss. I need to be going back home for my tea. Mam and Da don't know I left the bakery, and I'll be in even more trouble if they've found I've hoofed it."

What to do, what to do? Maureen Prescott thought to herself as she paced up and down in the stable. Roberts had vouched for Billy Morris' cunning, but from what she could see, the boy was a dunderhead. Now that she was so close, she could not let her plan fall apart—certainly not because of two mere children.

Finally, Maureen stopped pacing and said, "Take me to this other boy." Nodding her head at Roberts, she said to Billy, "You are not going anywhere for the time being." As she said these words, Roberts grabbed Billy and pulled him with them to the stall Rat was in. Even then, Billy did not fully realise his peril and put up little resistance.

When Rat first saw the mistress in the doorway to the stall, his initial thought was what a ridiculous outfit she was wearing. After the aborted horse ride with Tabitha, Maureen Prescott had felt quite out of sorts for some time. She always hated it when her plans were thwarted in any way. Roberts had ensured that Rainbow, the most high-spirited horse in the Prescott Manor stable, had been saddled too loosely, and the bridle left poorly fastened for good measure. It was to be the most distressing yet understandable accident when that so-called Lady Pembroke fell from her horse, trying to gallop after Maureen riding Jethro at a breathtaking speed and jumping some of the highest hedges.

After the outrageously presumptive interrogation to which she and her footmen had been subjected, Maureen had angrily, if perhaps short-sightedly, cancelled the ride. Then, only one thing could calm her nerves and reset her sense of world order: she must go and visit Cassie Williams. Maureen and Cassie were of an age and had played together somewhat as girls, then entered the Pembrokeshire social scene at the same time. Cassie, with her naturally golden curls and those oh so innocent-looking baby blue eyes, had, of course, been the catch of the season. No man had eyes for Miss Prescott's more subtle beauty and strong personality when her friend was in the room. Cassie could have aimed to marry at least a baron, but she fell in love with the younger son of a local doctor who was planning to follow in his father's footsteps.

Ten years later, Cassie's golden beauty had faded with the drudgery of marriage to a country doctor and motherhood to a brood of snivelling brats. There was nothing that raised Maureen Prescott's spirits more than dressing in all her finery and dropping in unexpectedly on her old friend Cassie, who was always far too polite to turn away her illustrious guest, no matter how inopportune a time it might be. For these visits, Maureen always made sure to dress in the very height of fashion, or fashion as she saw it, at least. This visit was no exception, and her dress, in multiple shades of blue with its excessive flounces, outshone only by the matching hat with not one, but three peacock feathers sprouting from its brim.

Maureen Prescott looked at the boy tied up in the stall. It was clear from the quality of his clothes that he was a member of the aristocracy. Maureen made sure always to get the new Debrett's each year and also had the London newspapers sent to her. She pored over the society pages to ensure she kept up on all the latest marriages and deaths amongst England's great and good. In addition, Miss Prescott was diligent in keeping up correspondences with various women she had managed to snag introductions to over the years. She used these communications to milk her reluctant acquaintances for all the latest gossip. She knew that Tabitha's marriage to Jonathan had been brief and hadn't resulted in any children. Wolf had ascended to the earldom too recently to have an entry in Debrett's. Still, the society pages did their best to report on the movements of London's newest and most eligible bachelor. So, she was reasonably certain that there had been no previous marriage or children. If that was the case, who was this boy?

Roberts had pushed Billy Morris roughly into the stall, and now his mistress indicated that he should take the rag out of Rat's mouth. "Do not even consider yelling, boy," she warned. This estate has many acres. The nearest house is too far for anyone to hear your screams, and my servants are loyal. No one will hear you or care if they do."

Rat considered the woman in front of him and his situation. At the moment, it was three against one, if he counted this woman. He didn't imagine that Miss Prescott's outrageous costume would allow her much mobility. Nevertheless, Rat was smart enough to know when the odds were stacked against him. At this point, he needed to buy himself time and lull his captors into a sense of security.

Nodding his head to indicate he wouldn't try to yell for help, Rat was happy to have the rag pulled out of his mouth.

"Now, tell me who you are and why you followed Billy here," Maureen commanded.

What was the best answer to give his woman? Rat wondered. There was a look of madness in her eyes that he had seen before during his time on the streets of Whitechapel. One woman in particular, a dollymop who sold herself in the dirtiest alleyways to any man willing to throw her a penny afterwards, called herself the Duchess of Whitechapel. She would tell anyone willing to listen how, after her wealthy father, the duke, had died, her wicked stepmother had turned her out onto the streets. Even at a young age, Rat had realised that the woman was insane. Sometimes, the duchess would share the stale loaves of bread she bought with her pennies, and so he and Melody had been willing to listen to her stories and indulge her madness.

As Rat considered the duchess, he decided that, just as then, the best course of action was to indulge whatever story this woman was most inclined to believe. "I am the ward of Maxwell Sandworth, the Earl of Langley," Rat proclaimed in his very best toff voice. He did not doubt that this woman would look kindlier on a member of the aristocracy than she would an orphaned Whitechapel urchin.

"Are you now?" Maureen said, "And so what were you doing following Billy?"

One of the lessons Wolf had taught Rat over the time the boy had helped him in his thief-taking work was to keep as close to the truth as possible. "Billy tried to pounce on me the other day when I walked down to Lamphey from the Hall. I managed to turn the tables on him and escape unharmed. But when I heard Lord Pembroke tell the others that he was going to the bakery to question Billy, I followed the carriage and waited around to see what would happen after he left. I saw Billy sneak away and trailed him here."

Rat was sure that his explanation contained little that wasn't already known or obvious. He hadn't mentioned the dowager's assignment, nor had he gone into any detail about Tabitha and Wolf's suspicions.

Miss Prescott seemed to find his explanation satisfactory and turned to Billy, saying, "It seems this entire situation is your fault, after all." Not waiting for Billy's answer, she turned to the groom and said, "Tie this fool up as well and gag them both while I think about how to fix this mess."

CHAPTER 30

By the time the dowager returned from the cottage, it was quite late in the afternoon and almost time to start thinking about changing for dinner. After her conversation with Elinor Hughes, particularly the last vague comments about a child at risk, the dowager felt even more guilty about the secrets she was keeping from Wolf and Tabitha. She wracked her brain for a way to share what she knew without giving away her secret. After asking Talbot where she might find everyone, she came upon Tabitha, Wolf, Lily, and Tobias in the Green Room. It seemed that Lily was still trying to craft the perfect letter to her parents. Tobias was sitting by her side, making not always helpful suggestions, while Tabitha sought to reinforce the dowager's message that Hamish and Jane would be thrilled by the betrothal.

Still worrying about Elinor's vision and with Melody's recent abduction fresh in her mind, the dowager immediately asked when anyone had last seen the little girl. "I came from the nursery just a few minutes ago," Tabitha assured her. "Why? Is something wrong?"

The dowager sank into an armchair, looking far more unsure of herself than anyone was used to. Turning to Lily and Tobias, she commanded, "Take your nonsense elsewhere. I must speak with Aunt Tabitha and Cousin Jeremy."

Whatever Lily might have felt about her fears about her parents' reaction being underestimated, she was always happy to escape her grandmother's presence. She and Tobias gathered up the notepaper and pen and scurried away.

"Do you have something to say to us that you do not wish Lady Lily and Viscount Tobias to overhear?" Tabitha inquired, bemused at what might be going on with the old woman.

Before she had a chance to answer, Langley entered the room. "Have any of you seen Rat?" he asked. "He was supposed to meet with me thirty minutes ago for another hour of study. It is most unlike him to miss a lesson; he is usually most diligent."

"Have you asked Talbot?" Wolf asked.

"I have. I even went to the kitchen and asked Mrs Budgers. I would not put it past the lad to have been so caught up waiting for fresh scones to come out of the oven that he lost track of time. She said that she last saw him perhaps two hours ago or so, leaving from the kitchen door."

"What can he have been doing all this time?" Tabitha exclaimed, jumping to her feet, already envisioning the worst. Melody's abduction was also very fresh in her mind. The fact that the man responsible for kidnapping the child, Lord Langley, had somehow so reformed himself in the views of them all that he was now included in an intimate family gathering still did not negate the fear she had felt.

"It is not like the boy to disappear for hours on end with no word," Langley acknowledged. "It will be getting dark soon and he is too responsible to cause us to worry intentionally."

Whatever confession the dowager may or may not have been inclined to make, Rat's disappearance now made her realise that she needed to reveal as much as she felt able. She hoped to be able to keep the darkest secret to herself but realised that even that may need to be told eventually. Sighing, she stood and said, "Let us move to the library. I have some information to share, and we may need to review the board afterwards."

Tabitha, Wolf, and Langley exchanged glances. Were they about to discover why the dowager had been acting so suspiciously since they arrived in Wales?

Resituated in the library, everyone except the dowager took a seat while she, uncharacteristically nervous, paced the same piece of carpet, fiddling with her fingers. Tabitha had never seen the woman like this; what on earth was going on? If she had been anxious on hearing that Rat seemed to be missing, now Tabitha could barely contain her worry.

Finally, Tabitha could not bear it anymore and said, "Wolf, pour everyone a brandy, and then, Mama, tell us what is going on."

Normally, the dowager would not countenance such a tone from anyone, particularly not Tabitha. Her silence was a mark of how distracted she was. This was not lost on the others, who exchanged worried looks. Wolf stood, poured brandies for everyone, and then settled back in the armchair.

The dowager took a big swig of brandy to fortify herself, then, taking a deep breath, began. "I received poison pen letters in the weeks before we came to Wales, all saying some version of, 'I know what you did'. They all demanded that I return to Pembrokeshire to pay for my sins."

"And you are only just mentioning these notes?" Tabitha asked angrily.

"Are these notes the reason you were so insistent that we come to Glanwyddan Hall for Christmas?" Wolf demanded.

"Only partially," the dowager insisted defensively. "I stand by my observation that you needed to show your face here sooner rather than later."

"That may be. However, even when I told you about the arson and the dead animals, you insisted that we still come. And now we know why," Wolf said, almost as angry as Tabitha. He did not enjoy discovering that the dowager had manipulated him—or manipulated him even more than he usually expected.

"We brought the children into a situation that you knew was dangerous, and yet you not only were adamant that we come, but you also kept all this pertinent information from everyone," Tabitha spat. "And now Rat is missing. If anything happens to the boy, it will be on your head!"

The dowager cast down her eyes and almost looked chagrined. Certainly, she was as shamefaced as she was ever likely to be. Rat's seeming disappearance cast her actions in a very negative light, even to her eye.

Langley, able to keep a cooler head than the other two, picked up on a threat they had swept right by, "What did the notes mean by knowing what you had done?"

This was the question the dowager had been waiting for, but now it was here, she had no more idea than ever how to answer it. Finally, she sat down, took another large gulp of brandy, and said, "I will tell you now that I have no intention of telling the full story unless it proves to be absolutely necessary. And I see no reason why that will be the case. However," she continued before Tabitha could jump in and berate her any further, "I will tell you what needs to be known."

Telling the story was proving to be more difficult than she had ever imagined. "Many years ago, before Jonathan was born, I was indiscreet. It was only once, but it seems there may have been a witness."

Indiscreet? What did that mean? Tabitha wondered. Her confusion must have shown on her face because Wolf said gently, "I believe her ladyship intends to convey that she was intimate with a man who was not her husband."

The dowager blushed deeply. Little ever made the woman blush, certainly not much over the last forty years or so. "Jeremy! Is it really necessary to use such language?"

Wolf considered the far less genteel ways he might have expressed the same sentiment, but he said nothing. Tabitha was not as inclined to silence and exclaimed, "Mama! Is this true?" She wasn't sure whether she was more shocked or pleasantly surprised. It was almost a relief to discover that the dowager countess had as much human frailty as the rest of them. The dowager didn't answer the questions, but her silence was response enough.

Picking the story up again, Langley asked, "And you believe that this witness has kept quiet for all these decades but is now threatening you with this information? To what end?"

"I do not know. I have puzzled over that myself, waiting for the inevitable demand for money to arrive, and yet it never has."

Now that the worst of her story was over, at least as far as she was concerned, the dowager relaxed somewhat and relayed most of her two conversations with Elinor Hughes. She had a little difficulty explaining why her maid had come to know of her adventures without also speaking of the pregnancy, but no one questioned why she had chosen to share such a confidence with Elinor.

As the dowager told her tale, or at least most of it, perhaps the most shocking part to her audience was that she put any faith at all in a so-called cunning woman. When she reached the end of describing her latest visit to the Hughes cottage, the dowager shared Elinor's last, worrying premonition," "I pooh-poohed it at the time, but to then return here and find that Rat is missing…" The dowager didn't finish her sentence.

"Tell us again exactly what she said," Wolf demanded.

"I have told you all I know. She said that she sensed that a child was in great danger. That is all. Trust me, Jeremy, I pressed her for further information, and she swore that was all she could sense."

Tabitha rose to get the notecards, but the dowager's head jerked up before she could reach the sideboard, "You will not be putting my personal history on a notecard for everyone to see."

Sensing that this sentiment was intractable, Tabitha tried to control her frustration as she asked, "Then what do we do next? At least we now have some idea of who our culprit is: someone who was a young girl forty years ago and is probably in her mid-fifties now. That is not very much to go on. Rat could be anywhere."

As she said these words, the library door opened, and Uncle Duncan stumbled in. By the surprised look on his face, it seemed he was not expecting to find them all there. "Ah didnae expect tae find onybody in here. It's a braw spot tae sit wi' a wee dram, then maybe hae a wee nap."

"Is that all you do, man? Drink and sleep?" the dowager snapped irritably.

"Ach, there are ither things I fancy daein' wi' ma time, if ye catch ma drift, lassie," the irrepressible rascal said with a wink in her direction.

The dowager stood, threw her shoulders back, and announced, "I will not stay here and be insulted by this scoundrel. If you hear any more on Rat, I will be resting in my room." With that, she stormed out of the library.

"Aye, but she's a bonnie lass, nae doot aboot it," Uncle Duncan said, taking the armchair the dowager had just vacated.

It was unclear to Tabitha and Wolf how serious Uncle Duncan's pursuit of the dowager was and how much the man just enjoyed riling her up. Either way, they had more important things to deal with.

"What's aw this aboot the wee laddie?" Uncle Duncan asked.

Uncle Duncan was blissfully unaware of the incidents at the hall and of their investigation into Glynda's death. No one saw any reason to change his state of ignorance. Instead, Wolf said, "Rat seems to be missing, and we are worried that something might have happened to him. We were just discussing what to do. We do not have the slightest idea where he might have gone, and no idea where to even start looking."

Uncle Duncan looked at them as if they were all simpletons and said, "Do ye no hae the wee doggie wi' ye still?"

"Dodo?" Tabitha asked. "Yes, she is still with us. Probably either in the nursery with Melody or in the kitchen begging for scraps from Mrs Budgers, why?"

Langley answered in Uncle Duncan's stead, "I believe that Mr MacAlister is suggesting that perhaps Dodo might be able to track Rat."

"Dodo?" Tabitha asked again. "She is not much more than a puppy and has hardly been trained to be a hunting or tracking dog."

"Well, while that is true, and it is also true that her breed has been bred more as lapdogs than anything else recently, she may still have retained some original canine instincts," Langley explained.

"Aye, that's it laddie," was all that Uncle Duncan had to say.

"We have no better idea," Wolf acknowledged. "But I do not even know how to begin."

Uncle Duncan chuckled, "Leave it tae me. I've done mair than my fair share o' huntin' in ma time. Go an' fetch the wee doggie, an' some clothes of the laddie."

CHAPTER 31

Roberts, the groom, had grabbed Billy and tied him up almost before the boy had a chance to protest. Another dirty rag was tied around his mouth, and he was dumped by Rat. The boy's eyes were wide with surprise at how his benefactor had turned on him. Miss Prescott stalked out of the stall, followed by her loyal retainer. Their voices got further away and eventually disappeared.

Rat waited another few minutes to be sure they were not returning, then, using his tongue, managed to pull down his gag. The first time it had been put on, he'd been unprepared. The second time he had been ready and had tried to make his mouth as wide as possible as the gag was secured. Once their captors had left, he relaxed his mouth, and there was enough slack for him to manage to get the filthy rag out of his mouth.

Billy watched him doing this enviously. The older boy was a brash bully, but in truth, he had very few real survival skills. Watching him sit there, looking as if he was about to cry, Rat concluded that Billy Morris wouldn't have lasted a day on the streets of Whitechapel.

"Billy," Rat whispered. "I need you to do exactly what I say, and we'll be fine." When the other boy barely reacted, he asked, "Are you listening to me, Billy? We need to get out of here now." There was no doubt in Rat's mind that it wouldn't take Miss Prescott long to conclude that the only way out of her immediate mess was to kill both boys. Between him and Billy, they knew far too much to risk letting them live. Perhaps if he were still just a street urchin, Miss Prescott might have hoped that her word would be believed over his. However, Rat was the ward of an aristocrat now and no longer a street rat whom no one cared about or believed.

Dusk was already falling, and Rat was sure that Miss Prescott wouldn't waste any time getting rid of her inconvenient witness once there was the cover of night. Using his legs to propel him, he scooted over to Billy. He positioned himself so that his legs were up abutted Billy's tied hands. "Billy, try to get one of your hands into my right boot. I have a knife in there," Rat whispered.

The other boy grunted in reply. Rat watched as Billy scooted a little towards him, then started to fumble at the top of his boot. Rat tried to guide him, and finally, Billy managed to get his hand in. Rat was grateful that these were new boots and that Lord Langley, grumbling at how fast he was growing, had bought them one size larger. They were also not knee-high boots and barely concealed the knife. Rat was glad it was sheathed because his leg would have been shredded otherwise as Billy managed to grab it and pull it out of the boot.

"Don't drop it," Rat ordered as Billy almost did just that. Rat considered what was most expeditious: did he get Billy to hold the knife while he rubbed his rope against the blade, or vice versa? Finally, deciding that he had far more experience using a knife than the other boy, Rat again scooted over so that he and Billy were back-to-back. He then somehow managed to unsheathe the knife and take it from Billy without cutting his hands too badly.

Finally, the knife was in Rat's bound hands, with the blade facing Billy's ties. Rat didn't realise until he got close to Billy that the groom, improvising in the moment, hadn't tied Billy's hands with the same strong rope that he had tied Rat's with. Instead, he had used much thinner rope that would be far easier to cut through.

"Hold very still, Billy," Rat ordered. "I'm going to try to cut your rope, but I can't see anything. Once I start, any sudden movement on your part and you'll be the one getting cut." A small whimper indicated that Billy had heard the warning.

Rat wasn't sure how long it took him to saw through Billy's bindings; it felt like forever. His arms and back ached, but he knew that if he relaxed, there was the risk of dropping the knife or losing the spot where he had made progress cutting. So, he kept going. Just when he worried that he truly could not keep going any longer, Billy squealed, and suddenly, there was no resistance and the knife went through the air, and he dropped it.

The first thing Billy did when released was to take the rag out of his mouth. It seemed to take him a while to undo the rope binding his feet, but eventually, he managed. Then, he came over and tried to untie Rat. That also took longer than Rat would have liked. Eventually, both boys were free. The entire thing must have taken quite a while, because Rat realised that it was now dark out and that the only illumination was from a full moon shining into the stable.

"Quick," Rat ordered. "We need to get out of here and get to the Hall before anyone comes back."

※ ※ ※

Dodo had been found in the kitchen, sitting under the large table, waiting patiently for any scraps that Mrs Budgers might drop. Wolf scooped the dog up and took her back to the library where they had agreed to meet. It had been quite a while since Dodo had first come to live at Chesterton House, and holding her now, Wolf realised she wasn't really a puppy any longer. He prayed that this meant that her exuberance could be contained better now and that they'd been able to focus the dog on the task at hand.

Tabitha had gone to fetch an old jumper that she knew Rat often wore. She had then gone to her room and had changed into the most practical clothes and shoes that she had brought with her, including a warm cloak, hat and gloves. She had quickly explained to Ginny that Rat had disappeared and the maid suggested that she go and round up the male servants to aid in the search. Tabitha thanked her for the help and then made her way back to the library.

The dowager was nowhere to be seen, and Tabitha assumed that she had retired for a nap as she had said she would. That was all for the best; she didn't put it beyond the stubborn old woman to insist on being part of the search party, and that was the last thing they needed. She contemplated going to find Tobias and Lily to recruit their help, but on second thoughts, she realised they would both be more of a hindrance than a help.

Wolf and Langley, also in warm outerwear, joined her shortly. "Are you armed?" Langley asked.

Wolf nodded, "Are you?" Langley answered by pulling a revolver from underneath his cape.

Looking at Tabitha, Wolf asked, "Is there any way I could persuade you to remain here?" She gave him a look that spoke volumes about what she thought of that question, and so Wolf merely handed her the dog and said, "Then take Dodo for now. She is wriggling too much for me."

Tabitha took the dog and sat with her in her lap stroking the silky ears while they waited for Uncle Duncan. After what felt like an eternity, the Scotsman appeared, also ready to brave the cold Welsh night.

"What do we do next?" Wolf asked, having never hunted or tracked with dogs.

"Ha'e ye got somethin' belonging tae the laddie?" Tabitha indicated the jumper she'd placed on a table when she had taken Dodo from Wolf. "Aye, right then. We'll tak' it ootside an' let the doggie get a whiff o' the clothes."

They left the library and made their way towards the servants' hall. Wolf had pointed out that they knew that Rat had left that way, so it made the most sense to start where he had. It was cold out, and Tabitha hoped that Rat had left wearing his coat that afternoon.

When they were outside, Uncle Duncan took Dodo from Tabitha and put her down on the ground, making sure there was a lot of slack in her lead. Then he gave the dog the jumper to sniff. At first, Dodo seemed quite interested in whatever the jumper smelled of. Tabitha remembered Rat wearing it the day before at breakfast and spilling some raspberry jam on it, so perhaps that was what interested the spaniel so much.

"Tell the dug tae find the laddie," Uncle Duncan said.

Tabitha realised that it was likely Dodo didn't understand the man's heavy accent any more than she did, and said, "Find Rat, Dodo. Find Rat." Tabitha had very little experience with dogs, but Wolf had remarked quite a few times that Dodo was more intelligent than the average canine. She knew that he'd been working with Melody to teach the dogs some basic commands, but wasn't sure if 'find', let alone Rat's name, were words Dodo would understand.

Dodo sniffed the jumper again, then turned from it and began walking in circles, sniffing the ground. Just as Tabitha started to worry that the entire enterprise was a waste of time, Uncle Duncan's arm was jerked forward as Dodo suddenly made off into the dark. They followed the dog through the gardens, grateful for the full moon, without which they would have no idea where they were going. Every so often, Dodo would stop, sniff the ground, sometimes turn around, but then, with encouragement from them all, would take off again into the night.

CHAPTER 32

The two boys left the stall, and with Rat leading the way and keeping in the shadows as much as possible, they started making their way towards the stable door. Rat realised that the moonlight that had been their friend earlier, now made it far too easy for them to be spotted. It was clear that whatever mischief he had caused, Billy Morris was not made for stealth manoeuvres; the boy didn't know how to tiptoe, and instead, every stomp of his feet seemed to echo through the stable. There seemed to be no one about, just the occasional whinny from a horse as they passed its stall.

Rat hadn't realised how large the stable was. As tempting as it was just to bolt, he knew the wisdom of being slow and careful. Finally, they reached the stable door, which the groom had closed when he left. Indicating that Billy should stay back, Rat pushed it open enough that he could peek out. There was no one around, so he turned and whispered to Billy, "It's all clear. Just follow me. We'll need to be careful until we reach the woods."

No sooner had he said those words than a large hand swung the door open, and Roberts appeared in the doorway. Narrowly escaping the man's grasp, Rat yelled, "Billy, just run for it," and bolted out the door. Rat had always been a fast runner; it was one of the things that had kept him safe in Whitechapel. Now, he ran as fast as his legs would carry him, hoping that the rather stout Billy was in his wake. As he ran, he heard voices yelling behind him but didn't look back. It wasn't until he was well away from the stables and the woods were in sight that he slowed down enough to look over his shoulder. Billy was nowhere in sight.

What should he do? Rat wondered. Perhaps Billy was just slow but had still got away. After running a little further, Rat looked back again and realised that wasn't the case.

Rat was tempted to turn and go back for the other boy, but he quickly realised that was a bad idea. Instead, he would make his way back to the Hall and alert the others. Yet again, he was grateful for the bright moonlight that he hoped would help him find his way back over the fields. Just as he started to feel he had got away, he heard the large clomping behind him that indicated someone, likely the groom, was in pursuit. From what Rat could remember of how he had gone to Lamphey earlier and then from trailing Billy to Prescott Manor, the quickest route back to Glanwyddan Hall was not through the woods but to strike out across the fields at a right angle.

Trying to size up his options as he ran, Rat realised that the fields provided little shadow and would enable the groom to follow him easily. On the other hand, the woods would give him trees to climb, leaves to bury himself in, and many other ways to hide from his pursuer. His brief interaction with Roberts hadn't impressed him with the man's intelligence. Rat did not doubt that he had the upper hand if it was a matter of matching wits rather than length of stride. Briefly, he questioned his decision, but then finally, knowing that every moment he hesitated brought the groom closer, Rat ran in the direction of the woods.

"When I get my hands on you, you brat, you'll be sorry," a nasty voice behind him yelled. It sounded as if the groom was closing in on him, and Rat, tapping into a last burst of energy, increased his speed towards the woods. He was so close and was almost amongst the thick copse of oaks and sycamore when his foot hit a rock, he tripped and fell. Cursing his luck, Rat tried to stand, and a bolt of pain shot through his leg. He must have twisted his ankle. Even so, he did his best to pull himself up and limp the last few yards to the relative safety of the woods.

Rat didn't realise just how much his fall had allowed the groom to close the gap between them until a hand bolted out and grabbed the scruff of his neck. "Gotcha!" a voice said in his ear.

The man's breath smelled of onions and something else that Rat didn't want to contemplate. "Thought you'd got away, did you? No such chance. The mistress has got a nice well just waiting for you and that red-headed idiot." As Roberts said this, he began to drag Rat back towards the stables, unaware or unconcerned about the boy's obvious injury.

"When I was a lad, two older boys fell down a well. Everyone thought it was a silly prank gone wrong. Broke their necks, they did. It was more than a week before the 'bodies were found. I don't think anyone will think twice if the same thing happens to dim-witted Billy and his little friend."

"No one will believe that I am friends with Billy," Rat snarled.

The groom laughed nastily, "By that time, it'll be too late for you. Boys will be boys, after all."

The pain in Rat's ankle was excruciating as Roberts dragged him across the field. Just as he'd given up all hope, he heard a bark in the distance and then voices yelling his name. Before Roberts could think to stop him, Rat was yelling, "Here, here, Wolf. I'm here."

"Shut up, you brat," Roberts said, but it was hard to drag Rat and keep him quiet at the same time. As the voices and barking got closer, Roberts decided that keeping the boy quiet was the priority and came to a standstill. He held Rat with one arm and put the hand of the other over the boy's open mouth. Rat didn't think twice before biting down as hard as he could. He was pretty sure he had bitten down through to the bone; he tasted the man's blood in his mouth.

"Just wait!" the man yelled. "It's going to be a particular pleasure to throw you in that well." As he said this, he unconsciously moved his hand away and loosened his grip on Rat just enough for the boy to squirm out of his arms. Rat's ankle was too painful for him to run, but he could yell, and that was what he did. He yelled at the top of his lungs. "Help! They're trying to kill me."

Roberts recaptured him quickly, but not quickly enough. As soon as they heard Rat's voice across the fields, Wolf and Langley took off, with Tabitha, Uncle Duncan, and Dodo bringing up the rear. Almost before Roberts had his arm tight around Rat again, he heard, "Stop, or I'll shoot."

The groom stopped, turned, and saw the tall figures of two men, both pointing guns at him. "You won't shoot at the boy," Roberts replied. If you don't back off, I'll break his neck. As he said this, he moved his arm up from around Rat's shoulders so that it was now tight across his throat.

"I am a crack marksman," Langley warned. "If I aim for your head, I will not miss."

Tabitha and Uncle Duncan reached them just as Langley made this threat. Her eyes wide, still panting from the run, she whispered to Langley, "Are you sure?"

Looking around at where Dodo had led them, Tabitha realised that the house in the distance must be Prescott Manor. What did that mean, and who was it holding Rat? The moonlight allowed her to get a good view of the large man with his arm around Rat's neck. The man looked to be some kind of outside servant, maybe a groom. How had Rat ended up here, and was this man somehow involved in Glynda's murder? The man didn't seem to have the confident swagger of a criminal mastermind. Whoever had set Rhys Thomas up for the murder of his wife had intelligence and cunning that, if appearances were to be believed, this man did not seem to possess.

Tabitha took a chance and called out, "If you kill the boy, there will be nothing to stop these men from either shooting you dead or capturing you. You will hang for this if nothing else. However, I do not believe that you are responsible for Glynda Hughes' murder. I think that you were merely a faithful servant doing what he was told. If you let the boy go, Lord Pembroke will speak to the magistrate on your behalf."

Wolf gave her a quizzical look; that was quite the leap of logic she was taking. This situation was likely nothing more than that Rat was caught trespassing. However, to his surprise, the man said nervously, "I didn't kill anyone. She did it all. Enjoyed doing it, I think. Said it was her revenge. The others told me how viciously she'd swung that hammer at Blackie Hughes' wife."

Amazed that Tabitha had guessed so accurately, Wolf continued, "None of this is your fault, and if you let the boy go, I will speak to your cooperation and plead for a reduced sentence."

These last words made the groom jerk his head up, "You promise I won't hang?"

"If you cooperate completely from this point on, I promise you won't hang." Wolf wasn't entirely sure he could make such a promise until they had more information about the crimes this man may have helped his mistress commit, but he would worry about that later once Rat was safe.

The man hesitated just a moment more, then relaxed his arm from around Rat, who collapsed onto the ground from the pain in his ankle. Tabitha rushed forward, throwing herself down next to the boy and pulling him into her arms. "Rat, are you alright?" she asked desperately.

"Yeah, m'lady Tabby Cat. I've twisted my ankle, that's all." Rat looked up at Wolf and Langley and said, "That woman is crazy. She has Billy Morris up at the stables and she was going to throw us both down a well." Rat pointed back in the direction he'd run from.

Wolf considered their next move. It was evident that Rat couldn't walk. Would Uncle Duncan be able to carry him back to the Hall alone? Rat was still a slight boy, but he had grown in inches and filled out since he had stopped living on the street and had started eating regular, wholesome meals. Uncle Duncan was a large man, but he wasn't young, and he certainly didn't seem fit. Wolf was sure that Tabitha couldn't carry the boy, and he needed Langley by his side.

Just as Wolf was pondering this, they heard voices shouting Rat's name coming towards them. Ginny had said that she would send the servants out to help look for Rat, and it seemed that she had. Wolf called out in reply, and a pair of his footmen and one of his grooms joined them quickly.

Relieved to see the tall, strapping young men, Wolf said to the groom, "I want you and Mr MacAlister to take the boy back. His ankle needs to be looked at." Then, turning to the footmen, he said, you two, come with us."

Tabitha noticed that Wolf hadn't mentioned her name. No doubt he wanted to order her back to Glanwyddan Hall but knew better than to expect her to comply.

The groom wasn't as tall as the footmen, but he was a young, strong man with broad shoulders and muscular arms. He scooped Rat up and began carrying him back to the Hall with Uncle Duncan and Dodo in his wake. Wolf and Langley kept their guns trained on Roberts as they said, "Lead the way back. And do not even think of trying to warn your mistress."

Roberts had served the Prescott family since Maureen was a child. Her love of horses had endeared her to the groom at a young age. Roberts wasn't entirely sure at what point his loyalty to his mistress had morphed from teaching her to ride and care for her horses to abetting her in murder and kidnapping, but somehow, he found himself here now.

There had been whispers amongst the servants when Mrs Prescott had finally been sent away to the asylum that her daughter would be next. Family retainers who had served the Prescotts ever since Mr Prescott made his fortune had long ago seen the early signs in the daughter that they'd recognised from the mother. As he walked up to the stables, Wolf's revolver at his back, Roberts reflected that perhaps the criminal acts he'd been coerced into helping with over the last few weeks should have been a sign that his mistress was finally as insane as her mother.

CHAPTER 33

Maureen Prescott was glad she had fetched the footmen, Shandley and Hectors. As Roberts chased after that brat from the Hall, Shandley held Billy Morris while Hectors went to find more rope to bind the boy again. "Make sure you keep one hand over his mouth until Hectors finds another rag." She'd heard voices dimly in the distance and didn't want Billy getting any ideas.

Pacing up and down just inside the stable door, Maureen considered her next move. How had her plan all gone so terribly wrong? Her mother, in her very last burst of lucidity had told her about what she had witnessed in the Glanwyddan Hall barn all those years ago between the then countess and her brother-in-law. Her mother seemed to need to speak this secret just once, though by the end of the telling, she was rambling again, so it wasn't entirely clear what was true and what was fantasy.

Miss Prescott had held the secret tight for some time, unsure how to make the most use of such valuable information. Ever since she was a child, she had understood the power of secrets. Whether it was a footman who she caught drinking his master's brandy or knowledge of Sir Jerome's byblow, secrets, when used wisely, were powerful.

When news of the new earl reached Pembrokeshire, Maureen could barely contain her excitement; the opportunity to be the next Lady Pembroke was within her grasp. Yet now, the situation seemed to be spiralling out of control. Roberts had assured her that Billy Morris could be relied upon, but the reality of the boy's incompetence threatened to thwart all her carefully laid plans.

How long did it take to chase and capture one small boy? Maureen wondered. The voices that she heard seemed to be louder now, and Maureen panicked. Whether Billy Morris could have been trusted or not, there was no doubt that the boy was now a liability. "Let us deal with this one first," she said to Shandley. "The boys don't have to go down the well at the same time."

The footman hesitated; just as with the groom, by the time he realised what his mistress intended to do to Glynda Thomas, he was too implicated in her crimes to do anything other than watch on helplessly as Maureen Prescott broke into the forge and then surprised the blacksmith's wife from behind with a hammer to her head. Both footmen then had to wait with her behind the forge until the blacksmith was seen returning and then help capture the man, supposedly after having killed his wife.

The footmen had been paid well for their help. They'd been complicit, but they hadn't killed anyone. Nevertheless, this was different; there was no doubt that she was expecting Shandley to pick this child up and throw him down the well. Shandley had grown up in Lamphey. He had saved his pennies so that he could buy apple turnovers from the bakery. Mrs Morris had always thrown in an extra pastry. These were good people, and he was about to murder their son.

Hectors returned with rope and a rag. "Tie him up," Maureen ordered.

"Miss, he's just a boy," Shandley said nervously. All the servants knew all too well what it was to spark their mistress' ire.

Seeing Shandley look at Hectors and lift his shoulders as if asking what the other man thought they should do, Maureen said irritably, "Fine! Give me the rope and I'll tie him up. If you want a job doing well…" the words tapered out as she grabbed the rope from the footman and began tying Billy's hands and then feet.

Hectors was the footman caught drinking the brandy. He was

a sharp young man who hoped one day to move to Cardiff or even London. He had big dreams. Perhaps Mr Prescott would let him go for the small infraction, but his master was a notoriously soft touch. Hectors had some money saved, so if Mr Prescott did take a sterner view of him drinking the brandy than expected, he'd just take off for Cardiff sooner than planned. Like Shandley, he had watched with growing horror as it became clear what his mistress had planned for Glynda Thomas.

The footmen had known that Rhys Thomas had come upon his dead wife's body, and yet they had followed Miss Prescott's orders to restrain the man and deliver him to PC Evans. Neither footman knew what the actual crime they had committed was and what the penalty might be, but they both were sure they had no intention of compounding it with murder.

Shandley let go of Billy and stepped away. "I'm right sorry, Miss Prescott, but I won't hurt the boy."

Rage surged through Maureen's body. Her mother had always told her never to dim her light. If her brilliance blinded others, it was for them to step back rather than for her to apologise. Looking at the two strapping footmen, she realised that they were not worthy of even standing in her shadow. She was not a fragile waif of a woman, and all the horse riding over the years had made Miss Prescott stronger than was perhaps fashionable for a woman. Yet she wasn't sure she was capable of hoisting a struggling eleven-year-old boy into a well. There was only one thing she could do: kill the boy in the stable and then dispose of the body later.

"Go back to the house. I will take care of this situation alone," Maureen growled. "Just keep your mouths shut, if you know what's good for you," she threatened.

During all this, Billy Morris remained so terrified that he probably couldn't have escaped even if his feet hadn't been bound. As soon as Miss Prescott had tied them, he'd fallen over and now sat on the stable floor, tears pouring down his cheeks. Maureen Prescott looked down at the boy in disgust. She had no problem with physical violence. Indeed, she had relished every moment of her attack on Glynda. What she didn't like was blood on her clothes. The murder of the blacksmith's wife had ruined an otherwise perfectly good dress, and the blue concoction she was wearing now was brand new. Perhaps there was something she could use as a more targeted weapon, less likely to cause a mess, in the tack room. Leaving Billy snivelling on the ground, Maureen went to see what she could find to kill him in a manner less likely to ruin her clothes.

As she disappeared into the stable, Billy heard voices calling his name. He tried to answer, but the gag was on far too tightly for him to make a sound. Suddenly, he saw figures silhouetted against the bright moon. The first person he saw was Roberts, the groom. Any relief Billy felt that he had been rescued disappeared at the sight of the man. Who were the men standing behind Roberts, and was that a woman with them? As the men came further into the barn, Billy released that one of other men was the toff who had interrogated him earlier that day.

"Untie the boy," the toff ordered. "Do not even think of trying anything. We will both be more than happy to shoot you."

The groom scurried over to where Billy lay and began to untie the ropes. He pulled the gag down, and Billy squealed, "She's gone to the back. She was going to kill me, she was."

No one had to ask who the 'she' was; Miss Prescott's complicity in the events of the last few weeks was evident, even if neither Wolf, Tabitha, nor Langley had any real idea why.

Langley kept his revolver trained on the groom, who was now untying Billy's feet, and said, "Pembroke, I'll keep an eye on this one. You go and find the Prescott woman."

Determined not to be left behind, Tabitha stepped forward to join Wolf. He looked as if he wanted to protest, but instead said, "Stay behind me. She may have a gun."

They walked stealthily through the barn, glad for the cover of the horses stamping their feet and neighing to each other. More than halfway down, they saw a light coming from a room off to the right. Wolf indicated that Tabitha should stay back, and then he stepped into the doorway, his gun out before him.

Maureen Prescott had been so busy selecting the perfect murder weapon that she hadn't heard the group turn up to rescue Billy. Her back was to the door, and she was rustling around in a box full of picks. It had occurred to her that if she could find a nice sharp one, she might be able to kill Billy quickly, easily, and most importantly, without too much bloodshed.

Hearing a noise behind her, Maureen turned around and saw Wolf. "Lord Pembroke, what a delightful surprise," she said, unable to keep the flirtatious tone out of her voice even though the gun the man was training on her suggested he knew some of what she had done.

"Drop what is in your hand, Miss Prescott," Wolf said, noticing the sharp implement she was holding.

"And if I do not, what will you do? Shoot me?" the woman said tauntingly.

"Without a second thought," he replied.

Miss Prescott dropped the pike and started to come towards Wolf. "You know, it doesn't have to be like this, Wolf. We were each other's first love, and as far as I'm concerned, nothing has changed."

What was the woman talking about?

"Miss Prescott, I am not sure what misconception you are harbouring. We have never met before the other night, and I am certainly not in love with you."

Maureen's eyes became hard and her tone cold as she said, "I speak of our first encounter, when we were young children, that first summer you spent at Glanwyddan Hall and I showed you the treehouse."

Was the woman delusional? "Miss Prescott, I can assure you that we did not meet as children. Glynda Hughes took me to the treehouse for the first time."

"Glynda, Glynda. It was always Glynda. Or Glynnie as she was then. I met you first, not Glynda. We met on the outskirts of the Hall's gardens. I had lost one of my dolls and you helped me search for it."

Wolf remembered the incident, but he was sure that it was

Glynda he had met that day and who had lost her toy. He had been so young, and it was so many years ago. Was it possible that the little girl had been Maureen Prescott instead? He cast his mind back, trying to remember. He did remember that they finally found the doll, and that they had then played for a while. The little girl had told him she had a secret place to show him and had taken him to the edge of the woods that separated Prescott Manor from Glanwyddan Hall. She'd shown him the huge, ancient oak, with the treehouse about fifteen feet up, accessible by a ladder. They had sat in the treehouse, pretending to have a tea party with her doll.

Wolf had only visited his grandfather for a week that first summer. The day he met the little girl was the last before he returned home. The following year, he went to the treehouse, hoping to reunite with his friend, and found Glynda sitting up there with a baby bird she had discovered and was attempting to nurse. It had never occurred to Wolf that this girl was not his friend from the summer before.

Seeing comprehension dawn on Wolf's face, Maureen said, "So, you do remember now. Do you also remember when I came upon you and Glynda in our treehouse, and she said that I couldn't play with you? You didn't stop her. You choose her over me!"

"Miss Prescott, we were very young children. I apologise for my behaviour at the time, but I hardly see how that justifies anything you have done recently, particularly Glynda's murder."

"She lorded it over me, you know; lorded the friendship over everyone. Oh, she'd pretend that she was not bragging, but I understood too well what she was about; she had stolen you from me and then spent years rubbing my nose in the fact. And who was she? Just a farmer's daughter. Nothing special." Maureen Prescott paused, then resumed in a more conspiratorial tone, "Did you know that I used to watch the two of you play? For years, I'd watch you come to meet her in my treehouse! The one I had introduced you to. As we all got older, I noticed the way she looked at you."

The venom in the woman's voice was awful, and the unhinged, wild look in her eyes was terrifying. "Then, the old earl died, and you never returned. I waited and waited, sure you would come back for me now you were able. I always knew that it was only Glynnie who kept us apart."

Maureen paused, then said in a conspiratorial tone that was somehow even more terrifying, "When it became clear that you did not intend to return, I thought about the secret Mama had told me about what she had seen the old crone dowager do all those years before in the barn with the viscount's brother. From all the gossip I received from London, it seemed that you allowed the hag unbelievable sway over your actions, and so I knew that if I forced her to return, she would bring you with. The pranks would merely reinforce the need for you to visit."

The conspiratorial tone then changed to something far nastier, "I never forgot you, but your darling Glynnie moved on almost immediately with the blacksmith's lad. Then, after all the effort I went to in order to get you to visit Pembrokeshire, the dead animals and the notes to that crone, I heard her in church talking about how much she was looking forward to seeing you after so many years. It could not have been clearer that history would be repeating itself and that she planned to keep you to herself again."

"And so, you killed her?" Wolf asked incredulously. "You had Billy do all those pranks and send the dowager countess those notes to lure me back here, and then killed Glynda out of some misplaced sense of proprietorship over my friendship?" Wolf felt nothing but intense sadness that a life had been taken so needlessly and that he was somehow the cause. He wanted to ask why she had bothered to have Billy throw the rock through the window, but the insanity blazing in her eyes was all the answer he needed.

Maureen Prescott smiled proudly. "I did indeed, and I was so close to removing your darling Tabitha from the picture as well. I would have been your countess before Spring." Wolf shuddered at the woman's words, unaware until that moment of the peril

SARAH F. NOEL

Tabitha had been in.

CHAPTER 34

Having untied Billy Morris, Wolf and Langley used the rope to tie Miss Prescott's hands. Wolf's first thought had been to take the woman back to Glanwyddan Hall and summon Squire Partridge and PC Evans. At Tabitha's suggestion, they instead took her to Prescott Manor, where a stunned Mr Prescott was confronted with his daughter's crimes. However, Tabitha thought it noteworthy that the man did not doubt their story for a moment, so perhaps he had more idea of the insanity his daughter had inherited from her mother than he was willing to admit.

Billy Morris confessed to his role, and Roberts confirmed everything. As promised, Wolf spoke up for the man and vowed to continue to do what he could to plead for leniency. By the time Mr Prescott called for the two footmen to answer for their role, it was discovered that their rooms were empty and that they had wisely left under cover of darkness while they were able. Billy spoke to their refusal to hurt him, and his belief that Maureen alone had murdered Glynda, and everyone agreed to let the two men go for now.

It was too late for the Pembroke Dock lock-up to send anyone over, but Squire Partridge assured everyone that he had brought some of his men with him to help take Miss Prescott into his custody. He had also taken Billy Morris, if only to strike fear into the boy's heart at the thought of being arrested.

Mr Prescott had given them the use of his carriage to get home. During the short ride back to Glanwyddan Hall, Wolf had told Tabitha and Langley about his extraordinary conversation with Maureen Prescott.

"Whether or not she was the little girl, nothing justifies what she has done," Tabitha exclaimed. "The woman is insane."

"Indeed, and because of that, I doubt she will ever see the inside of a prison cell," Langley explained. I am sure that her father has enough money and influence to ensure that she is sent away to an asylum instead of hanging for her crimes."

Wolf thought about the exchange with Maureen Prescott in the tack room, "I am not sure how we did not see it when we met her over the previous few days, but the woman is deranged. Her rantings about how she and I were meant to be together and how Glynda had taken me from her once and would not do it again were almost sad."

As they exited the carriage, Langley went on ahead, and Tabitha put her hand on Wolf's arm to hold him back for a moment. "Mama's secret. There is clearly more to it than just that one indiscretion. Do you think we should press her on it at this point?"

Wolf considered the question, "It seems that the only relevance it ended up having to this case was that Maureen Prescott learned it from her mother and used it to force us all to Wales. It seems to have had nothing to do with why she wanted us here or why she killed Glynda. If her ladyship chooses not to reveal the rest of her story, I believe we have no reason not to honour that wish." Tabitha nodded in agreement; this was exactly what she had been thinking.

They found everyone else in the large, east-facing parlour that had a particularly grand fireplace and was the warmest, comfiest room on a cold evening. It seemed that Mrs Jenkins and Mrs Budgers between them had taken care of Rat's ankle, and he was now seated in the most comfortable armchair in the room, drinking a hot chocolate and eating an iced bun, seemingly no worse for his adventure.

The dowager sat in the chair next to him and periodically patted his hand as if to assure herself that he was indeed safe and well. Bear had not been at the Hall when they discovered Rat missing, and so had not been part of the rescue party, but he had returned from the village in time to see the boy brought in by the groom. He was now sitting in a particularly large armchair with Dodo, the true hero of the hour, in his lap.

Lady Lily and Viscount Tobias were sitting side-by-side on a pretty Regency couch, still quite confused about what had happened over the last few days, let alone hours.

Tabitha, Wolf, and Langley took seats and gratefully accepted brandies, then started to tell the whole story. When they reached the part of the tale where Rat followed the Pembroke carriage to the bakery and then trailed Billy Morris to Prescott Manor, Tabitha scolded, "Whatever were you thinking, Rat?"

"I just knew that Billy Morris was a bad 'un," he explained. "I knew what I would have done if I were him and m'lord Wolf and Lord Langley had come and interrogated me. So, I waited after they left, and I was right."

"But why did you not just tell us that, lad?" Langley asked gently but firmly. "Did you think that we would not pay heed to your warning?"

Rat shrugged his shoulders. It was all very well for them to all say now that they would have listened to him, but he still had his doubts.

"Let us not lose sight of the fact that Rat was very brave and resourceful and that because of him, a wicked woman has been apprehended," the dowager said more approvingly than perhaps Tabitha wished.

"Indeed," Wolf said. "By all accounts, you showed a lot of ingenuity, and Billy Morris is alive because of you." His tone then became more serious, "Next time, Rat, speak up. I promise we will all pay attention to whatever you have to say."

Wolf sipped on his brandy and thought about the events of the evening. "I will go and see Elinor Hughes tomorrow," he said. "I must tell her the truth about why her daughter was killed and by whom. It is the very least I can do." He thought about the woman's warning of a child in danger, "Usually, I hold no truck with the ways of so-called wise women and magic. However, there is no doubt that Elinor's so-called premonition probably saved Rat's life."

No one disputed that, no matter how the blind woman had learned that Rat was in danger, without her warning, it was unlikely they would have found Rat in time. As they all sat silently for a moment, contemplating this thought, Talbot and one of the footmen entered the room with platters of sandwiches and sausage rolls.

Looking up at the grandfather clock, Wolf realised that dinner was long past time and that he was starving. He filled a plate with sandwiches, settled back in his chair, and said, "There are seven days until Christmas. Perhaps we can now put all this murder and mayhem behind us and focus on enjoying the holiday season."

"I do wonder if being the reason that one villager was murdered, another was falsely accused, and one neighbour is likely to be confined to an insane asylum will sour the good people of Lamphey on their new earl," the dowager noted drily. "I suggest that you double whatever largesse you were considering distributing at Christmas Eve, Jeremy. It never hurts to buy people's favour."

While Wolf was tempted to argue against the notion of bribing his tenants, as he considered the dowager's words, he decided that perhaps it would not be a bad idea to suggest to his steward that they increase whatever was planned for the Christmas boxes. Wolf didn't want the people of Lamphey and the areas surrounding the Pembroke Estate to have the events of the last few weeks be the lasting memory they had of the new landowner.

Looking around the room, Wolf realised that one person was missing, "Where is Mr McAlister?" he asked.

"It seems that he overexerted himself following you over the fields. The man came back, drank two large brandies in a row, and then took himself off to bed," the dowager said, just a little too gleefully.

"You know," Tabitha pointed out, "we have a lot to thank

Uncle Duncan for. It was his idea to use Dodo to track Rat's scent. Perhaps we can have a brief ceasefire in hostilities as a thank you," she suggested, looking pointedly at the dowager.

"I have no idea what hostilities you are talking about, Tabitha," the dowager said, followed by one of her signature sniffs.

EPILOGUE

Tabitha and Wolf stood side-by-side at the edge of the Hall's ballroom, watching the people of Lamphey enjoy their landlord's largess. Mrs Budgers had outdone herself and the smell of ginger and cinnamon filled the room as people enjoyed mince pies, mulled wine, spiced cookies, and more.

"All things considered, I think this is a great success," Tabitha said.

"Indeed," Wolf replied. "I even had Mrs Evans come up to me and say that it is better than the ones my grandfather used to throw. Apparently, he used to really scrimp on the mulled wine and the beer."

Tabitha laughed, then pointed out, "You know what this means, though, don't you?"

Wolf sighed; he knew exactly what it meant, "I believe that in resuscitating a tradition, I am now responsible for keeping it going."

"That is exactly what it means." Tabitha turning slightly to look more directly at Wolf. "I know that your early memories of Glanwyddan Hall were awful, and our first few days compounded those negative feelings. However, Pembrokeshire is beautiful, and the people of Lamphey are warm and welcoming. I think it is time to make new, wonderful memories here, Lord Pembroke."

"I could not agree more, Lady Pembroke," he said meaningfully. They had not discussed any further Tabitha's continued fears about marriage, but Wolf had a plan. A plan that he meant to begin to execute as soon as they returned to London in the New Year.

"Look at Lily and Tobias," Tabitha said, pointing to the young couple loitering near the glass doors leading out from the ballroom into the grounds. "For all that Lily claims that this will be a marriage of convenience, at least as far as she is concerned, I believe she may have stronger feelings for the viscount than she is willing to admit."

Wolf smiled at the sight of the couple standing next to each other, closer than necessary. Tobias was looking at Lily devotedly, but the expression on the young woman's face, while perhaps not as adoring, nevertheless, was certainly not one of cold disinterest.

"Lily came to tell me that she had received a letter from her parents in response to her one announcing her engagement. To no one's surprise, except perhaps their daughter's, Laird and Lady McAlister were thrilled at the news. I believe that a Spring wedding is being discussed."

Two hours later, the Christmas boxes had been distributed, the last mince pie had been eaten, and the good people of Lamphey had returned to their homes. Tabitha, Wolf, their extended family and friends retired to the cosy parlour. Melody had been allowed to stay up late for the party and now sat sleepily on Langley's lap, a final, half-eaten mince pie in her hand.

Rat's ankle was much improved, though the boy still insisted on using the spare cane that the dowager had lent him. He sat on the floor by the fireplace, feeling a little sick after eating far too many sugar plums. The birthday cake that had been rolled out as the crowning event of the evening's party had surprised and thrilled him. Now, he wondered whether two slices of the Victoria sponge had been a good idea.

Tabitha looked around the room. Uncle Duncan had changed his plans and had headed off to Bristol to stay with a golfing friend for Christmas. While Tabitha felt more affection for the loud, unrestrained Scot than the dowager did, she did acknowledge that their Christmas would be more peaceful with him gone. As she had days before, she reflected that she wasn't sure how such an unusual collection of people had grown to feel like family, but they had. Looking over at Wolf, laughing at something Bear had just said, it wasn't that her fears about committing to marriage again had disappeared, but she knew that somehow, she was meant to spend the rest of her life with this wonderful man.

※ ※ ※

Wolf and Bear, the duo you've grown to love, have a friendship and business partnership spanning over a decade. Curious about the beginning of their journey? Never fear. For this short story detailing their initial meet-cute, and more, **sign up for my newsletter o**r find the link at **sarahfnoel.com**

Want a sneak peek at book 7, **An Indomitable Woman** (https://books2read.com/AnIndomitableWoman)

Keep reading....

Finally, seated in the far more comfortable armchair, a cup of tea in her hand and the social niceties of small talk about each other's families out of the way, the dowager asked, "So, what can

I do for you, Tuchinsky?"

"You don't believe I've just come for a visit to see how the toffs live?" the other woman asked, laughing.

"I believe that you have a thriving business to run and no time to make social calls on a Wednesday afternoon that don't have a purpose," the dowager said in a matter-of-fact tone. As it happened, her more than-usual interest in Tuchinsky meant she would have been thrilled to receive a mere social call from the woman. However, she was astute enough to recognise someone on a mission when she saw them. Tuchinsky's impatience with the small talk had been evident; she had weightier issues she wished to discuss.

Putting down her teacup, Tuchinsky glanced away for a moment as she considered how she wished to phrase her request. Finally, deciding there was no better way to say it than bluntly, she answered, "Lady Pembroke, I want to hire you to find a murderer."

Whatever the dowager had been expecting, it was not that. In truth, ever since she had made the decision more than three months before to launch herself into the world as a private inquiry agent, she had been at somewhat of a loss for how to drum up business. Initially, she had tried milking her high society gossips, Ladies Hartley and Willis, for possible cases. She had thought that effort had surfaced a potential investigation. However, she had then been sidetracked when Mickey D, the Whitechapel Irish crime boss, had unexpectedly recommended her services to a madam. It was a matter of dispute between her and Tabitha and Wolf as to whether her subsequent adventures running a brothel in Villiers Street had been a reckless, ill-considered undertaking that had almost got her killed, or a brilliant and daring launch into the world of investigations. Whichever was closest to the truth, since then, she had been disappointed at the total want of subsequent potential clients beating their way to her door.

It had briefly occurred to the dowager to put an advertisement in one of the London newspapers. Indeed, she had considered how the title she had printed on her calling cards, *The Investigative Countess, Rapier Sharp Logic paired with Great Insight and Boldness, A Private Inquiry Agent,* might look in a broadsheet. However, on further reflection, that felt rather too akin to being in trade, and there was no greater horror as far as the dowager was concerned. Of course, if she had been pressed as to why setting herself up in business didn't feel like lowering herself to be no better than a solicitor or bank manager, but advertising the fact did, she might have momentarily been lost for words. Perhaps it didn't feel the same because she had never really considered the commercial aspects of her new chosen profession. She had no need for money and had set herself up as an inquiry agent solely to alleviate her boredom.

The dowager had considered how cases just seemed to crop up for Wolf and had hoped that she might be similarly blessed. Now, that actually seemed to be the case, and she was both delighted and, uncharacteristically, somewhat nervous. "A murderer you say? You want me to find a murderer?"

Order Book 7, **An Indomitable Woman**

Melody and Rat are the adorable Whitechapel street urchins Tabitha has taken under her wing. Would you love to know what they're like as young adults? Never fear, my new series, **The Continental Capers of Melody Chesterton**, will reveal all. **Book 1, A Venetian Escapade,** is available for **pre-order** now!

AFTERWORD

Thank you for reading A Discerning Woman. I hope you enjoyed it. If you'd like to see what's coming next for Tabitha & Wolf, here are some ways to stay in touch:

SarahFNoel.com
Facebook SFNoelAuthor
@sarahfNoelAuthor on Twitter
sfnoel on Instagram
@sarah.f.noel on TikTok

If you enjoyed this book, I'd very much **appreciate a review** (but, please no spoilers).

Order Book 7, **An Indomitable Woman**

Melody and Rat are the adorable Whitechapel street urchins Tabitha has taken under her wing. Would you love to know what they're like as young adults? Never fear, my new series, **The Continental Capers of Melody Chesterton**, will reveal all. **Book 1, A Venetian Escapade,** is available for **pre-order** now!

ACKNOWLEDGEMENT

Thank you to my wonderful editor, Kieran Devaney and the eagle-eyed Patricia Goulden for doing a final check of the manuscript.

ABOUT THE AUTHOR

Sarah F. Noel

Originally from London, Sarah F. Noel now spends most of her time in Grenada in the Caribbean. Sarah loves reading historical mysteries with strong female characters. The Tabitha & Wolf Mystery Series is exactly the kind of book she would love to curl up with on a lazy Sunday.

BOOKS BY THIS AUTHOR

A Proud Woman

Tabitha was used to being a social pariah. Could her standing in society get any worse?

Tabitha, Lady Chesterton, the Countess of Pembroke, is newly widowed at only 22 years of age. With no son to inherit the title, it falls to a dashing, distant cousin of her husband's, Jeremy Chesterton, known as Wolf. It quickly becomes apparent that Wolf had consorted with some of London's most dangerous citizens before inheriting the title. Can he leave this world behind, or will shadowy figures from his past follow him into his new aristocratic life in Mayfair? And can Tabitha avoid being caught up in Wolf's dubious activities?

It seems it's well and truly time for Tabitha to leave her gilded cage behind for good!

A Singular Woman

Wolf had hoped he could put his thief-taking life behind him when he unexpectedly inherited an earldom.

Wolf, the new Earl of Pembroke, against his better judgment, finds himself sucked back into another investigation. He knows better than to think he can keep Tabitha out of it. Tabitha was the wife of Wolf's deceased cousin, the previous earl, but now she's running his household and finding her way into his life and, to his surprise, his heart. He respects her intelligence and insights but can't help trying to protect her.

As the investigation suddenly becomes far more complicated and dangerous, how can Wolf save an innocent man and keep Tabitha safe?

An Independent Woman

Summoned to Edinburgh by the Dowager Countess of Pembroke, Tabitha and Wolf reluctantly board a train and head north to Scotland.

The dowager's granddaughter, Lily, refuses to participate in the preparations for her first season unless Tabitha and Wolf investigate the disappearance of her friend, Peter. Initially sceptical of the need to investigate, Tabitha and Wolf quickly realise that the idealistic Peter may have stumbled upon dark secrets. How far would someone go to cover their tracks?

Tabitha is drawn into Edinburgh's seedy underbelly as she and Wolf try to solve the case while attempting to keep the dowager in the dark about Peter's true identity.

An Inexplicable Woman

Who is this mysterious woman from Wolf's past who can so easily summon him to her side?

When Lady Arlene Archibald tracks Wolf down and begs him for help, he plans to travel to Brighton alone to see her. What was he thinking? Instead, he finds himself with an unruly entourage of lords, ladies, servants, children, and even a dog. Can and will he help Arlene prove her friend's innocence? How will he manage Tabitha coming face-to-face with his first love? And how is he to dissuade the Dowager Countess of Pembroke from insinuating herself into the investigation?

Beneath its veneer of holiday, seaside fun, Brighton may be more sinister than it seems.

An Audacious Woman

The Dowager Countess of Pembroke is missing!

While Wolf is contemplating whether or not he wishes to continue taking on investigations, it seems that the dowager has taken the matter into her own hands and is investigating a case independently. But why has she gone missing from her home for two nights and what mischief has she got herself into? Tracking down the elderly woman takes Tabitha and Wolf into some of the darkest, most dangerous corners of the city.

What on earth is the exasperating dowager caught up in that she seems to have become entangled with London's prostitutes?

An Indomitable Woman

The Investigative Countess, Rapier Sharp Logic paired with Great Insight and Boldness. A Private Inquiry Agent.

When the dowager countess receives her first assignment as a private inquiry agent from Tuchinsky, an East End gangster, she immediately throws herself into the case with gusto. Meanwhile, Lord Langley hires Tabitha and Wolf for an assignment that takes them deep into London's Jewish neighbourhood. Is there a connection between the two investigations? More importantly, can the two investigative teams work together?

Wolf has made his peace with continuing to take on

investigations and with having Tabitha partner with him, but how will he manage the dowager countess' continued meddling in such a dangerous case?

Printed in Great Britain
by Amazon